W9-CZX-332

Praise for the Midnight Breed series by LARA ADRIAN

BOUND TO DARKNESS

"While most series would have ended or run out of steam, the Midnight Breed series seems to have picked up steam. Lara Adrian has managed to keep the series fresh by adding new characters . . . without having to say goodbye to the original ones that made the series so popular to begin with. Bound to Darkness has all the passion, danger and unique appeal of the original ten books but also stands on its own as a turning point in the entire series with new pieces to a larger puzzle, new friends and old enemies."

—*Adria's Romance Reviews*

"Lara Adrian always manages to write great love stories, not only emotional but action packed. I love every aspect of (Bound to Darkness). I also enjoyed how we get a glimpse into the life of the other characters we have come to love. There is always something sexy and erotic in all of Adrian's books, making her one of my top 5 paranormal authors."

—*Reading Diva*

CRAVE THE NIGHT

"Nothing beats good writing and that is what ultimately makes Lara Adrian stand out amongst her peers.... Crave the Night is stunning in its flawless execution. Lara Adrian has the rare ability to lure readers right into her books, taking them on a ride they will never forget."

—*Under the Covers*

"...Steamy and intense. This installment is sure to delight established fans and will also be accessible to new readers."

—*Publishers Weekly*

EDGE OF DAWN

"Adrian's strikingly original Midnight Breed series delivers an abundance of nail-biting suspenseful chills, red-hot sexy thrills, an intricately built world, and realistically complicated and conflicted protagonists, whose happily-ever-after ending proves to be all the sweeter after what they endure to get there."

—*Booklist (starred review)*

DARKER AFTER MIDNIGHT

"A riveting novel that will keep readers mesmerized… If you like romance combined with heart-stopping paranormal suspense, you're going to love this book."

—*Bookpage*

DEEPER THAN MIDNIGHT

"One of the consistently best paranormal series out there.… Adrian writes compelling individual stories (with wonderful happily ever afters) within a larger story arc that is unfolding with a refreshing lack of predictability."

–*Romance Novel News*

Praise for Lara Adrian

"With an Adrian novel, readers are assured of plenty of dangerous thrills and passionate chills."

–*RT Book Reviews*

"Ms. Adrian has a gift for drawing her readers deeper and deeper into the amazing world she creates."

–*Fresh Fiction*

Praise for LARA ADRIAN

"Adrian has a gift for drawing her readers deeper and deeper into the amazing world she creates."

—*Fresh Fiction*

"With an Adrian novel, readers are assured of plenty of dangerous thrills and passionate chills."

—*RT Book Reviews*

"Nothing beats good writing and that is what ultimately makes Lara Adrian stand out amongst her peers . . . Adrian doesn't hold back with the intensity or the passion."

—*Under the Covers*

"Adrian has a style of writing that creates these worlds that are so realistic and believable . . . the characters are so rich and layered . . . the love stories are captivating and often gut-wrenching . . . edge of your seat stuff!"

—*Scandalicious Book Reviews*

"Adrian compels readers to get hooked on her storylines."

—*Romance Reviews Today*

Praise for Lara Adrian's books

"Adrian's strikingly original Midnight Breed series delivers an abundance of nail-biting suspenseful chills, red-hot sexy thrills, an intricately built world, and realistically complicated and conflicted protagonists, whose happily-ever-after ending proves to be all the sweeter after what they endure to get there."

—*Booklist (starred review)*

"(The Midnight Breed is) a well-written, action-packed series that is just getting better with age."

—*Fiction Vixen*

Look for these titles in the *New York Times* and #1 international bestselling

Midnight Breed series

. . . and more to come!

Hunter Legacy Series

Born of Darkness
Hour of Darkness
Edge of Darkness

Other books by Lara Adrian

Contemporary Romance

100 Series
For 100 Days
For 100 Nights
For 100 Reasons

Run to You
Play My Game *(Spring 2020)*

Historical Romance

Dragon Chalice Series
Heart of the Hunter
Heart of the Flame
Heart of the Dove

Warrior Trilogy
White Lion's Lady
Black Lion's Bride
Lady of Valor

Lord of Vengeance

EDGE OF DARKNESS

A Hunter Legacy Novel

NEW YORK TIMES BESTSELLING AUTHOR

LARA ADRIAN

ISBN-13: 978-1-711-735696

EDGE OF DARKNESS
© 2019 by Lara Adrian, LLC
Cover design © 2019 by CrocoDesigns

All rights reserved. No part of this work may be used or reproduced in any manner whatsoever without permission, except in the case of brief quotations embodied in critical articles and reviews.

This book is a work of fiction. Names, characters, places and incidents are either products of the author's imagination or used fictitiously. Any resemblance to actual events, locales, or persons, living or dead, is entirely coincidental. No part of this publication can be reproduced or transmitted in any form or by any means, electronic or mechanical, without permission in writing from the Author.

www.LaraAdrian.com

Available in ebook and trade paperback. Unabridged audiobook edition forthcoming.

EDGE OF DARKNESS

CHAPTER 1

The small bell above the diner's front door jingled as someone came in from the blizzard roaring outside. A gust of frigid air pushed in along with the late arrival. Tiny ice crystals blew against Leni Calhoun's nape as she headed into the kitchen with the emptied plates from what she'd thought was the last customer of the night.

"Sit anywhere you want," she said without slowing down or turning around.

Not that she actually needed to tell any of her regular customers that her tiny diner at the edge of the North Maine Woods was a seat-yourself kind of establishment.

Tonight's big storm meant business had been slower than usual, but steady. The timber truckers and hunters who made up the bulk of the traffic on the private, mostly unpaved, two-lane that rambled for ninety-odd miles between Millinocket near the Interstate and the Canadian border to the west knew Wednesday was pot roast day at the diner. Not even a fierce February Nor'easter would keep many of them away from a plate of slow-cooked beef and vegetables slathered in gravy.

Leni assumed she'd be ladling up the last of her gran's heirloom recipe for the straggler who'd just come in from the road. Grabbing the coffee carafe off the burner and one of the heavy white ceramic mugs still warm from the dishwasher, she walked back out to the dining area.

A couple of local men swung off their stools at the counter and told her goodnight as they shuffled toward the door. There were plenty of open seats left at the long bar, but the newcomer had bypassed them all to take the booth farthest from the half-dozen other patrons inside.

Leni didn't know him. He sat facing the entrance, his head lowered slightly and covered by the deep hood of his snow-sodden, black parka. Inside the faux fur-trimmed opening, she could just make out the squared edge of his beard-roughened jaw and a stern, unsmiling mouth.

He was a big man. Even seated she could tell he was tall and muscular. Beneath the heavy winter coat, his shoulders were wider and bulkier than a linebacker's. Probably a new guy pushing his luck trying to make a timber delivery to one of the sawmills before the week was out. Only seasoned local drivers and clueless newbies from away would even consider being on the unmaintained road in tonight's weather.

"Looks like another storm of the century out there," she said, making conversation as she set down the mug and began to pour the strong black coffee. "Then again, we seem to be getting one of these about every year, so—"

"No coffee." The deep voice was clipped and toneless, but the baritone rumble vibrated straight into her marrow.

"Okay, no problem." She stopped pouring and pulled the carafe back. "What else can I get you to drink, then? Coffee's the usual around here, but I've also got water or fountain soda. If you want hot tea, it'll take a few minutes for me to start a fresh pot of water."

He shook his head and some of the melted snow ran off his hood like rainwater. "I don't need anything to drink. Thanks."

The acknowledgment sounded rusty, though not insincere. He swept the parka's hood off his head with a big hand gloved in black leather. Leni wasn't one to gape, but damn, it was hard not to. The face staring up at her was nothing short of gorgeous.

From beneath a thick crown of brown hair a few shades darker than her own, penetrating blue-gray eyes met her gaze. His beard-shadowed, squared jaw looked even stronger under the wan yellow glow of the pendant light hanging over the table. Razor-sharp cheekbones should have made his face seem harsh, but instead all those unforgiving angles were set against a downright sinful-looking mouth that made her heart pound a little faster.

Being trapped in the hold of those stormy eyes didn't help.

Even though Leni with her brown hair and freckle-spattered cheeks had never been as pretty as her blonde, blue-eyed older sister, Shannon, she still got her fair share of second glances from men, both the locals and the ones just passing through. But this man studied her with an intensity that surpassed clumsy come-ons or garden variety ogling.

He looked at her as if he could see inside her with a glance. His gaze moved slowly over every feature of her face, from her hazel eyes and slightly upturned nose, to her mouth, which suddenly felt as dry as cotton. Then his gaze drifted lower, settling at her throat and sending her already drumming pulse into a gallop.

It should have unnerved her, the way he radiated dark power and a palpable, yet unspoken command. In a corner of her consciousness she was a little rattled, because it damn sure wasn't her nature to check her good sense into her panties every time a good-looking man came into the diner. Which, to be honest, wasn't that often. As in, never. And this man was unearthly handsome.

God, what was wrong with her?

Leni picked up the half-filled mug he wouldn't be using and rallied her focus. "All right, then. Nothing to drink. So, what else can I get you? I've got one serving left of my grandma's famous pot roast, and I guarantee you've never tasted anything like it."

The dark slashes of his brows furrowed a little over his unsettlingly intense eyes, even while the corner of his mouth quirked with wry amusement. "No pot roast for me."

"You sure? If you're thinking about heading for one of the mills near Jackman or St. Zacharie at the Quebec border, you'll need something that sticks to your ribs. You're looking at a hundred miles of dicey driving ahead of you." She gestured with her chin to the blizzard howling against the window. "What might take you four-plus hours in good weather will mean double or triple that time tonight. If you make it at all."

He grunted in response. "I'll take it under advisement."

She tilted her head, studying him now. He wasn't heading to either of those places. In fact, she didn't think he was a logger or a trucker, after all.

Working the diner for half of her twenty-seven years, first at her mom and gran's side, then on her own once both of them had passed, Leni had developed something of a sixth sense when it came to the types of strangers who passed through Parrish Falls on their way to somewhere else. But her first impression about this man had been all wrong.

He was unlike anyone she'd encountered before, and not only because of his soul-searching eyes and impossibly handsome face.

Something about him had tripped a lot of switches inside her, including a few she didn't want to acknowledge. When he took off his gloves and she spotted the unusual markings on the back of his strong hands, she understood why.

Holy shit. He was Breed.

Those tangled flourishes and swirls in a shade or two darker than his golden skin didn't occur in humans. They were otherworldly markings. *Dermaglyphs* that only appeared on the blood-drinking cohabitants of this planet who had lived in secret alongside mankind until about twenty years ago.

Leni had never seen one of his kind in person before, but she knew about the Breed. She knew enough to realize that the sheer size of him and the density and complexity of the *glyphs* tracking over his large hands and wrists meant the rest of him was sure to be covered in them too.

Which meant this male had to be almost pure-blooded, one of the most powerful, most lethal, of his race.

He retrieved some folded money from the inside pocket of his parka and peeled off a twenty. "I won't stay long," he said, pushing the bill to the edge of the metal-rimmed laminate table. "I just needed to get out of the cold for a while."

Leni stared into those turbulent blue eyes, astonished. Not only because she was having a conversation with a vampire in her diner, but because aside from the fact that he could take whatever he wanted from anyone he pleased—including their lives—he was sitting there offering to pay for a few minutes of kindness and consideration.

She shook her head. "Keep your money. Stay as long as you like."

As she spoke, the low diesel growl of an approaching heavy-duty pickup truck grew louder outside the restaurant. The black truck was rigged with a large snowplow blade tonight and had its lights set on bright. The twin beams sliced through the downpour of heavy flakes, practically blinding Leni through the window as the driver pulled into the middle of two open spaces out front.

Damn. Just what she didn't need.

Frowning, she bit back a groan. She'd gone the whole day without seeing the two men who climbed out of the truck. If she went the rest of her life without having to deal with Dwight Parrish or any of the rest of his clan, it would be too soon for her liking.

The Parrish family had been running this unincorporated patch of timbered, north country land for generations, longer than the state had been part of the Union. Over time, their line had thinned along with the fortune the earliest Parrishes had made in logging and fur trading. But the name still carried a lot of weight in the village and the surrounding townships, and there were few, if any, who dared to get on the bad side of old Enoch Parrish or his sons, Dwight, Jeb, and Travis.

Unfortunately, Leni was one of those few, although there wasn't a hell of a lot she could do about it.

The front door swung wide as Dwight and another local man, Frank Garland, came in and stomped off their snowy boots inside the diner. Assholes.

Leni's irritation must have been written on her face. When she glanced back at the Breed male seated in the booth, he was watching her. "Everything okay?"

"Just the usual." She forced a pleasant smile to her lips. "Like I said, take your time. Let me know if you need anything, all right?"

He gave her a vague nod before his hawklike stare swung to the pair of men now strolling up to the counter to chew the fat with the handful of customers seated there.

Dwight Parrish smacked his palm against the countertop, then his cigarette-roughened voice boomed over the rest of the diner. "What the hell's a person gotta do to get a cup of coffee in this place?"

CHAPTER 2

Knox hadn't arrived in the far-flung little village by choice. Probably not many people did. He'd only been in town for a few minutes, long enough to get the sense it wasn't a place that saw a lot of strangers—least of all, ones with fangs and *glyphs* like him.

If it hadn't been for the raging blizzard and a long-haul trucker with a weak bladder, Knox might still be sitting inside the warmth of a semi-trailer cab heading north on I-95. But when the ride he'd hitched in New Hampshire let him off several hours into Maine at a truck stop in Medway, his options were to either hunker down through the worst of the storm and the daylight to come, or keep moving. After five solid months of roaming and the occasional job since he left the only semblance of home he ever knew in Florida, Knox was no good at staying put.

He hadn't been for a long time.

Eight years and counting.

Not since Abbie.

He'd allowed himself to weaken where she was concerned, but no more. Not ever again. Now, he kept his life simple and devoid of emotional entanglements of any kind.

No obligations to anyone or anything.

As long as he kept moving, as long as he stayed inside the guardrails of his own discipline and the training that had made him a Hunter, one of the most lethal members of his kind, there was no time to think about what he'd lost. No room for pain or anguish. Or guilt.

So when the choice came down to cooling his heels for a few hours near the Interstate or hoofing deeper into the north country along the two-lane out of town, he'd chosen the latter. Thirty miles in, the picturesque but arduous trek had become largely uninhabited, other than a smattering of old farmhouses and mobile homes. He guessed he'd gone about twice that distance before he saw the dim glow of light coming from the diner a dozen yards on the other side of a weathered wooden road sign declaring he had just entered Parrish Falls.

He supposed he'd keep roaming along that same stretch of unpaved two-lane once he got back outside, possibly venture into Canada and see where the road took him from there.

The pretty brunette who'd offered him coffee and a hot meal before realizing what he was had mentioned that the border—and the promise of civilization—was roughly a hundred miles out by vehicle. Being Breed, he could cover that distance far faster on foot. Especially in weather like tonight's.

LARA ADRIAN

He had to admit, after nearly freezing his balls off in the blizzard, the idea of finding a soft bed and a warm, willing blood Host to take the itch out of his fangs and the other equally demanding part of his anatomy was a tempting one.

Those competing hungers pulled his gaze to the long, denim-clad legs currently walking away from his booth. In addition to having the loveliest, most honest face he'd seen in weeks, the brunette had a confident, direct demeanor and a smooth, slightly husky voice that had rubbed over his senses like velvet. And her list of assets didn't stop there. Tall and curvy, she had generous hips and a small waist that not even her baggy plaid flannel shirt could conceal. Thick dark hair that Knox guessed would probably fall halfway down her back was scraped off her neck in a loose knot on top of her head.

It had been all he could do to hold back his fangs as he'd stared at the bared column of her throat while she'd talked with him at his table. He'd gone a day or three too long without feeding, but it wasn't only the thought of her fresh red cells on his tongue that had his veins going tight as he continued to watch her now.

With his rejected mug in one hand and the glass coffee pot in the other, she returned to the long counter where the pair of men who'd pulled up with the snow-plow had now dropped into a couple of empty stools near the old-fashioned cash register.

She hadn't been happy to see them when they arrived. Her continued displeasure practically vibrated off her as she strode past them into the swinging door of the kitchen. She came back out with a pair of fresh mugs and poured coffee for each of the men.

"Anything else?"

She directed the question to the larger of the duo. Bulky, round-shouldered under a winter coat and several layers of all-weather fleece, he wore a grey knit cap and had a ruddy face covered in a reddish-brown lumberjack beard.

He took a sip of the hot coffee, eyeing the woman over the rim. "Ain't you gonna ask me about Travis, Lenora?"

"No. Why should I?"

One of those ham-sized shoulders lifted with his sneer. "He's coming home this weekend."

"I'm well aware." And from the flat tone of her voice, it wasn't welcome news.

"He's gonna want to see the boy, Leni."

She took a step back as if she needed to distance herself from the statement as much as the man who delivered it. Folding her arms in front of her, she shook her head. "Riley doesn't even know him. He doesn't know anything yet. And he's too young to understand."

"That's my brother's decision to make, not yours."

"His decision? Like hell it is," she shot back, scowling now. "I'm not going to let Travis anywhere near that child. You can tell him I said so."

The big man set his mug down. "You can't keep us away from the kid, not anymore. You know Travis won't stand for that once he's home. Maybe he'll come around the house and say hello when he gets back. Or maybe he'll want to head over to the elementary school next week instead and surprise his son with a little family reunion."

An older couple seated a few stools down from the confrontation evidently decided it was time to go. Tossing a few dollars' tip next to their half-empty plates, they ambled out of the diner, the cheerful bell jingling in their wake.

That left a pair of truckers and a slightly balding, middle-aged man in a camouflage hunting jacket remaining at the counter. The truckers hardly glanced up from their pot roast now. The man in the hunting jacket had polished off the last of his apple pie a few minutes ago and seemed intent on ignoring the drama taking place a few stools away from him.

And then there was Knox in the back booth, his hands flexing and fisting under the table, his battle instincts ratcheting tighter by the second as he stared at the overbearing asshole who seemed to have come inside with the sole purpose of causing upset.

Lenora, or Leni, as the man had called her, now exhaled a sharp breath as she planted her hands on the edge of the countertop and faced off against the overbearing behemoth.

"Dammit, Dwight. Hasn't your family done enough damage to mine?" She kept her voice tight and low, but Knox's acute hearing picked up every syllable and nuance of her fury. "Leave Riley out of this. He's not property."

"That's right, Lenora. He's flesh and blood. Ours."

Her chin hiked up. "Really? You couldn't prove that by me."

He scoffed. "Only because you've refused to allow the test."

She didn't so much as flinch. "That'll be two-fifty each for the coffees."

"Can I get mine in a takeaway cup, Leni?" It was the first thing the asshole's buddy said since they came in. He dug into his jacket pocket for his wallet, but froze in mid-motion when his companion slanted him a pointed look.

"We want something to eat too," the big man, Dwight, said. "I'll take a serving of that pot roast."

Leni clicked her tongue. "You're too late. It's all gone."

Dwight's glower narrowed at the lie. "Then gimme the meatloaf instead. With lots of gravy."

She shrugged and slowly shook her head. "Kitchen's closed now. On account of the weather."

"Bullshit." He uttered a threatening sound, something close to a growl, as he stood up. "Then get out my way, Lenora. I'm coming back there to make my own damn meal."

Knox wasn't about to let that happen. "Hey. Paul Bunyan. You heard the lady, kitchen's closed."

Every head in the place turned his way. Including Leni's. Her pretty hazel eyes went wide with surprise—and uncertainty—as she met his gaze from across the length of the diner.

The big human male's heavy brow furrowed. "Who the fuck are you?"

From his seat in the booth, Knox stared flatly at him, ignoring the demand. "Put your two-fifty on the counter, both of you, then go."

On a chortle, Dwight swung his head toward his nervous-looking buddy. "You believe this guy?" He started to approach. "The only one who's gonna be leaving is—"

Knox moved out of the booth and stood. His size had been somewhat diminished when he was seated. Now, his six-and-a-half-foot height and two-hundred-sixty pounds of muscle and bone was unmistakable. No doubt, so was the cold invitation to violence in his eyes.

Leni's aggravator stopped short, half a dozen paces between them. At the counter, the man in the hunting jacket suddenly jolted out of his willful ignorance of the situation. Scrambling off his stool, he inserted himself between Knox and the other man while the two truckers who'd been eating at the counter paid up and made a hasty exit.

"All right, everyone, let's simmer down." The man faced Knox as if he were the one at fault. His woodland camo jacket was unzipped, but he made a point of opening it wider to reveal the pistol holstered at his hip and the sheriff's badge clipped to his belt. "I don't believe I've ever seen you around here before, Mister . . ."

Knox let the prompt for his name hang unanswered, his eyes still on Dwight, who was clearly more than relieved to have the law coming to his rescue. Gutless pussy.

The fact that the apparently off-duty county sheriff didn't bother to step in while Leni was being verbally harassed annoyed Knox more than it should have. She wasn't his concern. Neither was the obvious protective bias the local cop seemed to have toward the arrogant man at his back. Still, suspicion stirred inside him.

The officer cleared his throat and tried another tack. "Hell of a storm out there. What brings you to Parrish Falls?"

"Just passing through."

The dodge earned him a nod and a narrowed look. "Where ya from, son?"

"Here and there."

Knox found it vaguely amusing that the fifty-something human hadn't yet clued in on the fact that he was Breed. Nor did he seem to realize that Knox was even more lethal than that.

He'd spent the entirety of his childhood, from birth to his teens, in the laboratory of a madman, being conditioned to kill without a speck of emotion just like the others in the Hunter program. Those hellish beginnings were training for the years he would spend under the collar of the same sadistic lunatic, doing his murderous bidding as one of scores of assassins who'd been bred in the lab.

It had been two decades since Knox and a number of other fortunate Hunters had been freed from their imprisonment in the program. That didn't mean he'd left his skills behind.

Far from it.

He was still a born-and-bred killer, easily the most lethal creature lurking in this isolated corner of the north Maine woods. Part of him hoped the chickenshit hiding behind the sheriff would give him an excuse to prove it.

"Didn't notice you drive up in a vehicle tonight," said the man with the badge and the gun. "Someone drop you off?"

"I walked."

The man gave him a dubious look. "Where you headed in weather like this?"

Knox shrugged. "Haven't decided."

"You sure don't talk much, do you?"

"Is that a crime in Parrish Falls?"

The sheriff grunted. Behind him, Dwight collected a small measure of courage, enough to scoff as he peered around the smaller, older man who separated him from Knox.

"Disrespect may not get your ass arrested but loitering can. So can being a public nuisance."

"He's not loitering," Leni said. Her gaze met Knox's and held for a long moment. "I told him he could stay in the diner as long as he likes. I've never turned anyone away and I'm not about to start. There's only one public nuisance in here tonight and it's not him."

Dwight sneered. "Sheriff Barstow, why don't you arrest this drifter for vagrancy? Maybe he'd prefer to wait out the blizzard in the county jail."

"You think there's a cell strong enough to hold me?" Knox spoke past the law officer, staring straight at Dwight. For good measure, he gave him a brief flash of his fangs.

"Holy shit!"

For a big man, it was amazing how fast he was able to leap back. The sheriff retreated a pace too. He held up a hand, which, to his credit, only trembled a little.

"Okay, now. Let's all relax for a minute." He spoke slowly, calmly, the way he might if he'd just been thrust into a hostage negotiation. Or a bomb scare. "No one's getting arrested. And no one wants any trouble here tonight."

"There doesn't have to be," Knox said. "If he apologizes."

The sheriff glanced pointedly over his shoulder.

"Sorry," came the muttered, insincere reply from the other end of the diner.

"Not to me." Knox stared at the man, then nodded in Leni's direction. "Apologize to her."

"What the fuck for?"

The sheriff exhaled impatiently. "For God's sake, Dwight, just do it."

"Fine. I'm sorry, all right?"

Knox pinned him with a cold look. "Now pay for the coffees and get out of here."

Dwight glared, but dug into the pocket of his jeans and withdrew a messy handful of crumpled bills and coins. His friend hurried to take out his money too.

"It's two-fifty each," Leni reminded them.

"Plus tip," Knox added.

The men paid up then left, Dwight stomping out the door like an angry bear. The sheriff followed them out and paused with the men near the pickup truck outside.

"Thank you for doing that." When Knox glanced Leni's way, he found a small smile tugging at her expressive mouth. "I don't think anyone's ever stood up to him before."

"You mean other than you?"

She lifted her shoulder. "Dwight Parrish doesn't scare me."

Knox scowled at the name. Parrish. No wonder the arrogant jackass acted like he owned the town. "What about his brother? Travis. Does he scare you?"

She stared at him for a moment, then dropped her gaze and shook her head. "It's nothing I can't handle."

"You sure?"

She nodded. When her head came back up, her expression was one of pure resolve. "Yeah. I'm sure."

He had doubts about that. He had questions he wanted to ask. Questions he had no business wondering about, never mind putting into words. And the longer he stood alone with her in the empty diner, the harder it was to ignore the frantic ticking of the pulse point at the

LARA ADRIAN

base of her smooth throat. Or the desire he had to feel other parts of her under his mouth as well.

Damn. His first order of business as soon as he reached civilization had better be a feeding and a good, hard fuck. Because the craving he had for this intriguing, far too tempting female was licking through him like a wildfire.

"I should go now."

"Okay. And thank you again."

He inclined his head. "You take care."

Her warm smile shot straight to his bloodstream. "You too . . . ah, I'm sorry, don't even know your name."

"Knox."

"Very nice to meet you, Knox. I'm Lenora Calhoun. Most people call me Leni."

She held her hand out to him. He took it reluctantly, bracing himself for the connection.

Not only because of the desire already spiking through him, but because touching her would also tell him things he had no right to know.

All of her sins, whispered to him through the power of his unique extrasensory ability.

But there was no jolt of revulsion. No hideousness flooding him like a slick of black, putrid oil.

There was only the warmth and honesty of Leni's smile as she looked at him.

Only the kindness of her intelligent hazel eyes.

"You stay safe out there, Knox."

He smirked, amused by her concern.

Outside, the roar of the pickup truck's engine intensified as Dwight Parrish hit the gas pedal and backed out onto the snow-filled road.

18

Knox let go of Leni's hand and pulled the hood of his parka up over his head.

Then he headed out to the frigid darkness, bypassing the sheriff as the man returned to the diner.

A hundred miles, give or take, stood between Knox and the Canadian border.

Maybe he'd take the trek slower than planned.

Several hours trudging through the blizzard might be the only way to cool the unwanted fire currently simmering in his blood.

CHAPTER 3

Standing behind the counter as Sheriff Barstow came back inside, Leni watched the swirling snow and darkness swallow Knox up.

She couldn't tear her gaze away, couldn't seem to inhale a single breath past the pang in her breast, until he had vanished completely.

And even after he was gone, she had the strangest compulsion to run after him and ask him to stay.

Or beg him to take her with him, no matter where he was headed.

It shocked her that she would even think it.

God, was she really that hard-up and lonely that a few minutes with a handsome drifter could turn her into a quivering puddle?

She probably didn't want to know the answer. And there was no need to do the math on how long it had been since she'd been in bed with a man. Or hell, since she'd even got within kissing distance of one she liked.

All she had to do was look at six-year-old Riley to be reminded of the length of her self-imposed abstinence. Not that she'd had much experience before the sweet baby boy had been dropped into her life and become her primary focus.

Leni hadn't given birth to him, but Riley was hers in every way that mattered. He was also the only family she had after her older, troubled half-sister had left town without a word to anyone only a few months after her son had been born.

Leni didn't regret a minute of her precious nephew's existence, nor her responsibility to provide a safe and stable, happy life for him. She would never wish him away, but sometimes she did long for more.

Did it make her a bad person that every now and then she just wanted to feel female and sexy? She wanted to feel alive, the way she had under the unsettling, penetrating intensity of Knox's stormy blue eyes.

Not going to happen. Not in a million years. About the only thing worse than thinking she could trust her heart—or her body—to any man in Parrish Falls or within a hundred-mile radius of the place would be getting involved with someone who was just passing through. Especially when that someone also happened to be Breed.

Knox was the most dangerous kind of male she could crave, and not only because she sensed the cold lethality in him. All it would take was getting naked with him just once for him to realize she wasn't entirely mortal herself.

It would take far less than that, probably. Because even though the small scarlet teardrop-and-crescent-moon mark she bore on her belly was concealed beneath her flannel shirt and a layer of thermal underwear tonight, there were other things that would give her away soon enough to someone like Knox.

Her singular blood scent. Her imperviousness to physical harm or injury, which was her unique gift as a Breedmate.

So, it was good that he was gone.

Lord knew she had enough problems to deal with already.

Sheriff Barstow collected his keys and gloves from the counter where he'd been seated before the confrontation between Dwight Parrish and Knox. The middle-aged man gave her a rueful shake of his head as he approached the cash register.

"You know, Lenora, the best thing you can do for yourself and that boy is find a way to make peace with the Parrishes."

"Make peace?" She blew out a short breath as she grabbed a cloth and a bottle of spray cleaner and began wiping down the countertop. "If you'll recall, I'm not the one who started this war."

"Maybe not. But do you really want to be the one to escalate it?" Barstow swept a hand over the thinning strands of his grayed comb-over. "I realize you're not happy about Travis coming home on Saturday."

"That's putting it mildly," she muttered, scrubbing the laminate. "Should I be happy that the man who went to prison for brutalizing my sister seven years ago is getting out early for so-called good behavior?"

"He's served his time, Lenora. He feels terrible about what happened to Shannon, but he's said all along that their off-and-on relationship was a volatile one. All due respect, your sister was no angel, either. She was a rebellious, troubled girl."

"Only after she got involved with Travis."

"She'd been in and out of rehab most of that year, Leni."

"Are you really trying to justify what Travis did by blaming Shannon? As if it matters, I know for a fact that she'd been sober for months the night he assaulted her."

Sheriff Barstow held up his hands. "Be that as it may, according to Travis's testimony, Shannon struck him first. He had the bruises and scratches to prove it."

Leni scoffed. "He had bruises and scratches, Amos. Shannon's skull was fractured in three places. He hit her so hard he almost knocked out her front teeth."

And despite all of that, her sister hadn't wanted to press charges. She probably wouldn't have, but after a trip to the county emergency room with a concussion revealed she was eight weeks pregnant, Shannon had pushed past her fears of retaliation from Travis or his family. All for the safety of her unborn child.

Now that responsibility rested on Leni.

"I'm Riley's legal guardian," she reminded the sheriff. "Until my sister comes home again, I'll decide what's best for her son. I don't suppose I'll be able to count on you to make sure that man doesn't come anywhere near Riley."

The sheriff's furrowed brow and sheepish stare was answer enough. "Travis Parrish is coming home a free man, Leni. So long as he stays on the right side of the law, I can't prevent him from going anywhere he wants to."

"You mean you won't."

It was a well-known fact that Amos Barstow's allegiance to the Parrish family went way back. His father had been one of old Enoch Parrish's closest friends before the elder Barstow died about a decade ago. Now, Amos was more than willing to look the other way over a lot of things when it came to the old man and his three sons.

His gaze gentled as he considered her now. "I'm sorry for what happened to your sister, Lenora. I truly am. I'm sorry she left all this burden on you when she abandoned her child and never looked back. This mess shouldn't have been yours to clean up."

"This mess?" Leni's voice rose along with her outrage. "Riley's not a mess I'm cleaning up. He's not a burden. As for my sister, she didn't abandon her child. She would never do that. I don't know where she is or what made her leave, but it wasn't by choice. She's going to come home one day. I know she will."

The sympathetic look on the seasoned law officer's face said this wasn't the first time he'd heard someone plead a case for an errant family member's honor. She could see his doubt. He didn't have to say he expected Shannon was gone for good—or possibly not even alive. His prolonged silence conveyed that clearly enough.

Leni couldn't take it another second.

"You mind turning the sign on the door around on your way out, sheriff? I'm going to close up now."

Besides, Riley was waiting for her to pick him up at her best friend's place. Although Leni and he lived in the house behind the diner where she and Shannon grew up, on weekdays her friend Carla Hansen brought Riley home with her after teaching at the elementary school he attended.

After her confrontation with Dwight Parrish and the reality of Travis's return tomorrow, she needed to see her little nephew's sweet face and know that he was tucked in safe and sound at home where he belonged.

Sheriff Barstow zipped up his jacket, then put his gloves on. "You be careful out there on the road tonight, all right?"

Leni inclined her head. "Goodnight, sheriff."

She continued her cleaning and watched him leave. His SUV turned left out of the diner parking lot, heading back toward the neighboring town where he lived.

A few minutes later Leni locked up, shrugged into her heavy wool peacoat without buttoning it up and trudged out to her old red Bronco. She cleared off the eight hours' worth of snow that had buried it during her shift, then hopped in and cranked both the heat and the wipers to full blast.

As the vehicle warmed up, she tapped Carla's number on her cell. "I just closed up and I'm about to head your way," she said after greeting her friend. "How was he today?"

"Great, as usual," Carla said, a smile in her voice. "We made snow angels in the yard after school, and then we spent a couple of hours looking at the blizzard on weather maps online and learning all about the biggest snowstorms. Did you know the world record for most snowfall in twenty-four hours was set in Colorado in nineteen-twenty-one?"

Leni laughed. "Huh. Nope, can't say I knew that."

"Seventy-five-point-eight inches, in case you're curious. Riley couldn't believe it was enough to bury two of him stacked together, so I got out the tape measure to show him. I think he's measured everything in my house now."

"No wonder you're his favorite teacher," Leni said, taking a right onto the two-lane that would carry her northwest a dozen or so miles to her friend's place near the school. "I'm sorry I couldn't get away sooner to come and pick him up."

"Don't worry about it. He's asleep. School's closed tomorrow, so he's welcome to stay the night if you like. The snow's still coming down with a vengeance out there. You should stay put."

"I'm already on the road. And I don't mind the drive." Leni put the call on speaker as she tried to talk over the rhythmic thump of the wiper blades. "I just . . . I really need to have Riley close and where I can see him tonight."

"What happened?" Carla knew her too well than to miss the note of anxiety in Leni's voice. "You sound rattled, and you never get rattled. Are you nervous about tomorrow?"

"I didn't think I was, but then I got a visit from Dwight Parrish at the diner tonight."

"Ugh. I should've guessed he wouldn't be able to resist gloating over his brother's early release."

"Dwight made it very clear I'm going to be in for a fight when it comes to shielding Riley from Travis. I'm really afraid they're going to try to take him from me."

"Then you'll take the fight to court. I know a great lawyer in Bangor who does a lot of pro bono work on family cases, especially when it comes to the protection of children. I'm sure she'll be willing to help you if you need her."

Leni let out a sigh. "Thanks, Carla. But you and I both know the Parrishes aren't the kind of people you take to court."

"Shannon did. Her testimony put Travis in prison for these past seven years."

"And look what happened to her."

Leni couldn't prove anything, but in her gut she knew her sister hadn't simply walked away from her life and everyone in it. The trial had barely begun when Shannon vanished without a word or a trace. Given her troubled background and her history as a runaway in her teens, her missing person case had gone largely ignored by local law enforcement and the rest of the community.

Leni didn't want to think what might have happened to keep Shannon away from her child, or from seeing her assailant's trial through to the end. All these years later, Leni wasn't ready to accept what everyone else in Parrish Falls seemed to think about her sister—that whatever had happened, she was never coming back.

Leni refused to believe that.

Emotion pricked the backs of her eyes, making it even harder to see through the heavy slant of the snow blowing in front of the vehicle. The Bronco's yellow headlights barely pierced the relentless swirl of flakes as she drove past the crossroad and the lone gas station in thirty-five square miles.

"I should hang up," she said, her tires slipping in the new snow already filling the road since the plow had been through. "I'm probably fifteen or twenty minutes away in this mess. Don't wake Riley before I get there.

I'm going to put him straight into bed when we get home."

"All right. Drive safe. See you when you get here."

Leni ended the call and leaned over the wheel, peering straight ahead. With the moon obscured by the storm, the unpaved road was treacherous and dark the farther she drove.

Drifting snow crowded the edges of the two-lane, narrowing it to roughly one and a half.

No more signs of civilization to light the way. No more houses on either side. Only thick hardwood forest and a steep ravine that followed the frozen stretch of river running parallel with the winding road.

She pushed onward for a handful of miles before headlights ahead of her cut through the darkness. The vehicle was moving fast, coming toward her. A large pickup truck. One she recognized immediately.

The sharp blade attached to the front of it shoved large heaps of snow into her side of the road. Instead of slowing, Dwight Parrish's truck picked up speed as if he didn't see her. Or as if he meant to challenge her.

Holy shit.

Leni swerved as his bright headlights filled her windshield. There was no shoulder to cling to, only soft snow on the ledge above the ravine.

And zero traction.

Her outside tire slid into the formless shoulder, too sharply to correct. The heavy Bronco kept going, veering out of control. She pumped the brakes, but the snow gave way beneath her, rendering them useless. The treads of her tires had nothing to grip.

Oh, God.

The front passenger side of the vehicle lurched at the edge of the steep drop.

Then it pitched forward, taking her over the side of the ravine.

Down and down and down.

Above her on the road, Dwight Parrish's pickup roared away without stopping.

CHAPTER 4

Inside the small gas station's convenience store, Knox put a few dollars on the counter for a packet of air-activated hand warmers he didn't actually need.

"Thanks for looking in back for these," he told the attendant behind the register.

The scrawny, tattooed twenty-something with ginger-colored dreadlocks bobbed his head, mild disinterest in his dull gaze. "No problem, man."

It would take a few minutes for the human's faculties to fully come back online after the blood Knox had just drained from him in the store room. The mind scrub he'd given him afterward ensured the local youth wouldn't even recall Knox had been there at all.

The precaution was more habit than anything else. In general, he didn't bother with Breed feeding laws or curfews, but his Hunter training had conditioned him to exist on the fringes of civilization. He preferred to navigate his world with speed and stealth, and leave no trace behind him.

Slipping his purchase into the pocket of his parka, Knox walked outside. The blizzard hadn't let up any during the few minutes he'd had his fangs sunk into the kid's wrist. Not that there had been much hope of that.

The unplanned detour had been more about taking the edge off the stirrings of his hunger for a very different blood Host.

He had been thinking about Leni's creamy throat and delicate skin as he'd taken the attendant's wrist to his mouth. It was a piss-poor substitute. The blood was thin and tainted with the acridness of a recent dose of opioids, but the drugs had no effect on Knox. The youth was also hiding a host of sins, everything from petty thievery to a handful of violent assaults. His guilt over those crimes tasted as bitter to Knox as the kid's addiction.

As for the red cells, they'd served their purpose. Nevertheless, sated from feeding and eager to be done with the trek to the Canadian border, it was no small aggravation that he was still thinking about the woman. Still wondering if she might have welcomed him into her bed, if he'd had the inkling to stay in Parrish Falls for the rest of the night.

Which he didn't.

Staying for the night would mean staying until the following sunset, when it would be safe for him to be outside again. He hoped to be hours into Quebec by then.

And miles away from the sweet, freckled nose and sharp, forthright hazel gaze of a woman he didn't think he'd ever forget.

Fuck, maybe he needed a mind scrub. Too bad he couldn't give one to himself.

Somewhere in the dark a diesel engine rumbled, drawing nearer. The soles of Knox's boots vibrated with the low sound, and with the metallic complaint of a snow plow's blade scraping over the narrow two-lane.

Dwight Parrish's heavy-duty pickup barreled past the gas station, sending clumps of snow and ice flying in its wake. He was alone in the cab, having apparently dropped his buddy from the diner somewhere along the way.

Knox scowled from within the deep hood of his jacket as he watched the truck roar up the road. He was sorely tempted to follow him. Roughing up a dickweed like that would give him great satisfaction, and not only because it seemed like more than one of the Parrish brothers could use a lesson in humility. Not to mention a brush with their own mortality.

But they weren't his problem.

Parrish Falls wasn't the only town saddled with a clan of self-important assholes running roughshod over anyone they pleased. It wouldn't be the last, either.

As for Lenora Calhoun, she wasn't the only beautiful woman who'd turned Knox's head during his rootless trek across the country. Why she had woken something in him after only a few minutes in her company, he didn't want to know.

He was finished thinking about her too.

Damn it, he had to be.

Putting his head down against the frigid push of the storm, he set off in the opposite direction of the diner and walked for a while. A forest of thick pines and spruce stood tall on either side of the sloping, snowy road. The decline grew more pronounced on his right, carving a deep ravine that followed the winding outline of the frozen river below.

And farther ahead, near the bottom of that same ravine around a mile away from where he was now, he saw a dim orange glow. Vehicle taillights.

The muffled sound of a running engine hit his acute senses at the same time. The stench of steaming, dark gray clouds of exhaust on the cold night wind. A hard creak of a door hinge as someone crawled out of the driver's side, stumbling and slipping in the tangled mess of the thicket.

A woman.

Holy shit, it was her.

Knox didn't run. Every ounce of his Breed agility and speed kicked into high gear as he flashed down the ravine.

Rapid-fire memories of another accident battered him in that short span of time. A wreck that happened eight years ago in the Everglades. One he had been helpless to stop. A death that still clawed at him today.

The recollection tore into him with talons even sharper than the spiky branches he crashed through now.

In less than a second, he reached the old red Bronco hemmed in place by trees near the bottom of the ravine and the woman who had staggered out of it.

Leni grasped the broken trunk of a young pine as he skidded to a halt at her side. Her head came up in surprise. "Kn-Knox?"

Her voice was shaky and small. Her dark hair was a loose tangle, most of it obscuring her face. But she could speak. She could move.

Thank God, she appeared to be all right overall.

He shook off the rusty memories that clung to him, focusing on the here and now. On Leni.

"Are you okay?" He couldn't keep from reaching out to move some of the disheveled tresses away from her cheek to check her over. No bruises on her face or brow. No cuts or contusions.

Miraculously, he saw no damage of any kind, not even a minor scratch. Just unmarred, satiny skin and those beautiful, long-lashed eyes that were staring at him in confusion and shock.

"Wh-what are you doing here? I thought you left town. How on earth did you find me?"

"Doesn't matter," he said, his voice rough as he took quick visual stock of her condition. "Are you hurt at all?"

She gave a faint shake of her head. "I'm fine. I, um, I had my seatbelt on."

He cursed under his breath. "A seatbelt wouldn't have saved you from the river if your car had gone any farther down this incline. Jesus, you might've been killed."

"I'm okay." The hand that had been holding on to the tree now came to rest on his forearm. "Really. It was nothing. I'm good."

Her touch felt hot against him despite the thick layer of his sleeve. Her gaze felt even warmer, fixed on his as the blizzard churned all around them in the darkness. In that moment, the attraction he'd felt toward her in the diner swelled into something more. Desire, yes, but he was also concerned. And more relieved than he had a right to be that Leni was standing before him in one piece, evidently unharmed.

He glanced away first. Using the power of his mind, he silenced the running engine of the Bronco. Then he looked back toward the disturbed embankment and the gouged shoulder where her vehicle had gone over the edge.

"What happened?"

"A truck was coming toward me in the opposite lane. I couldn't move over and he didn't slow down. I must've turned the wheel too hard. My tires slid off the shoulder and the next thing I knew, I went into the ravine."

"This truck that didn't slow for you," Knox said, scowling as he glanced back at her. "It was Dwight Parrish, wasn't it?"

Her brows rose in surprise. "How could you possibly—"

"I saw him pushing his plow, heading back the other direction." Knox's concern deepened. "Did he know he ran you off the road? Son of a bitch. Did he do it deliberately?"

Leni shrugged as if it was no big deal. As if this kind of thing could happen anytime. "He just likes to harass me. He thinks he can scare me."

"You don't look scared. Maybe you ought to be."

Her mouth took on a determined tilt. "Dwight Parrish has been a bully his whole life. Deep down, he's just a coward. All of the Parrishes are."

Knox arched a brow. "You're one tough lady."

"I am when I need to be." She hooked some of the snow-sprinkled brown waves of her hair behind her ear and sent a dismayed look at her Bronco. "Shit. I'm never going to get a tow truck way out here in this weather. I need to make a call."

"You mean to the county sheriff to report this?"

She scoffed. "There's no point in reporting this. The Parrishes are good friends with Sheriff Barstow. Dwight will claim he knows nothing about this and the sheriff will tell me to stop trying to pick fights on behalf of my sister."

Knox considered in silence. He'd gotten a glimpse of the lax attitude the sheriff seemed to have toward Leni's tormentor earlier tonight. "So, your sister has problems with this family too?"

"She did," Leni said. There was sadness in her eyes as she spoke. A quiet sense of loss. Knox would know it anywhere. "Shannon's the reason Travis Parrish has been in prison these last seven years. He assaulted her. Beat her almost unconscious. She had him arrested for it, mainly to protect her unborn child."

Knox clenched his jaw at the ugly details. Some of the pieces he'd been trying to put together after the incident in the diner now clicked into place. "The boy Parrish mentioned, the one he said is his brother's son. You're not the mother?"

"No. Riley's my nephew. I've been looking after him since Shannon disappeared a few months after he was born."

"Disappeared." Knox stared at her. "What happened to her?"

"No one knows for sure." Leni's haunted gaze said she had her share of suspicions. "I don't have time to get into any of this right now. I need to call my friend Carla and let her know I won't be able to pick up Riley tonight after all."

"The boy is with your friend now?"

"Yes. He and I live in my family's old house behind the diner, but Carla brings him to her place after school on weekdays so I can work. She's his first-grade teacher. I was on my way to pick him up when this happened," she said, gesturing toward the steep ravine.

Knox's sigh rolled between his lips, the steam of his breath drifting on the cold night breeze.

He couldn't leave Leni standing at the bottom of a thorny incline in the snow—no matter how much he wanted to assure himself it was the best thing for both of them if he did.

He watched her reach into her jacket pocket to pull out her phone.

"There's no need to call your friend."

"What are you talking about? I have to—" Leni's argument cut off on a gasp when Knox scooped her into his arms. "What the hell do you think you're doing?"

"Taking you out of this storm," he said. "Then I'm going to get your truck out of the ravine so we can go pick up the kid."

CHAPTER 5

When Knox said he was going to get the Bronco out of the ravine, Leni didn't realize he meant he was going to do it with his bare hands.

After carrying her up to the road via some kind of Superman move, it shouldn't have surprised her to realize the Breed male also possessed immense, inhuman strength.

It probably shouldn't have turned her on, either, but it was impossible to not be impressed and more than a little awed by him. Knox had treated her so gently, yet those same strong hands and muscled arms were capable of moving in excess of a couple tons of metal and machinery as if he'd been pushing a kid's toy.

Uphill.

In the middle of a punishing blizzard.

He'd done it all without her asking, and without seeming to expect a thing in return.

At least, so far.

Leni couldn't keep her gaze from straying to him where he sat grimly behind the wheel, navigating the drift-filled track of road. He had insisted on accompanying her to pick up Riley, even though she'd argued that Carla's house was less than a dozen miles from where she'd gone off the road.

"You really don't need to do this, you know. The Bronco's had better nights, but I'm perfectly capable of driving myself."

He didn't answer, just kept steering the truck through the snow and darkness, heading in the direction she'd said she needed to go. She got the sense he wasn't exactly thrilled to be chauffeuring her through the storm, but he hadn't been willing to leave her on the side of the road, either.

She would have been fine on her own. The accident had looked worse than it was and she'd walked away without a scratch, thanks to the shield of her secret ability. Not even the jagged branches that tore part of her flannel shirt open as she'd stumbled out of the vehicle had left a mark on her body.

Knox hadn't been overly talkative in the diner. Now, there was a gruffness about him—a stony detachment— that she couldn't ignore. It had set in almost immediately after he'd helped her away from the crash. As if his mind was somewhere else, his thoughts a thousand miles away from Parrish Falls.

Leni wondered if it had something to do with the name he'd shouted as he'd leapt into the ravine.

Abbie.

Was that the name of his Breedmate? He didn't seem settled enough to share an entire night with someone, let alone an eternal blood bond. In fact, settled was just about the last word Leni would use to describe him. Solitary. Restless. Unreadable. Remote.

But as she studied his stoic profile in the dim illumination of the dashboard, she mentally added another word to the list. Empty.

Because of Abbie, whoever she was?

Leni didn't think it was her place to ask. Nor did she expect he would tell her, even if she did bring it up.

His eyes were laser-trained on the slippery road ahead. His mouth a stern line above a square jaw that seemed to have been carved from granite. Normally, she was fine with a little silence, but there wasn't much that was normal about tonight.

"You know, if anyone had told me one night I'd be on the receiving end of a vehicular rescue by a Breed vampire in the middle of a Nor'easter, I would've told them they were crazy. Do you always go around saving damsels in distress?"

He swung a hard glance at her, something grim and dark in his eyes. "Never."

"Just my lucky night, huh?"

He grunted, about as chatty as a Terminator. She didn't miss his scowl in the second before he turned his gaze back to the road.

"You still haven't told me how you were able to find me back there. After you left the diner, I thought you'd be long gone from Parrish Falls."

"So did I. I had to make a stop on my way out. To feed."

Leni stared at him. "You mean you needed blood. From a living, breathing human."

He gave a nod, and the image of his mouth locked

on to someone's neck while he drank flooded her mind in an instant.

Not just anyone's neck. Hers. Although why she should imagine that, and why she should feel the mere idea of it like a current shot into her own veins, she didn't want to know.

Leni swallowed past the unnerving sensation, but only barely.

"Awfully quiet over there all of a sudden." He sounded vaguely amused as he glanced over at her. "I thought you didn't scare easily."

"I'm not scared." It was nothing close to that. Fear she could understand. Fear would be perfectly reasonable, given that she was alone with a strange and dangerous man on a dark, empty road. A man who had just reminded her in unmistakable terms that he was one of the most lethal predators in existence.

Instead, what she felt was an unfurling curiosity. Not only about Knox as a Breed male—the first one she'd ever met—but about the man he was as well.

"So, did you . . . um, feed?"

"Yes."

"From who? There aren't any houses between the diner and where I went into the ravine, and there definitely couldn't have been anyone walking around outside. Which only leaves Milo Cobb at the gas station."

"Skinny guy with questionable hair choices and a prescription drug habit?"

"That's him." Leni pivoted in her seat. "You could tell he's an addict?"

"Among other things."

"What do you mean, other things? How do you know?"

"Everyone wears their sins on their heart. Including Milo."

"Such as?"

"He's been stealing from his grandmother for years. First, it was the pain pills she needed following her cancer surgery. Now, it's cash and her social security checks."

Leni swore softly. "He lives with her. Sarah Cobb is one of the nicest people you'll ever meet. She's been taking care of Milo since he was a baby."

Knox's dispassionate shrug said he was merely reporting the facts.

"And you know all of this just by drinking his blood?"

"No. I'm not a blood reader. That's not my ability. When I touch someone, I see their sins. I'm not talking about the small things. I mean the ones that scorch a soul. I feel all of their deepest shames that never go away."

God, it sounded like a terrible gift to have. What kind of burden must it be for Knox to have spent his entire existence saddled with that kind of knowledge? Or to be aware that every touch could open a door onto hideous truths he had no choice but to see?

"I think if I had that ability, I'd never want to touch anyone."

He didn't answer. And in his silence, she couldn't help recalling that back in the diner, he had touched her too. She could still feel the hum of electricity their brief contact had spurred inside her.

"We shook hands earlier tonight. Did you feel all of my sins too?"

She was almost afraid to ask. Especially when she

was hiding the fact that she, too, had an unusual, unique gift. Aside from that secret and the fact that she'd been born a Breedmate, Leni had to believe she'd committed hundreds of small sins in her twenty-seven years.

Including more than a few impure thoughts tonight alone when it came to Knox.

He swiveled his head toward her, studying her for a long moment. "When I touched your hand, all I felt was you."

While she was relieved, he sounded anything but happy. In the semidarkness of the vehicle, his icy blue-gray eyes smoldered with banked embers. On a curse, he yanked his attention back to the road. He drove in silence again, a tendon pulsing beneath the dark whiskers that shadowed his cheeks.

His grip was bare on the steering wheel, his gloves folded on top of the dashboard. The *dermaglyphs* on the backs of his strong hands had first caught Leni's eye in the diner. Now they drew her gaze again. She knew the changeable Breed skin markings functioned as emotional barometers. At the moment, Knox's *glyphs* were filling with traces of dark colors, making the interlocking swirls and flourishes appear to come alive.

As cool and in control as he seemed there was an undercurrent of violence to him, even in his stillness. Like a viper waiting to strike.

He was the most dangerous thing to blow through Parrish Falls in all her recollection, and yet tonight he'd proven to be her biggest ally. Even if he seemed less than overjoyed about that with every passing minute.

She thought back to his conversation with Sheriff Barstow, all of his cagey non-answers about where he'd come from and where he was heading. No doubt, a man like Knox didn't have to explain himself to anyone. But still, she wondered.

She glanced at his nearly pristine black parka and his big boots, also new-looking, which seemed more suited for a hiking trail than a hundred-mile trek into the harsh back country.

"What are you doing this far north, Knox? It's obvious you're not from anywhere around here."

"Is it?"

"Yeah, it is." She pivoted on the seat to face him. "So, where'd you come from?"

"Medway, over at the Interstate."

"I mean before that." On a short exhalation, she tilted her head in challenge. "You don't sound like you're from Maine or anywhere else in New England. You don't look like it, either."

"That so." At first, she thought it was all the reply he was going to give her. For a long while he said nothing, his silence unreadable as he steered the truck past a drifted section of the narrowed two-lane. "I've been on the road for the past five months."

"That's a long time."

He shrugged dismissively, still staring at the road ahead of them. "I prefer to keep moving."

Looking at him, she found it hard to picture him idling anywhere for long. His big body radiated a restless, almost volatile, energy. Like a force of nature, something wild and unstoppable. Something untamed.

The exact opposite of her.

She had always been the steady one in the midst of turbulence and trouble, the one who took care of others first.

The one who stayed.

She studied Knox's stoic profile in the darkness. "I've never been anywhere else but here. I can't imagine being away from my home for so long."

It was impossible to say that without thinking about her sister. She'd been gone nearly five-and-a-half years now. Long enough for everyone in town to have written her off for good. But not Leni. She couldn't bear to think Shannon could truly be gone.

And so she stayed.

Even when in her heart she knew the only way to truly shield Riley from his violent father and the rest of the Parrish clan was to take him as far away from Parrish Falls as she could.

But where would she go?

How would Shannon ever find them if Leni and Riley didn't wait for her?

She would stay as long as it took for her sister to come home. And until that time, she would do whatever she had to in order to keep her sister's child safe. Even if she had to take on Travis Parrish, his family, and the whole damn town.

With her thoughts turning too dark, Leni swallowed past them. "So, where is your home, Knox?"

"Wherever my boots take me."

He said it matter-of-factly, no emotion at all. Yet his eyes said something different. Haunted, focused on some nebulous point in the distance. And now, she wondered. Was all of his relentless forward motion merely a habit to keep moving as he'd claimed, or a reluctance to reflect on what lay behind him?

Just when she was tempted to ask, his deep voice broke the quiet.

"The longest I've ever stayed anywhere by choice

was Florida."

She gaped at him. "The Sunshine State? That's a risky choice for a member of the Breed, especially one with the kind of *dermaglyphs* you have. You're Gen One, aren't you?"

He swiveled a narrow stare at her. "I didn't expect you to know so much about my kind."

She shrugged. "Just because you're possibly the first Breed male to come through Parrish Falls in recent memory doesn't mean we've never heard of the internet or national news."

He chuckled. It was a rusty sound, but she liked it. She liked the way his lips quirked with the hint of a smile as he resumed his focus on the drive.

Leni had her own reasons for taking an interest in his kind, but Knox didn't need to know anything about the Breedmate mark she'd been born with. Her mother had cautioned her all her life to keep that part of her a secret from the outside world.

Apart from her mom and her best friend, Carla Hansen, Leni's grandmother and sister were the only other people who knew that her father had been something other than human. Not Breed, but another kind of immortal. Leni never knew him. She had grown up knowing she was different, knowing she belonged to two worlds, yet feeling somehow separated from either one.

Knox was the closest she had ever come to glimpsing that other side.

In the diner she had placed him close to her age, despite the jaded, world-weary air about him. If he was first-generation Breed, he easily could have been born centuries ago.

"Are you really old, Knox?"

He exhaled a wry noise. "You sure like to talk. You ask a lot of questions too."

"Sorry." She shook her head and leaned back in the passenger seat. "You don't have to answer. I'm just . . . curious."

"I'm not as old as most Gen Ones," he said after a moment. "I was born a Hunter."

Leni swallowed. She knew the awful term—and the basics of what it implied. "You were part of that secret genetics program?"

He scoffed under his breath. "Genetics program. Is that what they call it on the news and internet? Dragos's labs were a prison. My Hunter brothers and I were enslaved to the program."

"I'm sorry, Knox."

He lifted his shoulder. "No reason to be."

But she was. Leni knew only the cursory details, but it was enough to send a chill into her veins. Young Breed boys created and raised in a laboratory, deprived of caring or contact, punished for any show of emotion. Shackled into obedience by collars containing concentrated ultraviolet light, which could be detonated on their master's whim or command.

The Hunters were bred to be the strongest, most merciless Breed soldiers in existence. Trained killers. A madman's personal army.

Brutal, highly skilled assassins.

No wonder Knox hadn't flinched with Dwight in the diner tonight. No wonder he seemed to generate a cold, unmistakable menace simply by being in the room. She could only imagine what a man like Knox could do to anyone who truly crossed him.

He was more than dangerous.

He was death.

Why the idea didn't send a jolt of terror through her, she didn't want to know.

Nor did she want to admit all of the hundreds of questions that were now swirling in her mind. Things she had no right considering and couldn't ask.

Terrible, selfish wishes she didn't dare speak out loud.

Pulling her gaze away from Knox, she stared out the window into the endless night that surrounded her. She had never been afraid to face the dark on her own before.

She told herself she wasn't now, either.

No matter what the haunted reflection staring back at her seemed to say.

CHAPTER 6

If he'd been looking for a way to silence her probing questions and curiosity, Knox figured he'd found it. Leni clammed up tight after he told her he was a Hunter.

She'd hardly blinked in the diner when she realized he was Breed, but the newsflash that he had been born one of the most feared and reviled members of his race had caused an almost palpable shift in the air between them. Then again, there were few people—human or Breed—who would relish the idea of sitting beside one of Dragos's notorious Hunters.

And Knox had been one of the best, most prolific, assassins deployed by his Master's command.

That part of his life was ancient history now. Not so ancient that he didn't feel a strong urge to deliver some payback on Dwight Parrish for sending Leni and her vehicle off the road.

The fact that she'd come out of it miraculously unscathed was about the only thing keeping the murderous side of him in check.

Barely.

Knox glanced at her. She stared out the passenger window, looking vulnerable and alone for the first time since he'd met her. No question, she knew how to take care of herself. He'd seen that in the diner. She was obviously smart and capable, with the spine and stubbornness to match.

But none of that had kept her out of the ravine tonight.

What would happen once Dwight Parrish's brother came home from prison? A man willing to assault her sister probably wouldn't hesitate to hurt Leni if things took a bad turn between them.

Fuck. Knox didn't even want to think about it. His hands tightened on the steering wheel, rage simmering in his veins.

Not good. Leni and her problems had nothing to do with him. He meant it when he told her he wasn't in the habit of rescuing damsels in distress. Hell, far from it.

Abbie was proof enough of that. He hadn't been there in time to save her. Memories of that night were never far from his thoughts. The tropical storm, the awful road conditions . . . the eighteen-wheeler that lost control and plowed into her vehicle.

He had allowed himself to care for someone, to feel, only once in the two decades since his escape from the Hunter program. He had let his guard down with Abbie and fate had kicked him in teeth by ripping her away from him. So, no. He had no interest in getting tangled up in anyone's problems. He had no intention of allowing himself to be that weak ever again.

Which meant the sooner he could put his boots on a path away from Parrish Falls, the better.

Knox navigated the slippery track of road, the Bronco's engine droning under the slap of the wipers and the tick of icy snowflakes hitting the windshield.

"That's my friend's place up there on the right."

Leni pointed to an old gray-shingled Cape Cod. It had only a handful of neighbors, each with a couple acres of land and dozens of tall pines. Flood lights illuminated the short driveway and the blanket of snow that covered the ground in all directions.

"Park on the side of the house. If Carla sees you or the condition of my truck, I'll have a hundred questions to answer before she lets me leave. Right now, I just want to get Riley home safe and in bed."

Knox drove to where she instructed, and she hopped out as soon as the truck came to a stop. Jogging through the dark and the flying snow, she slipped into the house through an apparently unlocked front door.

Knox scowled. Lax security was a given in small towns, but that didn't mean he had to like it. He stared holes into the house, his combat instincts on full alert for the handful of minutes it took before Leni appeared at the door again.

She returned carrying a sleeping blond-haired boy he guessed to be about five or six years old. The kid was draped over her shoulder like a sack of potatoes in his winter coat and pajamas, out cold as she hurried outside with him back to the truck.

Knox stayed behind the wheel as she'd asked, watching her fasten the unconscious boy into the booster contraption behind the passenger seat. Nothing seemed to stir the kid until Leni arranged his head against a plush teddy bear as a makeshift pillow. His eyes fluttered open, still heavy with the sleep of childhood.

"It's okay, buddy." Leni soothed him with a gentle kiss to his forehead. "We'll be home in a minute."

The sound of her voice instantly settled him. Letting go of a deep sigh, he drifted back into a deep sleep.

Knox felt anything but relaxed as he observed Leni's tender care with her nephew. She was patient and warm, her kindness toward the child tugging at a place inside Knox he didn't want to acknowledge.

"All set?" he asked gruffly, his deep voice sounding more annoyed than intended.

Leni nodded, then closed the back door and climbed into her seat up front. They made the drive back to the diner in silence. Her house stood behind it, a tidy old two-story, hip-roofed farmhouse with white wood siding. He parked in front of the detached one-car garage around back, then got out and followed her to the rear door of the house to make sure she and Riley got inside safely.

He should have stopped there.

He should have walked right back out the door as soon as Leni disappeared through the kitchen and went upstairs to put the boy to bed. Instead, he prowled the lower level of her home, checking all points of entry and frowning at the lack of sufficient security.

No deadbolts on either door. Aged hardware on what appeared to be ancient, original windows in each ground-floor room of the cozy, but easily breachable, old farmhouse.

The place had likely been standing for several generations much the same as it was now. Sturdy and lived in, a comfortable home filled with modest furnishings and rug-covered wood-plank floors that had probably felt the traffic of countless footsteps over the decades.

What Knox saw was an unprotected domicile that wouldn't hold against the local dogcatcher, let alone a convicted felon with an ax to grind. He wandered farther inside, his eye drawn to the numerous collections of photographs that decorated each room in the house.

Leni evidently lived alone with her young nephew, but she had surrounded herself with mementos of a loving, happy family. Snapshots of smiling faces preserved in whimsical frames on the fireplace mantel and in small groupings on end tables and other surfaces. Crafts and artwork created by a child's hands. Soft, homemade knit blankets draped neatly over the backs of the sofa and the antique rocking chair that sat in the corner of the living room.

Knox bit off a low curse. He felt like an intruder invading her private space, interrupting her life.

He'd seen her and the boy home safely. It was long past time for him to be gone.

He turned, intending to head back into the kitchen and into the night before Leni came back down. But at the same instant, floorboards creaked quietly on the stairs. For a moment, he considered using his Breed genetics to speed him out of there, but it wasn't in his DNA to run away from danger.

Not even when it took the form of a beautiful, hazel-eyed brunette.

"You're still here." She descended off the last step and approached him in the living room. "I thought you might've left already."

"I was just on my way."

"Okay." She gave him a faint nod, but the way she held her mouth made him think she had something more to say. "Where will you go?"

"Haven't decided. Montreal, probably."

"Do you have friends there? Someone you'll stay with?"

"No." He wasn't sure if she was asking for a reason, or if this was merely her seemingly endless curiosity sparking back to life. "No friends there. In case you haven't noticed, I'm not really the social type."

"I've noticed." She glanced down, and the retreat of her normally forthright stare put a tick of concern in his veins.

Lenora Calhoun was nervous, uncertain. More than that; she was afraid. Since she was trying to make conversation, he didn't think her fear extended to him right now, but there was no mistaking the current of anxiety rolling off her.

"Knox, if I wanted to reach you for some reason . . . is there some way I could find you?"

He felt a tendon begin to pulse in his cheek. "Why would you want to do that?"

"I mean, if I needed your help."

He didn't like the sound of that. The pulse in his cheek became a dull throb. "My help."

At his toneless echo, those clear autumn-hued eyes lifted, meeting his glower. "I've been thinking about what you said in the truck. About what you are."

54

He said nothing, holding her gaze and all but daring her to say the words.

"You told me you're an assassin, Knox."

"Was. I left the program behind me twenty years ago."

"But you still have those . . . skills?"

"What exactly are you asking, Lenora?"

She pivoted away from him without answering, drifting over to a decorative table in the corner, the one that had a collection of photos documenting her nephew's birthdays. Leni and a pair of older women were in several of the earlier pictures. Notably absent in the little boy's annual celebrations was the pretty blonde holding him in a hospital snapshot taken on the day he'd been born.

Knox hadn't been able to purge Leni's description of what had been done to her sister. A beating so violent it left her unconscious.

It was all too easy for Knox to imagine the same thing could happen to Leni.

She absently touched the frame of the photo of her sister and the sleeping infant in her arms.

"I'm not worried about myself. Honestly, I'm not. But I'll do anything to protect Riley." She glanced over her shoulder at him. "I can't let Shannon's attacker ever get his hands on that child. I won't, Knox. I don't care what it takes."

He stared at her. "Are you asking me to kill Travis Parrish for you?"

She winced. A short sigh gusted out of her as she immediately dropped her gaze. "I don't know."

"You don't know." Christ, she couldn't even force herself to say the words. How did she think she'd be able to live with the reality of calling for someone's murder when she didn't have the stomach to speak as much as the idea out loud?

Knox wasn't about to agree to her request, no matter how much personal pleasure he might take in ridding the world of a man who apparently had no qualms about brutalizing an innocent woman. And Knox had no doubt that eliminating the threat of Travis Parrish would only invite more trouble on Leni and the boy.

"You think the rest of the Parrishes would just roll over if Travis was gone? You think they'd just stand down, let you and the boy go on living your lives in peace?" He moved closer to her, needing her to look him in the eye and understand—truly understand—what she was asking. "I'd have to kill them all, Leni. I'd probably have to kill anyone loyal to them too. That's what it would take. Nothing less."

"Oh, God." She swallowed, already shaking her head as he spoke. "No, that's not what I want. I may not have much reason to like any of the Parrishes, but I don't want to be as bad as they are. Or worse."

"I know you don't." Knox took another step toward her. "And I won't be the one to put that sin on your conscience, even if you ask me to."

He meant that. Yet even as he said it, there was a part of him that was ready to protect her. He was no hero by a longshot, but was he the kind of cold bastard who could walk away and leave an innocent woman and child to their own defenses? He wanted to tell himself he was. For his own peace of mind, if nothing else.

But there would be no peace of mind if he abandoned Leni and never looked back.

After feeling her goodness when he touched her hand in the diner, after seeing her with Riley, he didn't know how he was going to turn a blind eye to the situation. Despite what he told her, the trained killer in him wouldn't take much convincing to tear through the entire Parrish family and the rest of the town if any of them posed a threat to her.

Fuck.

Her battle wasn't his to fight. Her troubles didn't belong to him, no more than she did. The smartest, easiest thing he could do for himself right now was get back on the road, and soon.

Then again, he wasn't the only one who should be thinking about leaving Parrish Falls.

"If making sure the Parrishes can't get their hands on the boy is really what you want, then you can't stay here. Find somewhere else to go, Lenora, somewhere you can start over. And I mean do it before Travis comes home."

She frowned. He didn't like seeing that stubborn glint sparking in her eyes. "I'm not leaving. I've lived in this town all my life. Five generations of my family have lived in this house. My grandparents built that diner out there."

"They're just buildings," Knox said. "Parrish Falls is just a town, like any other."

"No." Her chin tilted upward, her mouth pressing flat. "I won't leave. I can't."

"Yes, you can. You can do it right now. Pack a bag, put the boy in your truck, and go."

"I'm not going to run."

"Not even if staying means you might get hurt? Or worse?"

"I told you, I'm not concerned about something happening to me. I can handle whatever Travis or his family thinks they can do to me."

Knox scoffed. "Come on, Leni. You're smarter than this. You got lucky out there on the road tonight, but you have to know pride won't protect you or Riley in the long run."

"It's not about my pride," she fired back, desperation edging into her voice. "I can't leave. I need to stay for my sister. Until Shannon comes home, Riley and I are staying put right here where she can find us."

Her breathing had increased along with her pulse. Knox was close enough that he could hear the rapid pound of her heartbeat, the rush of blood racing through her veins. Yes, she was afraid. Maybe not for herself, as she'd insisted, but definitely for her little nephew.

And now he realized just how afraid she was for her sibling too.

"You're waiting around for a sister you haven't seen or heard from in years?"

"Yes. I am."

Knox let go of a curse. He had to admire her loyalty, no matter how futile it might be. "You said she left a few months after her son was born."

"Shannon didn't leave. She vanished. There's a difference."

"Only in the semantics. The net outcome is the same." He couldn't curb the cold frankness in his tone. Nor the sharpness of the truth she seemed reluctant to accept. "She's gone, Leni. After six years, I'd say she's not likely coming back."

She flinched as if he'd physically struck her. "Fuck you. You don't know that. You don't know a damn thing about me or my family."

No, he didn't. But his soldier's mind dealt in logic, not emotion.

If Leni needed reassuring, unfortunately she wouldn't get it from him. He wasn't the type to coddle or soothe. He didn't know how. And he sure as hell wasn't going to prop her up with false hope. Not when she was so afraid of Travis Parrish's return that she was willing to appeal for help from someone like Knox.

"I should go."

She stared at him, her gaze bleak. Wounded. "I think that's probably a good idea, Knox."

It was. He knew that. Yet his boots remained rooted where he stood.

Damn it, why hadn't he just kept walking right on past her diner earlier tonight? He'd already be across the border into Canada by now, instead of standing alone with Leni in the heat of her warmly lit living room, her beautiful face flushed with anger and a mounting regret.

He needed distance now, before he let his attraction to her spiral any further out of control. Leaving was the best thing for him to do for both of them.

Instead, he moved toward her, not stopping until there were only scant inches separating her body from his.

She didn't retreat. Maybe if she had, he would have found the scrap of discipline he needed—the smallest measure of honor—to prevent his hand from reaching up to stroke her cheek.

Her skin was as soft as velvet, infinitely warm.

His Breed gift had made him reluctant to touch from the time it first manifested in him as a child. Its silence when he was touching Leni felt like a balm. So much so, it was next to impossible for him to draw his hand away from her now.

He couldn't shake the memory of finding her staggering out of her crashed vehicle in the ravine. Unresolved fury for the bastard who'd done it simmered like acid in his veins.

Knox had killed for less offenses than Dwight Parrish's tonight. Leni had dismissed the incident as if it were merely par for the course, but he couldn't deny the urge to make the asshole pay in blood for the way he'd antagonized her.

Which was just more evidence that it was long past time for him to get out of her life.

Because what he'd told her was true. With men like that, taking on one meant going to war with the entire clan. As satisfying as he might find both prospects, it would only create added problems for Leni and her nephew. Especially when she was so stubbornly determined to remain in Parrish Falls.

And every minute he allowed himself to get lost in the stoic, unshakable grace of Leni's eyes, the more tempting it was to wake the killer inside him and let the ashes fall where they may.

But she wasn't his to protect. Not his to savor right now, either.

With a low rumble of warning curling up from his chest, Knox pulled his hand away from her cheek.

"You take care of yourself, Lenora Calhoun."

A quiet sigh leaked out of her. She nodded, crossing her arms over her chest. "Goodbye, Knox."

He stepped back, needing the space more than he cared to let on. For the first time since she walked into the room, he let his gaze drop from her face. His sight snagged on the tattered hem of her plaid shirt. The flannel had several long gashes in it near her abdomen.

He hadn't noticed it until just now.

"Did that happen in the ravine?" When he glanced up at her face again, her cheeks went ashen. "You told me you weren't hurt."

She shook her head abruptly. "I wasn't."

He knew that was true. He would have smelled her blood if she'd been cut. Yet her ruined shirt indicated otherwise. It had been ripped by jagged branches, a few stray pine needles still embedded in the flannel.

She started to turn away from him.

"Leni." He reached for her arm and pivoted her back around to face him. "Let me see."

"No." She pulled out of his loose grasp and her arms went in front of her like a shield. "I told you I was fine."

His vision flashed amber at her lie. "I know what you told me. I want to know what you're hiding now."

"Nothing."

He took her in both hands now, forcing her to face him. Then he lifted the torn hem of the shirt and his burning gaze settled on the creamy planes of her belly. Desire flared in him as he ran his fingers over her stomach, searching for the answer to a question he was reluctant to ask.

Then he found it.

A small red mark, the only flaw on her otherwise pristine skin.

Not an injury. That much had been true.

Nothing close to an imperfection, either.

His fangs erupted from his gums as he stared at the diminutive teardrop-and-crescent-moon symbol.

"Holy hell." He glowered up at her. "You're a Breedmate."

CHAPTER 7

Leni couldn't move, not even when it seemed like the smartest thing for her to do.

"A fucking Breedmate." Knox growled the words as he stared at her, his expression shocked, confused. Furious as hell.

His eyes gripped her in their molten glow. She'd never seen amber fire burning up someone's irises before. She'd never seen a pair of pupils transform from humanlike circles to otherworldly, vertical slits. Behind Knox's parted lips, the sharp tips of his fangs glinted bright white, as sharp as daggers.

No article or image she'd ever seen could have prepared her for the reality of facing a livid Breed male in the flesh. But it was the anger in the man who scared her more than the outward evidence of what he truly was.

"Jesus Christ, Leni. Were you going to say anything to me about this at all?"

"No."

At her denial, he cursed again, more vividly this time. He still hadn't let go of her. With one hand grasped around her arm and the other now fisted in the shredded hem of her loose flannel shirt, Knox drew in a breath through flared nostrils.

Everywhere he'd touched her Leni's skin felt seared, stretched too tight. Part of her bristled at his arrogance as he had run his fingers over her bared stomach, searching for the mark she'd been foolish to try to conceal from him.

He'd had no right. Not to touch her, nor to glower at her in accusation.

He'd had no right to lay his palm so tenderly against her face in the moments before, either, but the heat that touch had stoked inside her had less to do with outrage than she cared to admit.

She hadn't missed the crackle of hot sparks in his eyes when he'd caressed her cheek. Had he wanted to kiss her? She felt certain he had. Despite his outrage, every instinct in her body clenched with the anticipation that he might want to kiss her now, too.

Kiss her or kill her, she couldn't be sure.

Either option should have given her plenty of reason to be afraid.

Knox released her on a snarl. Under his lowered brows, his fiery eyes were narrowed and scorching. "This is why you don't have a scratch on you. Your Breedmate gift. It's self-healing, isn't it?"

"Not healing. It's different from that."

"Different how?"

"I can't be harmed." She lifted her shoulder, uncertain how to explain the extraordinary power that had been part of her all her life. "Whenever I'm in physical danger, my body creates a kind of shield around me. Nothing can penetrate it."

He scoffed. "No wonder you're not afraid of anything."

"That's not true." She shook her head. "I am afraid, Knox—for Riley. My ability is no use to him. It only protects me, not anyone else."

"Fuck." He took a step back, and she could feel his displeasure and frustration rolling off him. "What about your sister? Was she a Breedmate too?"

"Shannon is human," Leni said, refusing to talk about her missing sibling in anything but the present tense. "We're half-sisters. Her father was a local man. Mine was something . . . other."

Knox grunted. "Are you in touch with him?"

"No. I never knew my father."

"Where is he now?"

"I have no idea. My mom was in Portland on vacation with some friends when she met him. He was living on a large sailboat then, traveling the world. Apparently, he wasn't the type to stay put in one place for long. Why do you want to know?"

"Because you and the boy need somewhere safe to go. You need to be with someone who can protect you."

"I already told you, I'm not going anywhere. I'm not leaving Parrish Falls."

Knox's gaze flared brighter with the curse that gusted between his teeth and fangs. "You're a fool if you stay, Lenora. From everything I've heard and seen tonight, you and I both know it's going to be that kid upstairs who pays the price if things escalate between you and the Parrishes."

Leni's hackles rose as he spoke. In her heart, she knew he was right. For six years, she'd known eventually she would have to choose between keeping her sister's memory alive and keeping her nephew away from the brutal man who'd fathered him.

But dammit, she wasn't ready to let go of Shannon.

She wasn't ready to allow herself to imagine her sister was truly gone.

"I'll find a way to keep Riley safe."

"What about yourself?" he demanded. "Just because you can't be physically harmed doesn't mean there aren't other ways to hurt you. How are you going to feel when that boy is ripped away from you? Because you know it's going to happen. If you didn't, you wouldn't have asked me to kill Travis Parrish for you."

God, she hated the sound of that. Hated to think how low she might be willing to stoop out of love for the sweet little boy sleeping so innocently upstairs. But she couldn't deny it. She couldn't pretend she wouldn't be capable of anything if it meant keeping him safe.

"I'll manage on my own. I always have." She folded her arms, squaring off against the fuming Breed male in front of her. "Thanks for the advice, but we're not your problem, Knox."

He scoffed under his breath. "Yeah. That's what I've been telling myself all night. I should've kept walking right past this damn town. My first mistake was stepping inside your diner tonight. My second one, stopping to pull you out of that ravine. But the biggest mistake of the night is all yours, Leni."

He took a step toward her, furious and immense. Seething with a dangerous, animal rage.

A low growl rumbled deep inside him, yet another reminder that he was far from human. Especially now, when his reaction to her Breedmate mark still had him pulsing with aggression and barely contained rage.

"You knew what I was," he said, his deep voice deceptively calm, given the intensity of the rest of him. "You recognized I was Breed as soon as you saw the *glyphs* on my hand. You should've steered clear, Leni. You should've told me to get the fuck out of that booth, not invite me to stay. I would've left this town and never looked back."

She swallowed as he closed the meager distance between them.

Apparently, she had lost all grip on her sanity tonight. Because instead of fearing the predator in Knox now, she stood firm against him. Refusing to back down.

God, even worse, she couldn't stop wondering what it might feel like to be caught in those strong arms, pressed against all of that power.

Yep, crazy. Along with reckless and stupid.

He was right. She had made a terrible mistake tonight. She had enough problems in her life right now without inviting this snarling, dangerous new one any closer.

Not that he wanted that, either.

His fury pulsed off him, palpable and hot.

Leni lifted her chin. "I want you to leave now, Knox."

A wry smile twisted his mouth as he slowly shook his head. "No, you don't. But you damn well should."

Another step forward and there was no room between them. Nowhere to run. No space to mask the rapid tempo of her breathing or the heavy thud of her heart beating in her breast.

When she thought he might reach out to her face, instead his hand stayed low, moving aside the torn hem of her shirt. He stared at her Breedmate mark once more, a tendon going tight in the side of his dark, beard-shadowed cheek.

His gaze lifted to hers, those molten irises scorching her all over again. They mesmerized her. Unearthly and terrifying, yet beautiful. Just like the man himself.

No, she corrected, needing to find some distance here, not only from the intensity of his nearness, but from the unsettling heat of the reaction he awakened in her.

That uninvited warmth licked along her limbs and up her nape, while inside her, awareness pooled, sending that same fire into every vein and fiber of her body. It was electric, the energy that ignited so swiftly between them. It was undeniable. Perhaps even for Knox.

As he stared at her, a low curse fell from between his parted lips. Then he backed off, allowing a chill to fill the space he'd just occupied.

"We've both made enough mistakes we can't take back now," he uttered tersely. "I'm sure as fuck not going to add another one to that list now."

If he expected her to answer, she couldn't. Breathing was about all she could manage with the way her heart was galloping against her ribs.

Knox swore again, scrubbing a big hand over the roughened shadows of his jaw. "Lock your doors, Lenora. Stay put."

He gave her the curt order, then pivoted away from her and started walking toward the back door in the kitchen.

She followed after him, confused. "Wh-where are you going? Knox, what are you going to do?"

He didn't answer.

He didn't even bother to turn around before he stalked out of the house and into the howling blizzard outside.

Leni rushed to the door behind him, but he was already gone.

Vanished in that next instant, nothing but darkness and blowing snow in his wake.

CHAPTER 8

Cold wind buffeted him as he took off on foot through the storm.

His boots chewed up the snow-drifted terrain between Leni's house behind the diner and the vast expanse of wild, open forest that surrounded it. He needed the frigid air to batter him, snap him back to his senses. Flying ice crystals and bracing gusts sandblasted his uncovered head and face as he ran. He relished the needle sting accompanying his every step.

Knox craved every bit of punishment the blizzard could deliver.

Anything to cool the unwanted desire he felt toward the woman he'd left confused and upset behind him.

Twice, he'd almost kissed her tonight. He hadn't counted that one among his list of mistakes he'd rattled off where she was concerned, but when it came to grenade-level bad moves, getting physically entangled with Leni had to rank right up at the top. Especially now.

Christ, what if he had decided to tap her carotid instead of feeding from the tattooed loser working at the gas station? One sip of Leni's blood and Knox would be shackled to her for as long as either of them continued to breathe.

A Breedmate, for fuck's sake.

He snarled at the notion, furious over the fact that she'd wanted to conceal it from him.

Right now, there was a part of him that wished like hell she'd been successful because everything changed when he spotted that mark.

He couldn't unsee it. Just like he couldn't deny that as special and rare as Lenora Calhoun seemed to him earlier tonight when he'd assumed she was fully human, that tiny teardrop-and-crescent moon stamp on her belly was irrefutable evidence that she was even more extraordinary than he could have ever guessed. A female to be protected, and cherished, no matter the cost.

It would take a Breed male with a more bankrupt sense of honor than his to pretend those things didn't matter.

He'd been wrestling with the idea of walking away even before he saw what she was. Afterward, none of his arguments for leaving held any weight at all.

He couldn't turn his back on Leni now. Nothing would convince him that she and the boy would be safer somewhere else—anywhere else—than Parrish Falls. Obviously, persuading her toward that fact was going to be a challenge. Unfortunately for him, until he could bring the stubbornly loyal female around to his logic,

Breed honor dictated he do whatever was in his power to ensure her protection.

Even if that was the last damn thing he wanted or needed in his life.

"Fuck." The curse exploded out of him on a puff of steam as he pushed deeper into the uninhabited woods, his path following the general direction of the main road through Parrish Falls. The land was treacherous, dense forest and jagged ledges that grew steeper as he neared the cut of the river.

Knox didn't slow for anything. He wasn't only trying to burn off the heat of a bad impulse; he was on the hunt.

Vibrating under the rush of the cold air and snow swirling around him, he caught the distant rumble of the prey he was after. The sound of the pickup's diesel engine carried on the night wind, the lone sign of life for several square miles in the midst of the howling storm.

Knox followed his ears, taking off in the direction of the engine's monotonous growl.

He found Dwight Parrish on the two-lane, rambling away from town at a steady clip on the newly plowed stretch of road. Knox used his Breed agility to keep pace with the vehicle, observing from atop a long ridge that ran parallel with the road below.

The plow blade was up, no longer in use. High-beams sliced the darkness, swerving back and forth with the careless, weaving motion of the truck. Inside the cab, music blared. Evidently, Parrish was finished for the night and heading home.

Or so Leni's tormentor might have thought.

Knox sped up on his jagged promontory over the road, a blur of motion that no human eye could track, especially not in the dark. He paused about a mile ahead of Parrish with plenty of time to look for the detour he was about to deliver.

And there it was. He smirked, eyeing the thick trunk of a fallen pine that leaned against its neighbor up ahead of him on the wooded ledge.

Knox waited until the pickup's headlights approached below.

Then he hefted the heavy, snow-sodden obstacle and threw it down onto the road, blocking the truck's path.

Parrish laid on the brakes so hard he nearly fishtailed right over the edge of the ravine on the other side of the narrow two-lane. Taillights flared bright red in the dark. Snow kicked up in an arcing fan behind the rear bumper while the protesting tires steamed and screeched as the truck stuttered to a halt on the ice.

Inside the closed cab, Parrish's scream rose over the thumping bass of the sound system.

Now that he was stopped, he lifted his head to peer out the windshield at the large projectile that nearly totaled him. At the same instant, Knox leapt down to the road in front of the truck. He tried not to smile at the look of stupefied shock on the human's bearded face.

Instead, he lowered his head in a charging stance and flashed the bastard his fangs.

Parrish's eyes went wide at the threat. Panicked, he dropped the silver liquor flask he'd been holding in his right hand and scrambled to reach for the gearshift. "Holy shit!"

With few options for escape that didn't involve taking out his front end trying to get past the tree trunk blocking the entire span of the road in front of him, or risking the steep drop into the ravine and riverbank on

LARA ADRIAN

the other side, Parrish chose to reverse course. The truck lurched backward, gasoline and exhaust smoke acrid against the freshness of the blizzard.

But it was going nowhere fast.

Knox had already leapfrogged to the back of the truck. Boots planted firmly, he pushed against the rear bumper, forcing the wheels to spin and whine on the ice.

Parrish gave up, grinding the gears as he started to put the truck into drive again.

Knox didn't allow him that chance to escape, either.

He flashed around to the driver's side window and dropped his knuckles against the glass. Parrish jumped, swiveling a cornered look at him.

"How does it feel, asshole?" Using the power of his mind, Knox locked the truck's doors and jammed the transmission into neutral.

"What the hell do you want from me?" Parrish yelled on the other side of the glass.

He was a big man, one not accustomed to being on the losing side of an argument. Beneath his fright, he was pissed off. The twist of his lips within the thick growth of his dark beard gave away his contempt. Although right now, it was fear that overrode everything else.

He dived to the other side of the cab as if he thought he could escape out the passenger door, but it was no use. The locks held firm under Knox's will. So did the gearshift, which didn't budge no matter how hard Parrish tried to yank it loose.

"Son of a bitch! What do you want?" Parrish barked from inside. He gestured aggressively, despite the look of worry in his glare. "You want to kill me, vampire? Just fucking do it!"

"You'll know when I've come to kill you," Knox replied with utter calm.

He started pushing the truck toward the opposite side of the two-lane, toward the sharp drop-off into the ravine and the deep, frozen river below.

"What are you doing?" Parrish asked, his big head swiveling to gauge Knox's intent. "Oh, fuck. You can't—"

"I can," Knox said.

He kept pushing, pivoting the heavy front end of the truck and its plow blade right to the edge. Then a bit more. The front bumper teetered there, one nudge away from a head-first crash down through the bracken.

"Before you think about causing any more problems for Lenora Calhoun, understand that there will be consequences now."

Parrish swallowed, anxious, impotent in his anger. His shiny new truck groaned as the edge of the shoulder began to give way beneath it.

Knox did smile now, baring the tips of his fangs. "I've decided to stick around town for a while, so that means you Parrishes are going to answer to me if anything happens to Leni or the boy. We clear?"

"This is about her?" Parrish sneered. "What the fuck does she mean to you?"

It was a good question, one Knox wasn't prepared to answer. Least of all to an asshole like Dwight Parrish.

Finished with their conversation, he gave the truck a hard shove. It dipped forward, a rocking lurch that wrung a low moan out of Parrish. Then gravity took hold of the truck and the man inside it. The shiny black pickup crashed down the embankment, branches raking the sides, bracken and old stumps crunching beneath the tires and undercarriage as the heavy vehicle rolled all the way down to the bottom of the incline and onto the frozen edge of the water.

Knox didn't free the locks until he heard the ice pop and crack as it began to give way and the front tires started to sink into the river. Parrish poured out as soon as he'd been freed.

Knox stared, unmoved. What he'd told the human was true. He hadn't come to kill him tonight.

Whether he would on another night would be up to the Parrishes.

Because he meant what he said to Leni back at her house. One dead Parrish would mean war with all of them.

Knox wouldn't go there unless they pushed him to, but he had just sent the first shot over their bow.

If they were smart, they'd heed it as the warning it was.

CHAPTER 9

The sun came up too early for Leni that next morning.

She'd barely slept, tossing and turning in her bed until only a short while before dawn. Every time she closed her eyes, she slipped into nightmares revolving around Travis Parrish. Wide awake, her thoughts returned repeatedly to the Breed male who'd entered her life as unexpectedly as he'd apparently left it last night.

It wasn't only her thoughts Knox had dominated. He had commandeered all of her senses too. Without trying, she could still feel the warmth of his hand pressed against her cheek. She could still see the molten amber of his transformed irises as he'd gazed at her, glowered at her, growled at her.

She could still see the torment in his handsome, unearthly face in those fraught seconds when she couldn't tell whether he wanted to take her in his arms or get as far away from her as he possibly could.

She figured she had his answer now. After waiting up confused and uncertain for a couple of hours following his furious departure, Leni had finally turned off the lights in the house and gone to bed.

Knox had to be miles into Canada by now. She told herself it was for the best.

She cringed in shame for what she'd asked of him last night, or tried to. Knox may have been raised and trained to kill, but that didn't give her the right to treat him as if he were some kind of weapon at her disposal. He'd been right to refuse. He had said no to prevent her from living with the guilt, but it didn't erase the fact that she'd asked.

As for the rest of it—the other impossible things she wanted from Knox, things he'd also refused her, much to her humiliation—she simply wanted to forget. Forget her selfish needs and desires, forget Knox, and move on.

God, what had gotten into her? Her first concern, the only one that truly mattered, was the little boy who depended on her for everything.

She sat up in her mussed bed, her thin cotton sleep tank askew over her bare breasts. She straightened it, then swung her legs over the edge of the mattress. From downstairs, the muffled sound of Riley's voice drifted toward her open bedroom. It wasn't unusual for him to walk around talking to himself, or, rather, to his favorite stuffed animals and an ever-changing roster of imaginary friends. Leni had learned to play along, even when it meant setting extra places at the dinner table or waiting a few extra minutes on those school day mornings when one of Riley's invisible friends had delayed him getting ready to leave.

There was no school today. The storm had passed overnight, but the weather had shut down services across the county for the rest of the week. Her phone had buzzed with a closed-classes notice sometime before dawn.

She didn't expect she'd have many customers at the diner today, either. Since she couldn't recall the last time she'd taken a full day off, Leni decided what she needed more than anything right now was some uninterrupted Riley time.

Gathering her dark hair into a messy knot atop her head, she slipped into a pair of loose cotton pajama bottoms and her fluffy winter slippers, then shuffled into the bathroom to brush her teeth and run a wet washcloth over her face. She groaned at her haggard reflection. It would take a hell of a lot more than toothpaste and cold water to fix the dark circles under her eyes and the sleep-deprived sag of her cheeks.

Maybe she could persuade Riley that their day of fun together should begin with a good, long nap. Yeah, not likely. His energy was about as tireless as his sharp little mind.

On a resigned sigh, she snatched a thick pink terry bathrobe from its hook near the door and pulled it around her as she headed downstairs to get her nephew's morning started with some breakfast and her own with a giant mug of strong coffee.

A tiny race car and a scattered handful of plastic action figures lay on the rug at the bottom of the staircase, evidence of an unfortunate traffic incident and a nonstop child's short attention span.

In the kitchen, she heard her nephew talking in between slurps and crunching while his spoon clicked against a hard plastic bowl. "Fred doesn't like cereal 'cause the milk gets warm too quick. Sometimes, Aunt Leni lets me put honey in my bowl when I share with him. Then he eats it all up, 'cause honey's his favorite thing ever."

Fred being his cherished stuffed bear, who had recently informed Riley—and by extension, Leni—that he was too grown up to be called Freddy Bear anymore. Leni stooped to pick up the mess at the bottom of the stairs, smiling in spite of herself. She wondered which imaginary friend had decided to join them for breakfast today. Would it be Tyler the invisible T-Rex, or someone new?

With the collection of toys gathered in her hands, she headed for the kitchen, trying to look serious.

"Riley, what did I tell you the other day about leaving toys where someone might step—"

She stopped short, her words drying up as her gaze collided with Knox's stormy blue eyes. He stood there as if he belonged, leaning casually against the sink across from her nephew who was seated at the small breakfast table, hunched over his cereal bowl.

Riley gave her a sheepish look. "I'm sorry, Aunt Leni. I forgot."

"It's um, it's okay, sweetie." She glanced away from him to stare incredulously at the Breed male in her kitchen. "What are you doing here?"

"That's my new friend, Knox," Riley said. His blond head tilted in question. "You mean, you can see him too, Aunt Leni?"

"Yes, I can see him," she said, trying to keep the confusion—and the disapproval—out of her voice. "How long have you been here inside my house? And how did you get in? I locked all the doors and windows after you left last night, just like you told me to do."

One dark brow arched in response. Of course, locks would be no use against him, against one of his kind. That probably should have given her more pause than it did.

At the moment, all she felt was surprise . . . and an annoying prickle of awareness as her eyes drank in his broad chest and shoulders under his dark shirt and the massive arms that were crossed casually under his pecs.

If Riley had seemed the least bit nervous around him or afraid, Leni would have already shown Knox to the door. But he seemed perfectly at ease, munching away on his cereal as if he and the immense Breed male were fast friends. Typical for her nephew. The boy had an uncanny openness, a trusting innocence, that Leni would do anything to preserve.

Railing in front of him at Knox for barging into their home might make her feel good, but it would only upset Riley.

She gave Knox a look she hoped would convey her feelings as she set her armful of toys on the table. An open box full of tools and bagged hardware supplies sat there too, dusty and faded with age. Leni recognized it immediately, and her chest squeezed at the reminder.

"What are you doing with these things?"

Knox took a step toward her. "I found them in the garage out back last night."

"I know where you found them. I asked what you think you're doing with them."

"I'm going to install them for you. A box of new deadbolts and window locks isn't doing anyone any good packed away in storage."

His deep voice was level and calm, no doubt for Riley's benefit, but she heard the gravity in his tone. She couldn't miss the sober warning in his eyes.

Something happened after he left her last night.

Something involving the Parrishes.

A chill seeped into her veins as she held his grim stare.

Riley abandoned his empty cereal bowl, getting up on his knees in his chair to try to peek into the grit-coated box. "What is all that stuff?"

"Just some things from the hardware store," Leni replied.

Shannon had purchased all of the tools and new locks only a few days before she disappeared. Leni hadn't discovered the stash until afterward. By then she didn't see the point of having it installed. She didn't think new locks would prevent the Parrishes from coming after what they wanted.

There was only one thing that would do that. And as Knox had said last night, if she meant to go up against one of the Parrishes, she had better be prepared to fight them all.

"Riley, if you're finished with your breakfast, please go brush your teeth."

"All right." He settled back on his chair, then hopped down with Freddy Bear under his arm. On his way past Knox, he turned a hopeful glance up at him. "Can I help you 'stall that stuff?"

"You'd better ask your aunt," he murmured. "After you brush those teeth."

Riley gave him a nod, then raced out to do as he'd been told.

"He's a good kid," Knox said.

"The best."

Leni retrieved the empty cereal bowl and carried it to the sink. Knox stepped aside as she rinsed out the last drops of milk and a few soggy oat rings at the bottom. She didn't want to react to the heat of his big body so close to her, or the power that emanated off him even when he was standing still.

Nor did she want to think about the fact that while he was sending her senses into hormonal overload, she was dressed like a middle-aged hausfrau with bags under her eyes and her hair in a bedraggled rat's nest on top of her head.

Lovely.

Not that she needed to worry about looking good for Knox. They weren't together and this wasn't an awkward morning-after, no matter how much it felt like one.

Now that she was thinking about it, seeing him inside her house after having only met last night felt a lot less awkward than it should.

She had to remind herself that she was still pissed off and confused after their heated conversation before he'd stalked out the back door and vanished like a ghost. Just because she wasn't half as furious to see him again now didn't mean she wasn't due some kind of explanation.

"Where did you go last night?"

There was no way to ask without sounding like a suspicious lover who was overstepping her bounds. Especially given that she was standing next to him

LARA ADRIAN

indignant in her pajamas and about ten yards of terrycloth. But so be it.

When he didn't answer, merely held her in an inscrutable stare that left her to imagine a dozen different scenarios, she pivoted to face him full-on and fisted her hand at her hip. She didn't miss the subtle quirk of his lips as he took her in.

She cleared her throat. "I'm sure you didn't spend half the night turning my garage inside out looking for handyman supplies."

"No." A sober, unsmiling reply.

"So, where did you go? Did you do . . . something I should know about?"

"I just needed to blow off some steam, Leni." His gaze lowered to her parted lips. "I think it should've been obvious we both needed to let things cool off last night."

He was right. If he hadn't gone, she felt all but certain she wouldn't have been able to put the brakes on whatever was happening between them. Part of her still wasn't certain she was capable. Seeing him with Riley just now hadn't helped dim her curiosity about Knox, or her desire.

She looked at him and struggled to see the dangerous predator he was. Now, with his eyes the dark blue-gray color of a thunderhead and his pupils fathomless ebony pools, he looked like a man, not a lethal Breed male. When he'd been listening patiently to Riley talk about his stuffed animal as if it were flesh-and-bone, Leni couldn't imagine viewing Knox as the trained assassin he'd been bred and raised to be.

He was steady and strong, powerful and commanding. He was a man she wanted to know better.

A man she desired, after having gone a very long time without knowing the feeling.

She let her hands fall slowly to her sides. "The way you left last night, I didn't think I'd ever see you again."

He frowned. "I'm sorry for the way I reacted. You deserved more from me than snarling and barked orders."

"It's okay," she said quietly. "I'm sorry I didn't tell you about my mark. It's become a habit to keep it a secret. No one in Parrish Falls knows except my best friend, Carla. My mom told me from the time I was a little girl that I shouldn't let on to anyone that I was different, not if I wanted any kind of normal life. Especially here. There's not a lot of room for different in this town."

He grunted. "Just one of many things about this place that needs to change."

"Why did you come back?"

It took him a long moment before he answered. "Because I couldn't leave. If I did and something happened to you . . ." His voice faded out with his deepening scowl. "I'm not going to let that happen, Leni. I can't now."

She swallowed, her heart thumping hard in her breast. As stoic and detached as she'd seen him last night, as enraged as he'd been at discovering she was a Breedmate, there was no denying his concern now.

"I've decided to stay in Parrish Falls for a while."

"How long?"

He shrugged noncommittally, but there was no lack of resolve in his expression. "For as long as it takes for me to be certain you'll be safe. I need Travis Parrish and the rest of his family to understand that both you and the boy are under my protection. And if anything happens to either of you, all of them will pay."

That heavy drum of her heart galloped harder as he spoke. She had never needed or wanted the things he was pledging now. Her pride fought against the idea, a denial pushing its way to the tip of her tongue. It melted away under the ferocity of Knox's solemn expression.

She couldn't believe he would alter his plans just to look out for her.

After the way he'd responded to seeing her Breedmate mark last night, she thought she'd forfeited not only his trust but any trace of respect he might have felt toward her.

Now this.

She wasn't sure what to say, how to accept the gift he had just offered her.

"Where will you stay, Knox?"

"As close as possible." He cleared his throat, a frown deepening between his dark brows. "I can install new locks on all your doors and windows, but doors and windows can be broken. Nothing, and no one, will get through me."

She gaped at him. "You mean you want to stay here? In my house?"

"It's not a matter of what I want. What matters is you, keeping you safe."

Her breath snagged on the ferocity of his tone. She had never been the kind of woman who swooned and sighed over flattering words or unexpected kindnesses. But this was different. This was life-and-death, and until a dozen hours or so ago, Knox had been a stranger, someone who hadn't even known she existed.

Now, he was pledging his protection to not only her, but Riley too.

"Why?" she murmured. "Why are you doing this, Knox? Last night, you said it was a mistake stopping in Parrish Falls. You said it was a mistake helping me out of the ravine. So, why do you want to help me now? What changed?"

"You," he growled. "You changed the second I saw that mark on your skin."

Leni's racing heartbeat stumbled into a crawl. The blood rushing in her veins slowed, cooled. "The mark on my stomach changed what you think of me?"

"It changes everything, Lenora." He practically bit the words off, his deep voice low and controlled. "You're a Breedmate. That's as sacred as blood to my kind. Women with that mark, your mark, are the most precious thing we have in this world. You're to be protected at all costs."

"Not me," Leni said, needing to be clear. "Any woman like me. Any woman born a Breedmate."

"That's right."

She drew back from him, averting her gaze, looking anywhere but into his intense eyes. She glanced down at her fluffy pink robe and her well-worn slippers edged in faux fur, and could hardly hold back her scoff.

The most precious thing in the world to his kind. Sacred. Ridiculous.

That's how she must look to him right now, not only because of the way she was dressed but because of the embarrassment staining her cheeks. It wasn't her he was concerned about. It was any woman like her. Any woman born with the same mark.

She wanted to refuse his help.

More than anything, she wanted to relieve him of his obligation and demand he leave her to handle her own problems and damn him along with his misguided sense of honor.

If she were living alone, she would have said all of that and more.

But what about Riley?

He was the one who needed Knox's protection the most. She could take care of herself, but how would she keep Shannon's son safe until she finally came home to be with him again?

She couldn't. Not by herself.

And no matter how much she wanted to refuse Knox's offer, she had to accept.

What she didn't have to do was play along with his reasons, or think of him as anything more than a boarder for however long she had to endure his presence.

"All right," she murmured, forcing herself to look up at him again. "There's a studio apartment with its own bathroom in the attic." She gestured to the back stairwell, accessible through the kitchen. "My mom used to rent the room out from time to time. You can stay up there."

He gave her a slight nod. "That will suffice. Thank you."

She took another step away from him, pulling the edges of her robe a little tighter around her. "And Knox, while you're here . . . stay away from Riley. He's a sweet little boy who thinks everyone is a friend. I don't want you making him promises you have no intention of keeping."

CHAPTER 10

Knox tightened the final screw on the window in the living room and tested the new lock's hold. Rock solid, as secure as it could be. Just like the near dozen others he'd installed and the pair of deadbolts now gleaming on the front and back doors of Leni's old house.

He had spent the better part of the day securing the place. All morning, heavy, low-lying gray clouds had hung in the winter sky, blotting out the worst of the sun's rays as he worked inside on the locks. The tall pine forest hemming in the old house on all sides provided ample shade for the few minutes in the afternoon when he'd been forced to step out into the daylight to complete his tasks.

As a Gen One, his Breed skin could only endure about ten minutes of ultraviolet exposure before it started to singe and burn away. He would have preferred to work at night, but even the risk of UV burns was preferable to hours of idle time.

And he'd damn well needed to keep himself busy after his conversation with Leni that morning.

Seeing her come downstairs looking bed-rumpled and vulnerable had hit his senses more powerfully than if she had prowled into the kitchen wearing nothing but skimpy lingerie. Not that he wanted to be picturing her like that, either.

His mouth watered at the mere idea. His cock was equally enthusiastic, pushing against the zipper of his jeans. He'd been half-hard most of the day, his body responding every time he glimpsed Leni outside in the yard with her nephew or walking through the house doing her best to pretend she didn't know, or care, that he was there.

He'd pissed her off when they talked earlier.

Informing her that he intended to temporarily install himself in her home at the same time he was putting in the new locks probably hadn't been the smoothest method. What did he know about smooth? Born a killer, raised without emotion and brutally disciplined for demonstrating even the slightest humanity, he and his Hunter brothers were about as far away from diplomatic as he could get.

Still, he had expected her to be at least a little grateful for his offer of protection, no matter how inelegantly he'd delivered it. He had expected to see Leni's relief, if nothing else.

Instead, when he tried to explain how paramount her wellbeing was to the entire Breed race, she'd frowned at him and backed away as though he had insulted her.

Females.

Knox shook his head and blew out a sharp breath. Maybe it was a good thing Leni had purposely avoided him all day. If he was going to stay under the same roof with her for any amount of time, the less they spent at each other's throats the better.

Which would also mean the less risk he ran of pulling the stubborn beauty into his arms. Or into his bed.

Shit. That was a mistake he would not allow himself to make, no matter how much everything male in him disagreed. He wanted Leni before he spotted her Breedmate mark. If the night had played out even a little differently than it had, he was all but certain they would have ended up naked in each other's arms.

Until he saw her Breedmate mark.

And thank fuck he had.

There was hardly a better deterrent for him than the sight of that tiny scarlet symbol on her creamy, velvet-soft skin. That teardrop-and-crescent-moon mark meant forever. It meant she deserved a lot more than anything he was capable of giving her, especially when he only planned to stay in town for however long it took him to either neutralize the threat of the Parrishes or convince her to leave. He'd be glad to take whichever came first.

Until then, Lenora Calhoun was strictly off-limits. Keeping his distance from her physically and emotionally would be the only way to keep his sanity and his focus. In his head, he knew that was the best course of action.

Now, he just had to convince his body to get on board with the plan.

Knox cleaned up his work area and tools, then headed through the house for the kitchen to put everything back in the garage where he'd found it. The aroma of warm food and spices and buttery bread wreathed the air as he approached.

Leni had started cooking several hours ago. Now, she and Riley were seated in a formal dining room off the kitchen, eating a roasted chicken dinner and biscuits on crisp white china.

It was a cozy, unrushed meal complete with cloth napkins and serving dishes for each item on the table. An extra plate with a honey-drizzled biscuit on it was situated in front of Riley's stuffed bear, who sat in the spindle-backed chair next to the boy.

Knox couldn't help but admire the life Leni was providing her nephew. The impressive dinner she made for him came after a day devoted entirely to Riley's entertainment, from building a snowman in the front yard, to puzzles and board games over hot chocolate and a round of action figure army combat on the stairs.

Knox thought he might walk by the dining room unacknowledged, but where Leni seemed determined to keep her gaze rooted to her plate, Riley shot a wide grin in his direction.

"Hi, Knox!"

Fuck. So much for his Hunter's stealth.

The little boy pivoted around in his chair. "When are we gonna 'stall the deadbowls?"

"Deadbolts," Leni murmured, then sent a flat look over his blond head. "I think Knox took care of them all while we were having fun today."

"That's right." Knox indicated the collection of tools in his hand. "I just finished up, actually. Everything's secured now, sealed up tight from top to bottom."

Leni gave him a begrudging nod. "Thank you."

"No problem."

Riley grabbed Fred into his lap and motioned to the now vacated chair beside him. "Knox, come sit by me."

When he glanced at Leni, she shrugged faintly. It was about the closest thing to a truce they'd had all day. Riley patted the empty chair, his bright blue eyes imploring until he got what he wanted.

"Sounded like quite a battle on the stairs a while ago," Knox said as he put the tools on the floor and sat down. "Who won, the cowboys or the aliens?"

"The cowboys, a'course. Aunt Leni was in charge of the aliens and she always lets me win."

"Excuse me?" She set down her fork with feigned indignation. "Since when do you think I let you win, little man?"

"Since for always." Riley shrugged as he shoveled a large mound of mashed potatoes and gravy into his mouth. When Leni reached over and tickled under his arm he burst into a fit of giggles. After he calmed down, he brought his stuffed bear up to his ear, nodding solemnly. "Knox, Fred says you can eat his biscuit if you want. It's got lots of honey on it."

"I see that."

"Do you like honey too?"

Knox chuckled. "Not especially. How about we let Fred keep his dinner?"

Riley's pale brows knit. "You're not hungry?"

Knox glanced at Leni and saw she was waiting for his reply. There was no judgment in her steady hazel eyes, only curiosity and patient consideration. Whatever he wanted to tell the boy, she was leaving it up to him.

Knox opted for the truth.

"I don't eat the same kind of food that you and Fred do." He placed his arm on the table so Riley could see the *glyphs* snaking around his forearm and onto the back of his hand. "Do you know what these are?"

"Nuh-uh."

"They're called *dermaglyphs*. Only certain people are born with them, people like me."

"Cool!" Riley's eyes widened as he stared at the intricate tangle of markings. "Can I touch 'em?"

"Sure."

Tiny fingers traced the sweeps and flourishes before that inquisitive face tilted back up to look at Knox. "What kind of food do you like?"

Ah, Christ. He had to know Riley would come back at him with questions. He'd gotten a sampling of the boy's keen intellect and fearless curiosity that morning. But how the hell could he explain what he was without frightening or confusing him?

Leni's gaze seemed to be asking the same thing. She watched in guarded silence, trusting him—or maybe testing him. Either way, leaving him to dangle at the mercy of a six-year-old boy.

Knox cleared his throat. "You know how your buddy Fred over there only likes honey?" Riley nodded. "Well, I'm kind of like that too. Except, instead of drinking honey I drink something else."

"Milk?"

Knox smirked. "No."

"Root beer?"

"No. Not that, either."

"Good, 'cause soda's bad for you. Right, Aunt Leni?"

She smiled and gave him a nod, her warm eyes sparkling in the low light of the dining room. For a moment, sitting there with the two of them, Knox felt as though he had stepped into some alternate reality. A pleasant one, where he was a part of this little family and talks around the dinner table felt as natural as breathing.

Where the fuck had that feeling come from? He didn't want to know. Nor did he give it a chance to linger inside him. He drew his arm away from Riley's tickling exploration of his *glyphs*.

"I'm not like you or your aunt," he said, his voice gruff. "I don't eat the kind of food you do. I need to drink blood in order to live."

"Blood? Yuck." His petite nose scrunched up. "I wouldn't like that."

Knox chuckled. "Probably not. That's because you're human. I'm not."

"Then . . . what are you?"

"I'm Breed. People like me are born with *dermaglyphs* on our skin, like I showed you. Sometimes, our eyes change colors and our teeth get sharp."

"Why?"

"It's just the way we're born," Knox said, sensing no fear in the boy, only a quest to understand. "We're stronger than other people and we live for a really long time. There's only one thing that's stronger than people like me. Sunlight."

There it was. The basics of vampire life laid out in terms he hoped Riley's six-year-old mind would grasp. He figured it best to leave out the details of how Knox and his kind went about obtaining the blood that sustained them. He was trying to provide a level of understanding, not terrify him that his—or his aunt's— carotids were at risk.

Thinking about Leni's throat giving way under his fangs was an image Knox preferred to avoid envisioning too.

Especially in front of the kid. After struggling all day to hold back the part of himself that was pure predator and far too distracted by the beautiful brunette seated across the table from him now, the last thing Knox needed was to give Riley an up-close account of a Breed male gripped by the urge to feed.

To say nothing of the other animal urges Leni provoked in him.

She broke the prolonged silence that began to settle over the room. "It's okay to be different, right Riley?"

"Sure." He punctuated his agreement with a vigorous nod, then picked up his bear and began bouncing it in his lap. "Can me and Fred be 'scused now?"

"Fred and I," Leni corrected gently. "And yes, you may."

With the toy in hand, he slid out of his seat and tore upstairs.

"I'll be up in a few minutes to give you a bath and read you a story before bedtime," Leni called after him, but he was already long gone. She glanced at Knox and rolled her eyes. "You can see who really runs this house."

Knox smiled. "You're good with him."

"I'm spoiling him." She shrugged her shoulders and rose to begin collecting the plates. "Honestly, I don't have any idea what I'm doing. I'm just trying to do my best for him and get by until his real mom comes home."

Knox kept his opinion of that likelihood to himself as he stood and picked up a couple of the serving bowls. He thought she would refuse his help, but she said nothing as she carried her items into the kitchen. He followed, setting his things down on the counter next to the sink.

It had only been hours ago that they'd stood in this same spot, he dangerously close to acknowledging his attraction for her. At least, to himself. Right before he pissed her off and earned her cold shoulder for the duration of the day.

Her back was still up around him, the energy vibrating off her feeling guarded, even wary.

After they'd cleared the table and she filled the sink with hot, sudsy water, he returned to the dining room, bringing the collection of tools and leftover hardware supplies with him.

"I'll put that box back in the garage with the rest of these things."

"Thanks." She glanced over her shoulder and let go of a small laugh to see him holding up a hammer with a bright pink handle. "Shannon's favorite color. She was a girly-girl, but she was handy too. She went out and bought all of that stuff after . . ."

"After Travis assaulted her?"

She nodded, then turned back toward the sink to scrape the plates over the disposal and place the dishes into the water.

"Tell me about her, Leni. About the Parrishes."

Her shoulders lifted. "What's there to tell? My sister was the prettiest girl in town. Kind to everyone, smart like Riley. She was always so full of life. Travis took all of that away from her. She could've had any man she wanted, good men, here in Parrish Falls or anywhere else. She chose him."

Knox moved in beside Leni, knowing it couldn't be easy for her to talk about her sister. "I know he brutalized her, but was there more?"

"Yeah, there was." She scrubbed at one of the plates before letting it sink back into the water. "He got her hooked on drugs when she was a freshman. She kept it hidden from us for about a year. I was only eleven around that time. I didn't know what was going on. Mom and Gran tried to shield me from Shannon's problems. Eventually, things got bad enough that there was no hiding it."

"What happened?"

"She struggled with her classes, then started skipping them altogether. She spent some time in and out of rehab down at the county hospital."

"And Travis?"

"He's a Parrish," she said, swiveling a bleak look at him. "They're untouchable around here. Enoch Parrish and his sons own the lumber company on the edge of town. It used to be worth a fortune, but it's gotten hard to make a living in the timber-cutting and log-hauling business. Hard even for them, although you'd never know it. Rumor has it the family's still worth millions just for the twenty-thousand or so acres of farmable land they still own. And Travis was their golden son, at least until Shannon sent him away to prison."

Knox inclined his head, hearing the pain in Leni's voice. "Men don't just wake up one day and decide to beat a woman so badly she ends up in a hospital. Had he hurt your sister before that final time?"

Of course, he had. Leni's expression said it all. "She came home with bruises sometimes. And other . . . pains."

"Why didn't she press charges before it got worse? I don't mean that as a judgment, just a question. Had he threatened retaliation if she spoke out against him?"

"I don't think so. Shannon thought she was in love with him. Travis took full advantage of that fact. Once the trial got under way, his father and brothers spread lies about Shannon. They made sure the whole county believed she was combative and mentally unstable. They made it seem like she deserved what he'd done to her."

Knox bit off a low curse. As satisfying as it had been to send Dwight Parrish into the river last night, now he wished he'd drawn blood, broken bones. Choked the last breath out of the bastard. Of course, the true target of his lethal inclinations was the Parrish brother who'd be coming home the day after tomorrow.

The assassin in Knox wouldn't need to hear much more to feel justified in ending the son of a bitch. Or the whole miserable Parrish clan. If he thought Leni's life in Parrish Falls could continue with impunity afterward, Knox would be more than tempted to finish his business there the minute Travis's feet touched ground in town.

His first choice, however, the best one, was still to get Leni and her nephew out of the striking zone. He had thoughts on how he might accomplish that. He wasn't without a few connections, albeit distant ones. There were strings he could pull if he thought Leni might go along willingly.

And if she wouldn't go willingly?

Knox shook his head, refusing to consider the kinds of methods that would only leave her hating him. He wasn't ready to venture down those paths just yet, but if he got the slightest whiff of danger in these next couple of days . . . he would find a way to live with Leni's despisal.

"I can see why you don't want your sister's child anywhere near his father and his kin," he said, attempting to broach the subject from a different tack. "If she were here, I doubt she'd want that, either."

Leni nodded. "It was one of her biggest fears all through her pregnancy and into the trial. She told me countless times before she went missing to promise her I'd look out for Riley. I'm not going to let her down."

Leni must have sensed the direction of Knox's thoughts. Pivoting away from the dishes in the sink, she dried her hands on a towel and faced him square-on.

"Before you tell me again that I should run away or try to hide Riley somewhere far from Parrish Falls, it's not happening. I'm not going to let the Parrishes run me off. You've met Riley now. That little boy is innocent and everything that's good in this world. He has the bravest heart I've ever seen, and I'm not going to give him a reason to be afraid, or to think I believe for a minute that his mommy really is never coming home."

But Leni had her doubts.

She hadn't let her defenses slip in front of Knox until now.

"I realize you think I'm being stubborn by staying put here. Last night, you said I was being foolish."

He frowned, unable to deny either of those arguments. "What I'd like is for you to be careful, Leni."

Yes, because she was a Breedmate. But also because in the short time since he'd met her, he had seen the same things in her that she saw in her little nephew.

Lenora Calhoun was good and kind, even innocently so. She was brave. And he'd be damned if he wanted to stand by and watch while the Parrishes gave her any more reason to be afraid.

"What made you leave Florida, Knox?"

The question hit him blindside, jolting him away from the dangerous path his thoughts had gone. He'd hardly remembered mentioning anything about his life outside the Hunter program, but now their conversation in the truck came back to him. He wanted to forget he'd opened up to her about anything in his past, but she didn't seem inclined to let it go.

"Why do you want to know?"

"I'm just trying to understand how you can find it so easy to pull up stakes and live on the road for five months at a time."

"I've lived on my own for a lot longer than that over the past eight years."

"But Florida was the only home you knew after you escaped the lab where you were raised. That's what you said. So, how is it so easy for you to stay away? Don't you have any family?"

"Half-brothers," he said, then ran a hand over his tense jaw. "No one knows how many of us in total survived the program, but four of my brothers and I built a Darkhaven together in the Everglades."

"Do they have any idea where you are?"

He shook his head.

"Why did you leave?"

A curse gusted between his lips. "Long story. And an old one, besides. Doesn't matter."

"Now, who's trying to run away?"

He felt heat flare in his irises at her challenge. He wasn't accustomed to anyone standing up to him, not even with words. Yet Leni was willing to clash horns with him, especially when he was attempting to flex his authority or impose his will on a situation like the battle-hardened soldier he'd been brought up to be.

"We aren't talking about me, Leni. This conversation was about you, about your unwillingness to accept the facts."

"Is that right?"

"Yes. Like the fact that you are not equipped to take on men like the Parrishes on your own. Or the fact that no matter how long you plan to keep your stake planted in the ground here in this godforsaken corner of the North Maine Woods, it's not going to bring Shannon back."

"Maybe it won't." She narrowed a hard stare on him. If she'd been Breed like him, he had no doubt her eyes would be filled with amber fire. He knew she wanted to scream at him, but she kept her voice low and quiet, well out of earshot of Riley upstairs. "So, you think I should pack up and scramble away like a coward? How's that working out for you, Knox?"

"What the fuck are you talking about?"

"Abbie."

The name cleaved into him as sharp as a blade. He couldn't mask his confusion. His mouth went dry at the sound of Abbie's name on Leni's lips. It was disorienting, a feeling he didn't like one damn bit. "What do you know about her?"

"Only that you called her name when you came to help me in the ravine." Leni's brows knit. "You didn't know?"

Fuck. No, he didn't know that. He'd been jolted by the sight of Leni's disabled vehicle. He'd dreaded he might find her injured at the bottom of the steep incline—or worse.

But to call out Abbie's name?

Christ, he wanted the floor to open up and take him down. Anything but to see the soft understanding in Leni's eyes now.

"What happened to her, Knox?"

"She died." He said the words without emotion. Told himself he didn't feel the anguish gnawing inside his chest. Nor the guilt of how he'd failed Abbie. "There was a bad storm in the Everglades. She was driving in it. Her car broke down on the side of the road. A tractor-trailer collided with her. She was gone before I was able to reach her."

Bare facts, delivered in a staccato monotone. There was more he wasn't saying. Layers he wasn't willing to peel away from his heart just so Leni could prove her point.

Had he run away from the pain of losing Abbie? Hell, yes.

Did that make him a coward? Probably. In Leni's courageous, too-knowing eyes, certainly.

Knox started to turn away from her but she stopped him, reaching out to press her warm palm against his cheek.

"I'm sorry for your loss, Knox."

He allowed himself to feel her tenderness only for a moment before he drew away from her gentle touch. "I don't need pity."

"Do you think that's what I'm feeling for you?"

God, he wasn't sure he wanted to know that answer. If it was anything close to pity, he wouldn't be able to look her in the eyes ever again. If it was something else, something like the unflinching affection he saw gleaming in those melting hazel depths, it would be the flame that would ignite the tinderbox of desire he'd been refusing to let detonate from the moment he first laid eyes on her.

She gave him a soft, uncertain smile. "Hasn't anyone ever shown you kindness before?"

"Yes." He forced the word off his tongue, biting the syllable hard. "And she's dead now."

Leni let her hand drift slowly down to her side. "I'm not Abbie. I'm not going to break. I don't need your protection, Knox. And I don't want to be the recipient of your stoic sense of honor, no matter what you think my Breedmate mark obligates you to do."

A low growl built deep in his chest. "Maybe that small scrap of honor is all I've got left."

She scoffed quietly. "Maybe we're both trying to hold on to something so desperately because we know if we let go, we'll see how alone we truly are."

She walked past him as formidable as any warrior, leaving him standing mute and vanquished in the middle of her kitchen while her footsteps carried her up to the little boy waiting for his promised bath and a bedtime story.

CHAPTER 11

A rapid banging thundered through the house.
Leni jolted upright in the thin light of morning,
yanked out of a deep sleep she didn't even realize she'd
been in until every cell in her body was suddenly wide
awake. She must have nodded off reading to Riley last
night. The well-worn book about a mischievous boy in
a wolf suit and an imaginary forest full of wild things slid
off her chest onto the twin bed next to her sleeping
nephew as she sat up, trying to get her bearings.

The urgent knocking came again, echoing up from
the front door like machine-gun fire.

Her heart seized in her breast. *Oh, shit. What day was
it?*

It couldn't be Travis home already, could it? He
wasn't due for release until tomorrow.

She scrambled out of Riley's bed, still wearing her
long-sleeved henley, faded jeans, and cushy socks from

the night before. Not the way she wanted to go into battle, if that's what this early morning house call was about, but it didn't seem she'd have much choice.

Extricating herself from Riley's unconscious sprawl, she hurried down the stairs to see who was on her stoop.

Knox was already in the foyer, about two seconds from yanking open the door as Leni bounded down the steps.

God, he looked like malice personified. Huge and muscular, yet fluid as a cat in motion. He met her uncertain gaze, dark brows clashed together over grim eyes and a deadly expression. His dark, lethal presence ate up all the oxygen in the room.

It didn't help her breathe any easier that he also looked hot as hell, barefoot and dressed only in his jeans. He must have been fresh out of the shower. His dark hair was damp and glossy, his smooth, *glyph*-covered skin bared from the waist up and glistening with droplets of water.

Leni tried not to stare, but damn, it wasn't easy. She had guessed at the size of him when he'd been fully dressed, but her imagination had been no match for reality. Thick muscle bulked at his broad shoulders. Corded sinew wrapped his large biceps and strong forearms. His chest and torso looked as if they'd been sculpted from warm, lightly bronzed marble.

Although she didn't want to let her gaze travel any lower, it was impossible to keep from appreciating the hard ridges that defined his abdomen. That eight-pack and the tapered cut of his hips above the waistband of his jeans made her tongue tingle with the urge to lick every honed contour and beautiful *glyph*.

Another hard rap sounded on the front door. Then a woman's muffled voice. "Leni, are you in there?"

She mentally shook herself back to attention. Thankfully, it wasn't Travis Parrish waiting outside.

"My friend, Carla," she whispered to Knox, exhaling a relieved sigh. "It's okay."

His scowl eased only slightly. That air of danger vibrating around him took a bit longer to fade. He stayed where he was, as if he needed to see for himself that the person on the other side of the door posed no threat.

Part of her warmed to his protectiveness, however unnecessary it was at the moment.

Another part of her was annoyed to realize he had no intention of fading into the woodwork to let her speak to her friend in private, at least not until he was good and ready to.

Leni stepped in front of him and carefully opened a small wedge of space between her and the door.

"Finally, there you are," Carla said, exasperation written all over her face as she peered through the narrow crack. She made a quick visual assessment of Leni's appearance before she shook her head, her shoulder-length brown curls swinging. "I've been blowing up your phone since around eight o'clock this morning. Why didn't you answer?"

Leni leaned her elbow against the doorjamb and feigned a yawn. "I, um . . . I fell asleep reading a bedtime story to Riley. I just woke up. I didn't hear my phone. I must've left it in my purse or something. Is everything okay?"

Carla tried to look past her, into the house. "Do you know you've got a huge dent the front end of the

Bronco? And there are pine branches sticking out of the grille. What the heck happened?"

"Ah . . . it was just a fender-bender in the storm the other night. It looks worse than it is."

"That's good, because it looks like you've been off-roading in a Christmas tree farm." She stomped her boots, rubbing her mitten-covered hands together in front of her face. "Jeez, it's cold. Aren't you going to let me in, Rip Van Winkle? I come bearing gossip."

Leni swallowed, feeling a tense shift in the air behind her where Knox yet loomed. "What kind of gossip?"

Carla rolled her eyes. "Fine, I guess I'll tell you before you let me turn into a popsicle out here. I ran into old Willa Barnes and a couple of the other local fat-chewers at the post office this morning. They were talking about Dwight Parrish and how his brand-new pickup ended up in the river a couple of nights ago."

Leni nearly choked. "In the river?"

"Yep. With him inside it. He managed to get out, more's the pity, but apparently the truck is a goner. It sat half-submerged at the bottom of the ravine down by the falls until Sheriff Barstow got some of the county boys to make a special trip out there yesterday to tow it up."

Leni didn't think for a minute that Dwight's misfortune was any more accidental than her own plunge into the ravine. And while she couldn't see Knox, she could feel his cold satisfaction emanating from a few feet behind her. "Did you hear how it happened?"

"Apparently, Dwight's telling everyone who'll listen that he was attacked on his way home from plowing. By a vampire, Leni. Can you imagine? One of the Breed way up here in Parrish Falls? According to Dwight, the only way he escaped getting his jugular torn open was by ditching his truck in the river."

Knox's derisive scoff was quiet, but Carla didn't miss it. "Is someone in there with you?"

Shit. Leni wasn't ready to explain her unusual houseguest—or the circumstances that had brought him into her home. Carla knew about her Breedmate mark, but what would her friend think if she learned Leni had agreed to allow a Breed male she'd only just met into her home? Even worse, one who'd been born and raised a killer.

She tried to appear calm and casual. "I should go wake up Riley and get some breakfast into him. Call you later?"

"You're acting really weird right now, Len." So much for trying to dodge her best friend's scrutiny. Carla studied her, her expression moving from curious to concerned. "What's going on with you? Are you okay?"

"Yeah. Sure. Of course. Why wouldn't I be?"

"Well, for one thing, I know how upset you are about Travis Parrish coming home tomorrow. But for another, I just told you there's a blood-crazed Breed male on the loose somewhere in town and you've barely blinked."

Dammit. She had never lied to Carla and she hated to start now. Leni shook her head, letting go of a resigned sigh. "He's not blood-crazed."

"What?"

"Come in here, quick." She pulled her friend inside and closed the door behind them. "Carla Hansen, meet Knox. Knox, this is my best friend, Carla."

His stony expression hardly looked welcoming. He dipped his chin in vague acknowledgment. "The one who watches Riley for you."

"You know who I am?" Carla gaped at the huge, half-dressed vampire standing in the foyer. Then she swung a confused look at Leni. "You two know each other?"

"Knox and I met a couple of nights ago. At the diner."

Her brows arched high. "A couple of nights ago. You mean, the night of the blizzard. The night you came to my house to pick up Riley and didn't mention one single word about meeting a" —her gaze flicked back to Knox for a second— "a new . . . um, friend?"

Were they friends? Leni hadn't really considered what to call her relationship with him. After all, it had only been about thirty-six hours since he'd wandered into her diner and turned her life upside down.

So, why didn't it feel strange to see him in front of her now, looking for all the world as if he belonged in her house? Why did he seem like the one person who understood her better than anyone else, with the exception of Carla, whom she'd known literally all her life?

It wasn't friendship that made Leni's face heat under the intensity of Knox's gaze. For all the moments they'd clashed in the past couple of nights since they met, there was no denying the attraction that simmered between them. It crackled beneath the surface of every glance, every word they exchanged, even the angry ones.

She could feel that electric awareness now as Knox's gaze lingered on her. Heat licked through her veins, coiling somewhere deep inside her.

Based on the astonished expression on her friend's face right now, Carla seemed to be picking up on the charge in the air too.

Knox cleared his throat. "You have things to talk about with your friend. I'll be upstairs."

She nodded, but he was already in motion. Silent in spite of his size, he vanished into the kitchen to the back stairwell leading up to the attic apartment.

The instant he was gone, Carla's brows shot high on her forehead, her eyes wide as saucers. "Oh. My. God." She kept her voice barely above a whisper as she hooked her arm through Leni's and pulled her into the living room. "Did you see how fucking gorgeous he is?"

Leni exhaled a laugh. "I have noticed that, yes."

"What's he doing here?"

"Well, last night he put in some new locks on the doors and windows. Right now, I imagine he's upstairs in the attic apartment finishing drying off after his shower was interrupted."

"Do you realize how nuts that sounds? Where the hell did he come from?"

"Most recently? The Interstate over by Medway, according to him," she said, amused as she recited one of Knox's cryptic answers. She had to make a little light of the situation, because it sounded nuts to her too. "He told me he's been on the road for the past several months, going nowhere in particular. Apparently, he's got brothers living in a Darkhaven down in Florida."

"Brothers?" Carla wiggled her brows. "Do you suppose they all look like him? If they do, please tell him I and my virgin carotid will happily volunteer as tribute to any one of them."

Leni groaned. "You're awful."

She laughed. "I'm lonely. I'm withering on the vine up here in the frozen North. And so are you, Len." She tilted her head. "Or are you? Don't think I didn't see the way you were looking at your unusual houseguest just now."

"The way I was looking at him?"

Leni wanted to deny it, but Carla's shrewd gaze narrowed. "Holy shit. Have you broken your nearly six-year drought with a hot stranger you just met? And a Breed male, besides?"

"No. Of course, I haven't." Leni shook her head. "No way. With Riley under the same roof?"

"But you want to." Her face lit up with conspiratorial enthusiasm. "Holy hell. Yes, you totally do!"

"Shh." Leni felt her cheeks go red. "It's not going to happen. And keep your voice down, for God's sake."

"Does he know about you? About what you are?"

"Unfortunately," Leni replied. "I tried to keep it from him when he rescued me from the bottom of the ravine and pushed the Bronco back onto the road. But after we picked up Riley and brought him back to the house, Knox saw my Breedmate mark. Let's just say he wasn't happy about it. Then again, he wasn't happy about a lot of things by that time."

Carla stared. "Okay, we're going to circle back to the point about you pissing off two-hundred-and-fifty-plus-pounds of smoking hot vampire in just a second. First, let's unpack the part about him rescuing you from the bottom of the ravine. What are you talking about?"

Leni sighed, catching her lip between her teeth. "It's kind of a long story."

"Girlfriend, school has been out for two days and I've just discovered my best friend has a vampire handyman bunking in her attic. I've got nothing but time."

CHAPTER 12

Knox felt Leni's presence even before he heard her footsteps outside the old garage in back of the house that evening.

She let herself in without asking, bringing with her the scent of crisp snow, nighttime forest, and the sweeter fragrance of her freshly washed hair and skin.

He didn't know how he could have missed the fact that she was a Breedmate when he first met her in the diner. Every woman born with that symbol on her body possessed her own unique blood scent. Leni's was cedar and rich cream, an intoxicating mix that complemented the strength and warmth of the woman herself. It called to his senses like a siren's song, and he greedily breathed it in as she approached.

"It's cold out here," she said, her voice husky and soft. Every fiber in his body lit up with awareness as she joined him in the back of the dimly lit outbuilding. She wore a pale gray sweater that looked as soft as a kitten and a pair of black leggings that clung to every inch of her long legs before disappearing into her untied snow boots. "Is that the faucet from the attic bathroom?"

His nod felt as tight as the rest of him. "Yeah. Just making a few small repairs around the place while I'm here."

Today alone he had replaced several broken tiles in the shower, sealed some bad weather-stripping in the dormer windows, and tacked down a few loose floorboards at the top of the attic stairwell. At the rate he was going, he'd have Leni's entire house refurbished before the end of next week.

Not that he expected to stay that long.

A few days at most.

Less than that if he could help it. Since she'd made it clear that persuading her to leave wasn't going to go well, he would have to come up with another solution if things went south with Travis Parrish.

One that didn't require Knox to be in close proximity to the woman.

God knew he was having a hard enough time living under the same roof with her as it was. Every minute was becoming a test of self-control.

Seeing her in the foyer that morning had been yet another test. Only a minute before he'd been punishing his body under a cold shower, attempting to douse his uncooled desire for her. After a restless night spent prowling his quarters and trying to resist the urge to seek her out following their conversation in the kitchen, he had been itching for an outlet for his aggression.

He had almost hoped to find Travis Parrish or his brother on the other side of the door instead of Leni's

LARA ADRIAN

friend. He would have welcomed the opportunity to pound his fist into something more deserving than the attic's old walls.

But it hadn't been misplaced aggression pulsing through him when he'd heard the insistent rapping on the front door. It had been something deeper. Something more than basic concern for a female he was honor-bound to protect as a member of the Breed.

He would kill for Leni Calhoun, no question. In some rusty corner of his conscience, he had to admit— at least to himself—that he would do anything to preserve the simple, idyllic life she had made for herself and her nephew.

She pivoted around to lean her back against the workbench as Knox reassembled the repaired bathroom fixture. "Carla went home about an hour ago."

"I know. I was in here when I heard her car leave."

He had purposely made himself scarce during their visit. Maybe he should have said more than a handful of words to Leni's friend after she'd arrived, but it wasn't his job to be hospitable. He was there for one purpose, even if he had to keep reminding himself of that fact.

"Anyway, I promised Riley we'd rent that new superhero movie tonight," Leni said. "We're going to start it in a minute, if you'd like to come in and join us."

Knox exhaled. "I don't think that's a good idea."

"Why not?" She tilted her head, her tone playful as she watched him. "You got something against caped crusaders?"

"No," he said, setting down his work and meeting her gaze.

Damn, those eyes knocked him out every time he looked at her. So clear and steady. Fearless.

116

Right now, there was a hopeful gleam in them that seemed to carve a hollow in his chest as she stared at his grim face.

"You said I shouldn't make promises to the kid that I won't be keeping, Leni. I agree. I don't think it's a good idea for him to get used to me being around."

"Oh." She frowned and glanced away from him, giving a dismissive shake of her head. "Yeah, that's true. Good point."

It was. So, why did he feel like such a bastard for saying it?

"I shouldn't keep Riley waiting," she murmured. "Anyway, I really just wanted to come out and see if you needed anything. I haven't seen or heard from you since this morning when Carla was here."

"After our conversation last night, I thought keeping my distance from you would be best. For both of us."

Fuck. He instantly wished he hadn't said a word, just kept his mouth shut and let her go.

Because although she had started to move away from him, now she paused.

"Knox, about that . . ." She faced him, her expression pinched with contrition. "I'm sorry for prying about Abbie, about your life. I didn't have any right to say the things I did about what you've been through or the choices you've made."

He couldn't keep the low curse from slipping past his clenched teeth. Her charge that he was running away from his past while still clinging to it had been dead-on. He hadn't wanted to hear it. Hell, no one had ever dared say it to his face before.

Of course, Leni with her forthright manner and fearless heart wouldn't hesitate to put him firmly in his place, set him straight. He liked that about her. He respected her for having the guts to call him on his bullshit, even if it pissed him off to admit it.

"You don't need to apologize," he muttered. "You were right. About everything you said."

She studied him for a long moment then glanced down, toying with the edge of her roomy sweater.

"Carla told me what you did." Her gaze lifted. "You put Dwight Parrish and his brand-new truck in the river?"

"Only seemed fair."

Her mouth curved, those mesmerizing eyes lit with amusement. "You did that for me?"

He shrugged. "I wanted to convey a message, that's all. Announce my presence in Parrish Falls in clear, unmistakable terms."

"Ah." She nodded, but it was obvious she wasn't buying his excuse. "Well, I think you've done that. Carla says the whole town is already buzzing with the news that we have a Breed male in our midst. Dwight's making it sound like you're a homicidal maniac."

He grunted. "Not that far from the truth. I don't much care what anyone thinks or says about me."

"Normally, I don't either. But the Parrishes will use anything they can against me when it comes to Riley. It's not going to take long for tongues to start wagging about the fact that you're staying here with me."

"If you want me to leave, I will."

"No," she said, no hesitation at all. "I don't want that, Knox."

"You sure?" He almost wished she'd say the words, give him an out before he allowed himself to become any more involved in her life. "I'm not the only one of my kind who's capable of protecting you and Riley. I could make a call right now, send for someone else to step in and do this right. Hell, just about anyone would be better suited for babysitting duty than me."

"Is that what this is to you?" Her brow pinched. "Is that how you see me, Knox?"

Shit. He hadn't meant it to sound like a jab toward her. Far from it. "Do you really need to ask that?"

"Yes. I really do." She swallowed, inhaling a breath that seemed to fortify her. "I need to ask it, Knox. I need to know if you're only here out of some aggravating sense of duty, or because you want to be. I need to know if I'm the only one feeling like there's something building between us, or if I've just been alone too long to tell the difference. Because if I'm wrong, then I—"

Knox speared his fingers into her loose hair and pulled her against him, silencing her doubts with his kiss.

Leni melted into him on a moan. That throaty, uninhibited expression of pleasure and need went straight to his cock. Behind his closed eyelids, his vision bled amber. His fangs lengthened as he teased the seam of her lips with his tongue. She let him in on a shivery gasp, her mouth hot and wet on his, open for his taking.

With one hand cupping her nape, he let his other glide down the graceful curve of her spine. He took hold of her hip and dragged her closer, needing her to feel what she did to him. How hard she made him.

His blood raced like wildfire in his veins, throbbing and molten, just like the rest of him. It took all he had to break the contact of their mouths. His breath sawed out of him, desire all but ruling him just from a single kiss.

The glow from his transformed eyes lit her face as he looked at her. "Does that answer your question, Lenora?"

Her jagged sigh left no room for doubt, but he kissed her again, just to make things clear. This time, he claimed her mouth with all the heat and hunger he'd been struggling to hold at bay since he arrived in Parrish Falls and first saw her.

Her hands roamed over his back, her short fingernails raking across the bunched muscles that twitched and jerked under her touch. He wanted to feel her hands on his bare skin.

Fuck, he wanted her naked beneath him. If he didn't put the brakes on this kiss, that's exactly where they were heading.

He drew back on a rough growl. "You should've told me to go. Christ, you still should."

She shook her head as she gazed up at him, her lips kiss-bruised and glistening. "I don't want anyone else, Knox."

Were they still talking about keeping her and Riley safe? He wasn't sure. He wasn't sure of anything but the feel of Leni in his arms. He didn't want to let her go, but if he held on another second she wouldn't be going anywhere for the rest of the night.

"Your friend's going to be disappointed to hear you didn't agree to a substitute."

Leni gave him a confused look. "You mean, Carla?"

"She and her virgin carotid," he said, a smirk tugging at the corner of his mouth.

"Oh, my God. You heard that?" She gaped at him, and he could almost hear her mind replaying the entirety of her entertaining, and rather illuminating, conversation with her friend. "Please tell me that's all you heard."

He grinned. "I will, if that's what you need me to say."

She groaned. "You heard everything, didn't you?"

"Every last word." He arched a brow. "Almost six years, eh?"

She winced, then let out a laugh. "Dammit. I'm going to kill Carla next time I see her."

He lifted her chin on his fingertips, barely resisting the urge to kiss her again. "Don't worry, your secrets are safe with me."

"What about the rest of me, Knox?"

A promise lit on the end of his tongue. Solemn words he didn't have the right to be thinking, let alone give voice to. He held back his reply, but only with the force of both his teeth and fangs.

Pleasure, he could give her. Physical security? Without question.

He would even give his life for her, if it came down that.

But promises like the one she asked of him now felt far out of his grasp.

His tongue cleaved to the roof of his mouth as she stared up at him. Silence spread between them, awkward and heavy.

Back at the house, the kitchen door squeaked open. "Aunt Leni, where'd you go?"

She flinched, blinked. Cleared her throat. "I, um . . . I need to get back inside."

"Yes," Knox said, sounding as grim as he must have looked.

Leni pivoted around and hurried out of the garage. "I'm right here, honey. Are you ready to get that movie started?"

Knox didn't let out his breath until she was back in the house and the door was closed behind her.

CHAPTER 13

When Knox came in from the garage a couple of hours later, he found Leni asleep with Riley in the living room. She sat scrunched into the arm of the sofa, her chin tipped down on her chest at an awkward angle, while the little boy sprawled across the cushions in his pajamas, his pale blond head resting on a pillow on her lap.

Knox exhaled a quiet chuckle as he stepped into the room. On the television across from them, the movie's closing credits rolled to a triumphant score implying a resounding win for the heroes. He turned it off, catching his hulking reflection on the darkened screen.

The way he had entered the world, the things he'd been forced to do, Knox had never considered himself one of the good guys. He had never particularly cared to be, either.

Selfish. Solitary. Savage. Those were the things that best defined him.

Not softness. Not sympathy.

Not some twisted urge to be a savior to the fierce-hearted beauty and the innocent child sleeping so trustingly under the guard of a man who'd been raised a soulless monster.

Knox told himself he didn't feel any of those things now, as he stepped over to the sofa and simply watched the pair for a long moment. He couldn't leave them like that, even though he knew the smartest thing for him to do was head upstairs to wait out the remainder of the night in peace. Especially after that kiss with Leni.

He still burned from it, everything male in him greedy for another taste of her.

He wanted more than just a taste.

He watched her breast rise and fall with her breathing. He could hear her pulse thudding, could see the fluttering tick of it in the side of her bent neck. His fangs responded of their own will, hunger chasing through his own blood, his gums throbbing.

Fuck. This desire he had for her was dangerous.

Looming over her like some maniac with smoldering eyes and elongated fangs wasn't the kind of picture he wanted to paint for her or the kid tonight.

In the garage, Leni had asked if she was safe with him. After he'd overheard her admit to her friend that she wanted him—after learning no man had given her pleasure in nearly six years—safe was the last thing she should be feeling with him.

Knox mentally jammed a lid on his lust for Leni to deal with the unconscious child in her lap. He carefully lifted Riley off her and carried him up to his bedroom.

Leni didn't stir as he went back down to collect her too. Her heavy sleep was testament to just how exhausted she truly was. Knox knew how little she'd been able to rest these past few nights. He'd heard her roaming the house at all hours. Saw the fatigue and worry over Travis Parrish's homecoming tomorrow shadowing her eyes. She felt boneless in his arms, draped against him as helplessly as the child he'd just ferried up to bed a minute ago.

But Leni was no child.

As he tossed aside the coverlet and gently placed her on the mattress, he couldn't help but pause for a moment to soak in the sight of her. Leni was tall and lean, yet curvy in all the right places. She was no waif, but the thick-knit, oversized sweater and soft black leggings she wore gave her a fragile quality that tugged at him even as he longed to peel her out of her clothes and feel her nakedness against his hard, far-too-aroused body.

She must have finally sensed she wasn't alone. Just when he had almost convinced himself to get the hell out of her bedroom, her long lashes stirred, then lifted.

"Knox?" A look of surprise swept over her face. It morphed quickly into worry. "What's going on? Where's Riley?"

Knox sat down on the edge of the bed as she began to rise up in alarm. "It's okay. He's okay. The two of you fell asleep watching the movie. I just carried him to bed a minute before I brought you up here."

She exhaled her relief, letting herself fall back against her pillows. "You carried us both to bed?"

"It was either that or let you wake up in a few hours unable to move your head."

"Wouldn't be the first time. But thank you for that." Her brows furrowed as she stared at him. Then she groaned and covered her face with her hands. "Oh, God. I was having this awful dream that my friend Carla came over and made me admit some really embarrassing things." She spread her fingers a bit, eyeing him through the cracks. "Can we please forget everything that happened in the last twelve hours or so?"

He smirked. "No chance of that."

As much as he might wish it were possible to put the revelations about her sex life—or lack thereof—out of his mind, he'd been unable to think of much else in the time since her overheard her conversation with Carla.

Kissing Leni in the garage hadn't helped.

In fact, it had only lit a match to his unresolved desire for her.

He cleared his throat. "I should let you sleep. I brought you up here because it was obvious you were exhausted. Tomorrow's going to come early."

"Yeah."

She parted her lips as if she wanted to say something more, but then thought better of it. She glanced down. The move sent a tendril of her dark hair swinging into her face.

Knox should have let go. He should have let her keep whatever she was reluctant to say. Instead, he reached out, swept the stray lock out of her eyes and lifted her chin on the edge of his finger.

"You all right?"

She nodded, but her gaze told him something different. "The day I've been dreading since Travis Parrish was sent away is finally here. It's only hours away now." She swallowed. "I'm scared, Knox."

He knew how much that quiet admission cost her. He understood her apprehension about her sister's assailant coming home. He'd seen the fear in Leni over the thought of losing Riley to his father and the rest of the Parrishes. He had recognized Leni's worry the night she asked for his help. But this was the first time she'd said it out loud.

He exhaled a low sigh, sliding his hand from her chin to her nape. He cupped his fingers around the back of her neck, drawing her toward him. "There's no reason to be afraid. I'm here. I'm not going to let anything happen. Not to you. Not to Riley."

"What can you do if they try to take him from me? What can anyone do about that, Knox?" Emotion choked her voice. She slowly shook her head in resignation. "Half of him is Parrish. He belongs to them, more than he belongs to me."

"Bullshit. That's not even close to true. Blood has nothing to do with where someone belongs. It has nothing to do with the lengths someone will go to protect what matters."

As he said the words, he realized just how profoundly he meant them. Not only when it came to Leni and her sister's child, but how Knox felt about the woman he was looking at now.

Leni wasn't his. As a Breedmate, he fully expected that one day, the gift of her eternal blood bond would belong to another male, one who deserved her. That didn't mean he wouldn't protect her to his last breath.

Even without the mark on her belly, her life had become precious to him. It was worth fighting for. Worth dying for.

He was starting to believe she might even be worth living for, something he hadn't felt in a very long time.

"I'm not going to let anything happen," he said, the promise rough for the presence of his fangs. "I'm going to keep both of you safe and together. No matter what it takes."

She leaned against him and he brought his arm around her, holding her close in spite of every warning that thundered through his blood and body. He was treading into dangerous waters with her tonight. His need for her intensified now that she was cuddled into his chest, her sweet scent filling his senses.

He tipped his head back, searching for the strength to get up off her bed and leave the room. Leni's palm rested over his heart. She had to feel the savage drumming beneath her hand. She had to know just how close he was to breaking.

"Knox." His whispered name sounded like a plea.

She reached up to him, cupping the side of his face. His jaw was clenched so tightly, it was a wonder his molars didn't shatter. She coaxed him to look at her.

When the glowing coals of his irises met the unflinching desire in her gaze, he couldn't contain the growl that boiled up the back of his throat.

Leni pulled his head down to hers. She said his name again, then her mouth was on his.

That spark was all it took.

He had been holding on to his control by a thread. Now it went up like tinder, exploding out of his grasp. Leni's kiss seared him. She may have been out of practice, but there was nothing untried or uncertain in the feel of her lips on his.

Her fingers tangled in his hair, dragging him closer. He moved his hand at her back under the loose hem of her sweater, craving the heat of her skin. Christ, she was so soft. He couldn't get enough.

Their mouths joined and urgent, he reached around to the front of her and pushed up the edge of the thin lace bralette she wore. Her breast filled his hand, the nipple as taut as a pearl against his palm as he caressed her.

"I want to see you," he uttered against her parted lips.

Her moan was all the permission he needed. He bared her from the waist up, the hot amber light of his fevered gaze licking over every perfect inch of her.

The Breedmate mark on her abdomen should have cooled him. It should have slowed him down, at least. But seeing that delicate scarlet symbol on the creaminess of her skin only made his need to possess her burn brighter, hotter.

Dangerously so.

He eased her down onto the mattress beneath him, running his hands over each luscious curve and smooth plane. He needed to see more of her, all of her. Grabbing the soft black fabric at her hips, he peeled her out of her leggings, leaving her wearing just her panties. If he'd been expecting basic white cotton, he couldn't have been more surprised to find a skimpy scrap of black lace and satin covering her sex.

"Christ, you're beautiful, Lenora. Sexy as fucking hell." Glancing up at her, he arched a brow. "That long drought of yours ends right here."

She sighed, catching her lip between her teeth as he gazed at her. Her dark hair lay in a wild tangle behind her head, her body spread out before him like a feast.

And he meant to savor every delectable inch.

He levered himself up and started with another kiss, taking her mouth possessively, mercilessly. From there, he moved to the tender spot below her ear, then along her throat to the sweet hollow at its base.

She arched beneath him as he continued his sampling of her sweetness, his lips and tongue moving ever downward toward the prize he couldn't wait to claim.

When he reached the edge of the black lace at her hip, he nipped at it with his teeth and fangs. Leni's legs scissored, her spine undulating as he stroked her with his hands and played his tongue along the softness of her inner thigh.

Her cleft was wet and hot, the scent of her arousal drilling into his skull, making him wild with the need to be inside her. He drew her panties off with impatient hands, too far gone to pretend he had any patience now.

She was even prettier like this, naked and open for him. So drenched she glistened.

He stroked his fingers along the slick seam of her sex, his cock kicking in response to the tiny convulsions that swept over her under his touch.

"I need to have you on my tongue," he growled tersely. "I want to feel you come against my mouth."

"Knox," she gasped, her pelvis lifting when he lowered his head to her and suckled her. Her voice was tight, strangled with pleasure. "Oh God."

He wasn't sure how he found the discipline to keep his own need in check. It owned him, careening toward the breaking point as Leni quaked and shuddered against his mouth.

"That's it," he rasped, feeling her climax spiral tighter with each flick and thrust of his tongue. "Come for me, Leni."

"I can't." She moaned, and it sounded as full of anguish as it did pleasure. "If I come, I'm going to scream. I can't . . ."

Ah, shit. The sleeping kid down the hall.

Knox wasn't going to let a little detail like that get in the way. He intended this to be a total annihilation of her prolonged neglect. Anything less than her full surrender wasn't acceptable.

"Go ahead and scream, Leni." His mouth moved against the molten sweetness of her folds as he drove her toward the peak. "Let it all go, baby. I've got you, I promise."

She didn't last more than another moment.

And when the jolt of her release hit its crescendo, he moved up her body and caught her broken cry with his kiss.

~ ~ ~

Leni's world splintered apart behind her closed eyelids, ecstasy rippling through every cell and nerve ending. She had no choice but to let the pleasure come. Her shout tore out of her, jagged and unhinged, swallowed up by the heat of Knox's mouth on hers.

True to his word, he caught her. He let her break against him, held fast by the surrounding strength of his arms.

Her moan when he pulled his lips away from hers sounded like a protest, but she couldn't help it. She wasn't ready for him to stop kissing her. She wasn't ready for him to stop anything he was doing to her body right now.

What she wanted was . . . more.

His eyes blazed as he lifted his lids and stared down at her. The pupils were so narrow the amber all but engulfed them. His dark brows were heavy slashes, the golden skin over his cheekbones seeming to be stretched taut over the sharp angles of his face. The pointed tips of his fangs gleamed white and sharp behind the broad line of his sexy mouth with every hard breath he drew into his lungs.

Fierce and unearthly, that's what he was. The most formidably attractive male she had ever seen.

He kissed her again as he reached between her legs. "I love the taste of you. The feel of you. Christ, Leni . . . you're so soft and wet and sweet. I shouldn't have let this happen, because now I'll never get enough."

Leni could hardly fathom it. She wasn't the kind of woman who inspired this kind of lust in a man. Yet he was staring at her now as if she were the only woman he wanted. Vibrating with the intensity of his desire for her.

She felt that same unbearable need drumming through her. She ached with an emptiness that demanded to be filled.

Reaching for him, she fisted her hands in the fabric of his shirt. "I want to feel your skin against mine, Knox. Now."

His eyes flared brighter at her breathless order. Rearing back, he pulled off his shirt and tossed it aside. His *dermaglyphs* churned with dark colors, twisting vines of indigo and burgundy and deep gold. Their changing hues made them seem alive on his skin, captivating her gaze and making her want to chase the pulsing patterns with her tongue.

A low growl built in his throat as she devoured him with her eyes. "Holy fuck, that look on your face is burning me up."

"Hurry, Knox."

He chuckled, working swiftly to strip out of his jeans. She licked her lips when she saw he wore nothing under them. His cock jutted out proudly, thick and heavily veined.

She couldn't hold back her moan. If the *glyphs* on his torso and limbs made her womb clench with yearning, seeing the swirls and flourishes twisting around his immense shaft nearly make her climax on the spot.

The sight of Knox like this awakened something inside her, a yearning that had been dormant until now. Unrealized.

It had nothing to do with the length of her self-imposed dry spell. She craved him on an elemental level. The way she needed air to breathe and food to survive.

Right now, she had never wanted anything more than to feel him pressed down upon her, inside her.

"Knox." She writhed with that need, unable to conceal the depth of her hunger for him.

Undressed, he stood at the edge of the bed and drank her in. His searing gaze heated her flesh everywhere it touched her, as hot as a live flame.

His strong hands clamped around her ankles and he yanked her toward him, until her backside nearly slid off the bed. Then he knelt down between her parted legs, his hands rough against the sensitive skin of her inner thighs as he spread her wider, until she was fully open to him.

"So fucking beautiful," he uttered thickly. "Sweet as honey and cream."

He scooped his palms under her ass and lifted her to his mouth. Leni gasped at the scorching heat of his mouth on her again. He showed her no mercy at all, every hard tug of his lips and tongue on her clit igniting a fresh fire inside her.

Every graze of his sharp fangs over her tender flesh shot molten lava into her veins. When he drew the swollen bud of her sex between his teeth, the cauldron in her core boiled over.

Her orgasm streaked through her, white-hot and electric, as jagged as lightning.

Before it could shatter her completely, Knox rose up. He entered her in a long, slow thrust, filling her until she felt she might split apart from the bliss of his body invading hers. The pleasured scream that rose up her throat left her lips as a wordless sigh as Knox began to move inside her.

Sensation overwhelmed her, swamped her. It was too much. Too much bliss. Too much intensity after such a long period of emptiness. Not only her body, but her life. Her heart.

Knox had stormed in only days ago, yet being with him felt like coming home.

Tears pricked the backs of her eyes as she clung to him. She held them back, but he must have sensed the stillness that washed over her.

"Hey." His voice was rough, his expression taut with concern as he ceased moving. "Am I hurting you?"

"No." She shook her head, swallowing against her parched throat. "I'm not hurting at all. This feels good, Knox. I didn't realize how much I needed it."

The corner of his mouth quirked. "Six years is a damn long time."

"Yes, it is." She let go a quiet laugh, her hands stroking his bare shoulders, her fingers tracing the intricate lines of the *glyphs* that rode the bunched muscles. "But I'm not talking about how long it's been since I've gotten off without having to use my own fingers to do it."

"Christ," he hissed, heat flaring in his eyes. "Just hearing you say that makes me want to see it in person sometime."

He started rocking inside her again, his strokes slow and deep. Leni moaned, sinking into his rhythm, savoring the fluid glide of their bodies in perfect tempo.

"Tell me what you it is you needed, sweetheart."

"This. You," she said, sighing as the pleasure bloomed into something wild again. "I just needed to feel safe tonight. I needed to feel connected to something solid and warm and unbreakable. Just for a little while."

"Then hold on to me." He lowered his head and kissed her, unrushed, soul-searing.

When he drew back it was on a harsh sigh. His Breed irises radiated like a furnace. His pelvis rolled hard against her, stretching her to the limit.

He ground out her name as savagely as a curse, and maybe it was. He powered into her now, his thrusts hard and unforgiving. Her control seemed to snap its tether at the same moment his did. She held fast as he buried his face in the curve of her neck and the hard jolt of his mounting release rippled through his big body.

She had no choice but to hold on to him as he began to move with the ferocity of a storm. He pushed her higher, then higher still, toward the peak of a steep cliff that seemed to have no end.

She wasn't afraid of getting close to that sheer drop. She wasn't afraid of the tempest of Knox's need as he chased his own release. She held on to him, ready for the fall.

Welcoming it.

They tumbled over the edge together.

CHAPTER 14

Lowering his head under the cold spray, Knox braced his hands against the shower walls and let the water needle his shoulders and back.

He'd come back to his attic quarters a couple hours before sunrise, realizing the only way he was going to let Leni sleep in peace was if he put some healthy distance between them. Considering the rampant hard-on he sported under the icy punishment of this third shower since he'd returned, he didn't think any amount of miles or time would be enough to chill his desire for her.

He had spent almost all night making love to her, some dim part of his brain trying to rationalize that the sharpness of his need would smooth out once he'd had his fill. Problem was, feeling her beneath him, feeling her body respond to his, shatter with his, only honed that need into a razor-sharp hunger unlike anything he'd ever felt before.

Not even with Abbie.

That admission clawed at him. It shamed him, but he couldn't deny it. He had adored Abbie for her free-spirited nature and her seemingly endless capacity to love people and bring them into her world, her life. A shameless flirt, she had been impossible to ignore. Her irrepressible light had drawn him and every other male in her orbit as easily as moths to a flame.

Leni couldn't be more different. Calm, steady, responsible. Reserved and cautious, yet caring. When she opened herself to someone, it was a true gift. A rare one, from what Knox had observed.

And she had given that gift to him last night. In fact, she'd allowed him in from the first night he'd arrived in Parrish Falls.

Her kindness and quiet strength had attracted him even more than her fresh-faced beauty and sultry curves. Her fear for the welfare of an innocent child had all but guaranteed Knox couldn't walk away and leave her to deal with her problems on her own.

For most of the time since he'd laid eyes on her, Knox had been telling himself he regretted his decision to stop at Leni's diner. Last night blew that lie to pieces.

He was never going to regret seeing her lost to the pleasure he had given her. She had surrendered herself to him completely.

She had trusted him. Skin on skin, not a single barrier between their bodies or their connection to each other.

It humbled him, that she would accept him after such a long time without anyone else. He was far from deserving of a gift that precious. Just one more thing he'd taken from her and could not regret enjoying, bastard that he was.

Now, every gasp and moan, every shuddering tremor that had rocked her, was seared into his mind. Every ecstatic scream he swallowed with his kiss echoed in his blood, in his marrow. What they shared last night would never leave him, no matter how much time or distance he was determined to put between Leni and him.

Knox cursed as he closed his eyes and cranked the shower temperature from cold to Arctic.

He'd barely left her bed and all he could think about was getting back into it with her. If he'd thought a single taste would sate his hunger, he was realizing the depth of his mistake this morning. How he would manage to stay under the same roof with her now and not want to get her naked again was beyond him.

He didn't even want to consider the added complication of the boy.

Staying in Parrish Falls wasn't in the plan when he'd arrived there. Staying any longer than necessary was only going to make things worse—as if he needed to bury himself inside Leni in order to realize that.

Fuck.

He turned off the water, then stepped out to hastily towel off. His skin still felt overheated despite the cold, his cock still stubbornly refusing to back down. He stuffed it into the jeans he pulled on, hoping like hell he could get his thoughts—and his libido—under control for the rest of the day.

The upcoming night would be a battle he'd have to fight once he got there. It would be a mistake to let things get any more complicated or involved. A momentary weakness was bad enough. A repeat performance would not only be unfair, but cruel.

Leni had warned him not to make promises to Riley he couldn't keep, but what about her?

She obviously wasn't the kind of woman who took a new man into her bed whenever the whim struck. Lenora Calhoun was the kind of woman who put down roots and nurtured them. She was the kind of woman who would put her life on hold to look after a motherless child.

The kind of woman who deserved white picket fences and a life free of struggle or pain. Not to mention an eternal blood bond with a male who was worthy of her. One whose hands weren't already stained with a lifetime of blood and violence.

Christ, what the hell was wrong with him?

One night of spectacular sex and he was mentally waxing on about picket fences and blood bonds? If that wasn't evidence enough that he needed to get a grip on the situation—rein things in hard and fast with Leni— then he didn't know what was.

Impatient now, he yanked on his dark T-shirt and stalked out of the bathroom on bare feet.

Clamping a lid on what he was starting to feel toward Leni was imperative, but that wasn't going to solve the other issue he hadn't yet addressed.

She'd made it clear she wasn't willing to leave town if things turned any more dangerous with the Parrishes, so that left the problem in Knox's hands. He had to ensure he had somewhere to take her and Riley if their safety depended on it—even if that meant taking them there against her will.

She would despise him for it, he was sure. But her life was more important than how she felt about him, and he wasn't willing to leave it to chance.

He had been putting off making the call for long enough.

Walking over to the small closet near the bed, Knox reached inside the zippered chest pocket of his black parka for the burner phone he'd been carrying with him all these months on the road.

How many times had he been tempted to toss the damn thing and really disappear? Too many to count. Now, he was glad to have it. The battery was long dead, but he willed it back to life with a mental command.

He didn't know how any of his brothers would respond to hearing from him after all this time, but he'd deal with that as it came. There was only one male he trusted to help.

As the Florida Darkhaven's resident surveillance and tech expert, Razor had both the skills and the connections to put a plan in motion on little to zero notice.

He would have questions, of course. Razor dissected every problem with the acuity of his chosen name. It was simply his brother's nature, just as Knox's nature was to keep all of his shit locked up tight.

His involvement with Leni being no exception.

Before he could change his mind, he started tapping the digits that would connect him to the Darkhaven's secured line.

It hadn't even begun to ring when Leni's scream ripped through the morning quiet of the house downstairs.

CHAPTER 15

"Riley!" Leni raced into the kitchen, her heart slamming against her ribs. "Rye, this isn't funny. Where are you?"

Moving at a dead run, she nearly crashed into Knox. He came off the last step of the back stairwell as if he'd materialized rather than moved. He approached her looking grim with concern, dressed only in jeans and a dark T-shirt.

"What's wrong?"

"Riley. He's gone."

"What do you mean, gone?"

"I mean he's not anywhere in the house." She gestured wildly, panic clawing up the back of her throat. "I should've checked on him as soon as I woke up. I should've made sure I saw him before I got in the shower." The words tumbled out of her, her voice choked with guilt. The only thing heavier was the terror churning in her stomach. "Oh, God. Today of all days, I shouldn't have let down my guard for a second."

Saturday. Travis Parrish's release day.

The day she'd been dreading for years was finally here and she'd lost Riley the instant her back was turned.

"Hey." Knox's strong hands settled on her shoulders, his stormy blue eyes trying to reach her through her rising alarm. "It's going to be okay. Slow down, Leni. Tell me what happened."

She withdrew from his touch, bristling at the tenderness no matter how much she wanted comforting and reassurance.

"I overslept." It came out like an accusation, sharp with anger. She didn't blame Knox for her distraction as much as she blamed herself, but worry for Riley made every word grate over her tongue. "I just went in to get him up for breakfast after my shower, but he's not in his room. The blanket is missing off the bed. Fred's gone too."

Knox gave a measured nod as he listened. "He can't have gone far, Leni. He must be around here somewhere."

"What if he's not?" she snapped. "What if they took him while I was sleeping? Or last night, while we were—"

Sick with guilt, she could hardly finish the thought. Her morning had started off like a dream. She had awakened with a smile that she couldn't seem to erase from her lips, her body aching in all the right places after the incredible night she'd spent in Knox's arms.

All of that giddy joy and blissful fatigue evaporated in an instant. Ice-cold fear replaced it when she found Riley missing a minute ago. Her veins were still freezing with worry. Her throat was still raw from her scream, her heart still on the verge of exploding.

"Everything's going to be okay," Knox stated firmly. "The Parrishes didn't take him. They're just men, Leni, not ghosts. I promise you, no one came into this house last night or this morning. I would've heard them. I would have smelled them."

She stared up at him, miserable. "And yet Riley's gone."

Although she hadn't meant to fault Knox for her failure, his jaw tightened as if she'd struck him. She paced away from him, heartsick and furious with herself.

This was all her fault. She had let herself enjoy a few hours of pleasure, of normalcy, and this was the price. Riley's safety.

Her gaze flicked to the door leading out to the backyard. She drew in a breath.

"It's unlocked." She swung a look at Knox. "The deadbolt. It's open."

She had been so swamped with panic she hadn't noticed the detail until now. She glanced at the small pile of footwear cluttering the mat beside the back entry and realized Riley's favorite pair of yellow rain boots were gone.

"He's outside."

The realization snuffed some of her alarm, though not all of it. She wouldn't be able to relax until she had Riley in her arms. She dashed out in her slippers, no patience to fumble with her own boots or a coat. Dressed in the loose jeans and light sweater she threw on after her shower, she scrambled off the stoop and down into the thick blanket of snow that spread out behind the house and into the surrounding forest.

Morning sunlight nearly blinded her, beaming from a cloudless blue sky and sparkling off the pristine snow cover like diamonds. She followed a pair of kid-sized boot prints that made a meandering path toward the trees.

"Riley!" Her shout echoed in the tall pines. "Riley, where are you?"

A sudden gust of cold wind buffeted her from behind. It passed by her, a blur of energy and motion too fast for her eyes to track, especially in the harsh glare of the sun's rays.

But when she glanced down she saw there were now two sets of prints in the snow. Riley's distracted amble into the woods, and an arrow-straight path left by Knox's bare feet.

Oh, God. He'd come out into the daylight to look for Riley?

Her heart lurched at the thought. More than a few minutes of ultraviolet light was lethal to the Breed, especially a Gen One like Knox. Yet he'd just run straight into the brightest part of morning. For Riley.

For her.

Leni raced into the forest, following the trail of footprints. Out of breath, her heartbeat hammering, she felt as though she'd run more than a mile when she finally spotted Knox's hulking form up ahead near the ravine.

He held Riley in his strong arms.

"Oh, thank God."

The little boy was dressed like a superhero, the blue coverlet from his bed tied around his neck like a cape. Red long john pajamas and yellow rain boots completed the makeshift costume. His teddy bear dangled from one hand as Knox carried the boy and Fred up from bracken-tangled incline above the river.

Leni sprinted forward, swamped with relief. "Riley!"

Now that she saw he was safe, it was hard to keep her anger at bay. She had never raised her voice to him or had to discipline him, but he had never given her such a fright before.

That cold fear still leeched into her veins as she caught up to them. Some of it transferred to Knox when she noticed the blistering skin on his bare arms. The UV light was taking a toll already, singeing his face and throat too.

"Knox, you shouldn't be out here like this. Give Riley to me. I'll take care of him. You need to go back to the house before you burn up."

"Don't worry about me." His deep voice allowed no argument. And he kept his hold on Riley, all but dismissing the certain agony of his scorched skin. "I'm not going anywhere until I have both of you safe inside."

Leni held herself together as they hurried back to the house. Once they stepped into the kitchen and Knox set Riley down on the floor, the dam burst on all of her emotions.

She crouched to pull the boy into a fierce hug. A sob caught in her throat as she clung to him. She couldn't let go. She could hardly speak for the torrent of relief and anger and gratitude spilling over inside her.

His slim little body tensed. "Aunt Leni, are you crying?"

"Yes, I am. And do you know why?" She couldn't hold back the wet trails that ran down her cheeks as she set him away from her. With her hands clamped on his narrow shoulders, she looked into his confused face. "I thought something very bad had happened to you. You scared me, Riley. You scared me very much."

"I'm sorry."

She shook her head. "That's not good enough. Not this time. What have I told you about playing outside?"

He frowned, looking reluctant to add to her upset. "I don't remember."

"Yes, you do. Never alone. That's the rule." Leni expelled a sharp breath instead of the curse that leapt to the tip of her tongue when she thought of all the awful scenarios that had played through her head from the moment she woke to find him missing. "You do not leave the house by yourself. Especially not now. Not ever. Do you understand?"

"But I wasn't alone. Fred came with me." He held up the stuffed bear as if to prove his point. "And we made a new friend in the woods too, but I don't know her name 'cause she ran away when I tried to ask her."

Leni pinched the bridge of her nose. "I don't have the energy for this right now, kiddo. I can't deal with talking toys or imaginary friends. Not today."

"But Aunt Leni—"

"Enough," she bit off tightly. "This is real life now. You broke the rules today and I don't ever want you to do that again. Promise me."

He nodded, his sweet little face drooping with remorse. "Promise."

Leni lifted his chin and untied the corners of the small blanket draped over him. Divested of his cape, she took Fred out of his hands and set both items on the floor beside her. Next came his rain boots.

"Go on upstairs to your room now. I'll be up to talk to you about all of this in a few minutes."

"What about Fred?"

She shook her head. "He's staying down here with me."

"Why can't I take him?" he whined.

"Because both of you are grounded until I say otherwise."

"No!" He stomped his stockinged foot. "That's not fair—"

"I said go." She jabbed her finger in the direction of the stairwell. "Up to your room, Riley. Right now."

Her sharp tone clearly took him aback. He whirled away from her on a huff, then ran upstairs in a burst of tears.

Leni let out her breath in a long, heavy sigh. "I've never raised my voice to him before. I've never had to discipline him."

"You're doing it out of love. Every kid should be so lucky," Knox said, his deep voice devoid of judgment. "He'll survive."

"What about you, Knox?" She stood up and pivoted to face him. "Your burns—"

"Are nothing," he said, shrugging as if the extensive blistering and smoldering skin on his muscled arms and handsome face didn't faze him in the least.

What must he have endured in his life that agonizing injuries like this meant so little to him?

That he'd risked the exposure to help her and Riley made Leni's heart squeeze even tighter in her breast. She moved toward him, hating that she was the reason for his pain.

"You shouldn't have done it," she murmured. She reached for him, wanting to touch him but uncertain where her fingers could land without adding to his discomfort. She rested her hand lightly over the center of his chest, which had been shielded from the light by the fabric of his T-shirt.

He flinched under her fingertips. "Does this hurt?"

"No." The word sounded strangled and thick. His heartbeat thudded heavily against her palm. Leni looked up at him and found his blue-gray eyes fixed on her. Embers glittered behind the stormy hue of his irises. "You shouldn't stand so close to me, Lenora."

The points of his fangs showed behind his lip as he uttered the tight, low warning.

She didn't heed it. All she wanted to do was wrap her arms around him and never let go.

"Tell me what I can do to help you. Your skin needs care, Knox."

God, she could barely stand to look at the severity of his burns. They went beyond anything she'd ever seen before, closer to a prolonged dose of pure radiation than even the worst bout of sunburn. Just standing in close proximity to him she could feel the heat of his burns warming her own skin.

It was easy to think of Knox in human terms the longer she spent in his company, but this was a stark reminder that he was something different. He was more than a man, yet as strong and invincible as he was in so many ways, there were things that could wound him.

There were things that could kill him.

Things as mundane as a few minutes of sunshine.

"I should take you to the county hospital."

He frowned. "They can't help me."

"Then I'll run a cool bath for you in the tub upstairs. I can make some cold compresses—"

"None of those things can help, Leni."

"Then what will?" She stared up at his blistered, smoldering cheeks and brow. The sparks that had been igniting in his eyes a moment ago intensified as his gaze caught and held hers. The heat radiating off his big body seemed to shift toward something sharper, something verging on dangerous, predatory. "You need blood. Don't you?"

She didn't miss the flare of amber that lit his irises in response. But he shook his head. He took a step back from her, then another.

"I need time, that's all. A few hours and my body will heal itself."

"A few hours of agony," she pointed out. She didn't want to imagine how miserable that duration of suffering would be for him. "How long would it take you to heal if you were able to feed from someone?"

He shrugged. "Less than an hour probably. It doesn't matter. I can't risk more exposure now and I'll be healed before it's safe for me to head out and find a blood Host anyway."

Leni nodded, realizing he'd already considered and dismissed the idea. "I could go out and find someone for you." Even as she said it, a selfish, possessive part of her regretted the offer. But his suffering was harder to bear. She would do anything in her power to ease it. "I'm sure if I gave Milo at the gas station a few dollars he'd be willing to come. Or there's Carla. She'd be here in a minute if I asked her to help."

He visibly balked. "Forget it. The worst of this will pass soon enough. I don't need anyone's help."

"Not even mine?" She lifted her hand toward his ravaged face and let it hover there, wanting to give him comfort yet knowing anything she did would only make his pain worse. Except, perhaps, one thing. "What if you fed from me, Knox?"

"Jesus Christ." He nearly choked. "Don't ask me that. Don't even fucking think it."

"Why not?"

"Because it's not going to happen," he snapped. He scowled at her, and the glow of his eyes surged brighter. "One drop is all it would take to bind me to you. That means forever, Leni. There's no taking it back, no matter how much either of us will surely want to one day. It's a shackle that can't be broken, not ever."

He made the idea sound ominous and awful. She didn't want to feel so stung by his description of something she knew was sacred among the Breed.

She understood the bond between Knox and a woman born with a Breedmate symbol on her body would be an eternal one. She knew only death could sever the blood connection between a mated couple.

And yet she was willing to give that to him.

True, she was offering out of concern for his injuries, but there was something deeper behind the feeling. She cared for him. She had accepted him into her life and her confidence. Last night she had accepted him into her bed. She wasn't sure when he'd infiltrated her heart, but there was no denying it now.

It stunned her to realize that.

It stunned her even more to realize just how much it hurt to hear Knox dismiss the idea of drinking from her as though it was the last thing he would ever consider.

The feel of his fingertips under her chin jolted her. He lifted her gaze to his, his face a ruined mask of torment and pain. "I'm not here to add to your problems, Lenora. Letting things get out of hand between us last night was bad enough. I should've had more control. I owe you an apology for that."

His gentleness now only made his regret for what they'd done together seem that much more evident. She hadn't considered making love with him to be a mistake, but it was obvious he did. To hear him blame himself for the incredible night they'd shared broke something tender and vulnerable inside her.

She couldn't let him see the fracture. She had been the one with a lack of control last night. She had been the foolish one—then and now.

She withdrew from his touch and folded her arms in front of her. "Yeah, I guess we both lost sight of reality last night."

Standing here with Knox, she would have worsened the mistake exponentially by giving him her blood, her bond.

The awful truth was, if he wanted her, she still would.

God, that must make her worse than a fool.

"I need to go look after Riley," she said, working to keep the hurt out of her expression and her voice. "Thank you for helping me find him and bring him home."

He gave her less than a nod, a stiff, formal response.

Leni didn't wait to let him see any more of her humiliation.

Turning away from him, she strode out of the kitchen with a new resolve. From now on, she needed to protect her heart as fiercely as she was willing to protect her nephew's life.

CHAPTER 16

She avoided him for the rest of the day and the duration of the night.

Thank fuck for that small mercy, even though he'd won it from her by being an unfeeling bastard. Something he seemed to excel at, and not only since he'd met Leni.

He didn't know how to be anything else. Deep down, he would always be the disciplined laboratory rat, the born-and-bred soldier who'd been taught nothing but logic and combat from the time he was torn from his mother's womb.

Knox had needed both of those skills yesterday morning, when Leni had stood before him offering her blood to heal him.

Offering her bond, for crissake.

He had been sorely tempted. Not only because of the severity of his UV burns, although they had been hellish enough to warrant some relief. No, the temptation that had leapt to life inside him had little to do with any of the pain or injury he'd endured for most of the day until his body had finally healed itself.

His craving to take Leni's throat under his fangs had been born of something even more demanding than physical suffering.

It had been fueled by desire. Possessive need. A depth of caring that had nearly overcome him when he saw the sincerity of her offer in her eyes.

Her blood—and her eternal bond—had been his for the taking.

Her tender, courageous heart as well.

It humbled him, even now.

And it shamed him to reflect on how callously he'd rebuffed those gifts.

He'd had to shut her down hard and fast. Especially when everything Breed in him had been dangerous with the need to feed, to find some relief from the intensity of his wounds.

Shit. He should have taken her up on the offer to bring him a blood Host. Nearly twenty-four hours since he'd run headlong into the morning sunlight to look for the boy and now he was walking the edge of a ravenous thirst.

He would have to leave the house to address the situation as soon as night fell. God knew if he'd be up to the test of another night under the same roof with Leni, regardless if she continued giving him the cold shoulder.

But what about the next night? Or the one after that?

He knew the best solution for her, and for himself.

It was the one he'd been trying to ignore while he dealt with the agony of his burns. Now that he was healed, it was time to do what was right.

Before he could change his mind or delay any longer, he picked up his burner phone and called his brother's encrypted number. The call connected on the third ring, nothing but silence on the open end of the secured line.

"Razor, it's me."

A measured exhalation filtered into Knox's ear. Then a low, hissed curse. "Well, I'll be goddamned. Hell must've frozen over if I'm hearing from you, brother."

"Close," Knox said, glancing out the attic window at nothing but snowdrifts and ice crystals on the ground below.

"Where you at?"

"Maine."

Razor grunted. "What the fuck are you doing up there—and in the middle of ball-shriveling February, besides?"

"I've been asking myself that same question for almost a week." He took a seat on the edge of the narrow bed. "I need you to do something for me, Raze."

"As long as it doesn't involve me meeting you up there, I'll do my best. What's going on?"

"I need a safe house. Somewhere up here near the North Maine Woods, or even Quebec."

"I'll see what I can do. What kind of trouble are you in?"

"It's not for me. It's for someone else. A woman. Her name's Lenora Calhoun." He cleared his throat. "She's a Breedmate."

"Yours?" Razor asked, more than mild surprise in his voice.

Knox blew out a curse, but only because the swift denial he expected to issue had suddenly gotten trapped in the back of his throat. "I have no claim on Leni."

And he intended to keep it that way, before he fucked things up any worse.

"If you've got no claim on her, why is she asking you to find her a safe house?"

"She hasn't asked. This is my decision. It's for the best."

Razor scoffed. "Spoken like a man who has no claim on a woman. What the hell have you gotten yourself into up there?"

"You want to keep asking stupid questions, or are you going to help me?"

"I'm just trying to figure out what made you call for an assist after going on half a year without a word. Been a long time since you worried about anyone, Knox. Especially a female."

"She's a Breedmate," Knox muttered. "Isn't that enough?"

"You tell me, bro."

It was enough, and Razor damn well knew it. But the cagey former Hunter was like a bloodhound when it came to chasing down quarry, and right now he smelled Knox's weakness where Leni was concerned.

"You know what, forget it." Knox stood up, started pacing the tight confines of his quarters. "This was a bad idea. I'll find another way to handle this situation myself."

Razor chuckled. "Relax, asshole. I'm all over it already. I just put feelers out to a couple of my contacts while we've been talking."

Some of Knox's frustration simmered down. "I don't want to rely on any of your shady underground connections, Raze. No other Hunters for this, either. I need someone I can trust implicitly to keep Leni and her young nephew safe."

"She's got a kid?" Razor's dubious tone came through loud and clear. "Is the boy Breed?"

"No. He's human. Her half-sister's six-year-old son."

"That could complicate things."

Knox ran a hand over his jaw. "Tell me about it."

"I'll make it work."

"Thanks, man. I'll owe you."

"I know. Don't be surprised if I come to you to collect one day."

Knox wasn't sure what he meant, but his brother's tone hinted at private troubles he was in no hurry to confide. "I want a legit resource on this, Razor. Airtight security and confidence from whoever you bring in, all right?"

"Is the Order legit enough for you?"

Knox's track back and forth halted. "You've got contacts in the Order now?"

"I've got contacts everywhere that counts, brother." He paused, silent for a moment. "Say the word and it's done. But you and I both know once I open that door, I can't close it again. Lucan and his warriors don't fuck around when it comes to protecting unmated Breedmates. Especially ones who're in some kind of danger. That's what we're talking about here, right? You going to be ready to let your Leni go if the Order decides she'll be able to live a safer life away from you?"

"I told you, she's not mine."

So, why did it grate over his heart like jagged steel to imagine the Order taking Leni and Riley into their protection? He couldn't ask for a better, more capable alternative—other than one of his own brethren down in the Everglades Darkhaven.

"You haven't answered my question, brother."

"Just make it happen," he snarled.

"All right." Razor's reply was solemn and resolute. "Consider it done."

Knox ended the call without a reply, his attention snagged on the sound of Leni and Riley talking downstairs. The front door creaked open, then closed with a solid thump.

What the fuck?

Where was she going? How could he protect her when she hadn't even told him she was leaving?

Right. As if he would be any use to her in the full light of another morning.

"Son of a bitch."

He flashed down to the kitchen in an instant, met with the silence of an empty house. On the counter near the sink lay a note jotted in crisp handwriting.

Took Riley with me to open the diner. I need him with me, where I can keep a close watch and know he's safe.

When I get home, we need to talk.

—L.

Knox leaned against the counter and exhaled a curse.

She was right, of course. They did need to talk.

He only hoped she wouldn't despise him for what he'd just done.

CHAPTER 17

Opening the diner had been just the distraction she'd needed.

Business was slow most of the day due to the unmaintained roads surrounding Parrish Falls and the tinier bergs spread out around it, but she'd had a steady flow of customers that kept her hopping between the kitchen and the dining room from the minute she turned the sign in the front door.

The bell jingled as another patron, one of her favorite locals, came inside from the cold and took his seat at the counter. Leni grabbed the coffee pot and filled the ceramic cup in front of him, leaving room enough for the triple creams she knew the regular would be dumping into the strong brew. "How did you and Mable fare in the storm the other night, Claude?"

The old man nodded in greeting as he tore the foil tops off the creamers. "Power's still out and the road's a mess, but we're just fine. We were luckier than most. Heard on the satellite radio that the roads farther into the interior toward St. Zacharie are going to be all but impassable for the next couple of days."

"Well, I'm glad you were able to make it out. It always brightens my day to see you."

His gray-whiskered cheeks turned a little ruddier at her compliment. "Mable would've liked to join me, but her damn hip's acting up again. Thought I'd come in for coffee then bring us home something warm for lunch."

Leni smiled. "I just made a batch of chicken and dumplings this morning."

"Sold," he said, toasting her with his steaming cup. "I'll take two plates to go."

"Coming right up."

With the rest of the lunch customers already taken care of and Riley contentedly playing at the far booth with a handful of race cars she'd let him bring from home, Leni headed into the kitchen to prepare the new order.

She had settled into her usual rhythm in the hours she'd been back at work. It felt good having something else to occupy her thoughts, other than the complicated jumble her life had become in recent days. Working took her mind off the Parrishes and her unbearable sense of dread over Travis's homecoming. God knew she needed a break from that worry.

She should be relieved he hadn't made a beeline for her house the moment he was freed from the state penitentiary. She was glad to be spared the confrontation, but she also couldn't lull herself into believing he would stay away forever.

And while keeping herself busy allowed her to put that trouble on the shelf for awhile, it didn't help her stop thinking about Knox. It didn't help ease the hurt that had opened up in the wake of his cool rejection.

The full day and night she'd gone without speaking to him—without so much as seeing him despite the fact that he was living under the same roof with her—had passed at an agonizing pace. It felt as though a week had stretched out between them. She missed him as if it had been even longer than that.

What kind of naive idiot did it make her that she had let her heart get so tangled up in him after only a few days in his company?

A few days and one incredible night, although she didn't want to think about the feel of Knox's arms around her now. She didn't want to remember how consuming the feel of his mouth on hers had been, or how intensely pleasurable it had felt to have his big, powerful body moving over her naked skin, thrusting deep inside her.

A shiver of arousal swept through her, igniting her veins in spite of the hurt that lingered in her heart.

She had expected to feel some measure of satisfaction behind the wall she'd constructed between them. Instead, all she felt was alone. As for Knox, she couldn't even be sure he had noticed her determination to avoid him. Or maybe he'd been relieved.

Either way, the time apart had given her a chance to think more clearly—something she'd seemed incapable of doing ever since Knox arrived in town.

For most of her life, she had taken care of herself. For the past six years, she had taken care of Riley by herself too. She was perfectly capable of doing that now, and no one—not even Travis Parrish or the rest of his family—was going to stand in her way.

She had managed well enough before Knox showed up. She would manage after he was gone. She and Riley were not his concern.

As soon as she returned home after work, Leni intended to free him of whatever obligation he felt toward protecting them. In fact, she planned to demand it.

She'd been rehearsing the words in her head all day. Now, all she had to do was convince herself she truly meant them.

Forcing a smile to her face, she carried out the packed and bagged servings of hot lunch and set them down on the counter while she wrote up the bill.

"Here you go, Claude."

He glanced at the total and shook his head. "You're slipping, Leni. Forgot to charge for my coffee."

"It's on the house for everyone today. Seems the least I can do for all of you who've been braving the roads to come in and eat."

He grinned. "Well, in that case, thank you kindly."

"My pleasure."

She made a quick round with the carafe again, refilling his and the rest of the patrons' cups. Then she swung by to check on Riley, who was currently chatting up the elderly couple seated in the booth in front of his.

"The red one's the best, though. It's got doors that open and it goes really fast. Watch."

Leni caught the airborne muscle car in her free hand as Riley launched it off the table. "Okay, I think we all get the picture, kiddo. Cars need to keep their wheels on solid ground in here, all right?"

She glanced at her customers and offered an eyeroll and a mouthed apology. They didn't seem bothered in the least. Riley had that effect on most people, Leni included. She'd hated reprimanding him yesterday, and her attempt to ground him had been admittedly lax. Staying mad at the little charmer was next to impossible.

Rather like the bigger, slightly less charming—but equally devastating—male she'd left back at the house.

"I've got macaroni and cheese waiting for you in the kitchen," she said, placing Riley's car on the table with the others. "Are you getting hungry for lunch?"

He bounced on the seat, his face lit up with excitement. "Yes!"

"Then please put away your cars and go use the restroom. I'll bring your mac and cheese out to you. Make sure you wash your hands before you come out."

"Okay!" He swept the fleet of miniature race cars into his backpack before scrambling out of the booth and hurrying to the nearby men's room.

Leni couldn't hold back her smile as she finished her rounds of check-ins with the smattering of patrons, then returned to the kitchen to fetch his lunch. The normalcy of the day settled around her like a warm comforter. This was how things were supposed to be for her.

Steady, familiar, comfortable.

It should be enough.

It would have to be, because starting tomorrow Knox would be gone.

She didn't want to think about that, no matter how much she wanted to believe it was for the best.

She scooped a portion of the fresh-baked casserole onto a plate for Riley, then added a spoonful of applesauce and a couple of florets of steamed broccoli.

She had no delusions that the green veggies would pass his lips without a good deal of cajoling, but she figured it was always worth a shot to try.

With a glass of chocolate milk to complete the meal, Leni pushed open the swinging door with her hip and stepped out to the dining room with both hands full.

At that same moment, two men approached the diner's entrance from a large gold SUV in the parking lot. She didn't have to see the Parrish & Sons logo on the side of the vehicle to know who it belonged to. Leni recognized Enoch Parrish's bent, wiry frame even before he lifted his gray head and scowling face.

The younger man accompanying him looked vastly different than she recalled.

Travis Parrish had gone away to prison a tall and trim, slope-shouldered twenty-five-year-old. He was returning home twice as thick and bulky with weight-trained muscles. His rich brown hair was shorn tight against his skull and flecked with silver now, evidence of a difficult existence these past several years. But his face was unmistakable.

So was the flat, dark gaze that found her through the glass of the diner's front door.

Some cowardly part of her urged her to drop what she held in her hands and rush to bar the door before they could get in. But it was already too late for that anyway. The bells over the entrance gave a jaunty clamor as Shannon's convicted assailant and his sneering, elderly father came inside.

A handful of the locals turned to greet Travis like an old friend or a favored son. Maybe it was unfair for her to wish everyone despised the Parrishes as she did. To most of the town, they represented not only the founding family but the largest employer when the timber business had been booming. The Parrishes continued to bankroll various businesses and charitable causes in the county. They had been flexing their wealth and power for generations, and there were few who would cross them, even now.

Still, watching Travis stroll into her establishment to shake hands with her customers as if he belonged there—as if he hadn't been sent away for nearly killing her sister—set Leni's teeth on edge.

She put the plate and glass of milk down on the countertop near the cash register, her gaze wary and guarded. She didn't know whether to demand the two of them leave, or let them see that she wasn't going to be easily intimidated.

She chose the latter, at the same time praying they would go before Riley came out of the restroom.

Someone seated farther down at the counter called out to Enoch. "Heard what happened to Dwight the other night. Attacked by a goddamn vamp? What's the world coming to when we've got bloodsuckers pushing this far north?"

"My boy's doing just fine, considering," the elder Parrish said, swiveling his narrow gaze on Leni behind the register. "As for the creature that attacked him, we're gonna be ready for the bastard next time he dares show his face again."

Leni wanted to laugh at the sheer bravado of the statement. There was nothing Enoch Parrish and all three of his sons combined could do to Knox before he eviscerated every last one of them. She held the old man's gaze, refusing to let him cow her.

Another man chimed in from a booth near the door. "Takes more than a near brush with death to slow Dwight down. I passed him and Jeb driving a load of timber toward the border on my way into town this morning. They were hauling ass too, nearly plowed right into me."

Travis, who'd been busy basking in the welcome from some of the patrons, now swung a glance at his father.

Something peculiar flickered in the old man's eyes, but he shuttered it with a slow blink and a flattened smile directed at the local man who spoke. "We had an order that needed filling right away."

"Must've been important to brave the awful road conditions out that way."

Enoch chuckled dryly. "Money doesn't wait for good weather."

The man laughed. "Amen to that."

"Besides, Dwight has a vehicle to replace now." The Parrish patriarch turned his attention back to Leni. "What we ought to do is press charges against the Breed male who attacked him. Unless you can think of a reason we shouldn't."

"Maybe I should press charges against Dwight for running me off the road earlier that night. Whatever he claims Knox did to him, he had it coming."

With the diner buzzing with conversation now, Enoch moved closer to the register where she stood. Skewering her in a stare that made her skin crawl, he lowered his voice to a soft murmur. "He's gotten to you, hasn't he, girl? That blood-drinker. He got his fangs into you already. Or was it something else he stuck in you?"

Leni bristled. "How dare you speak to me like that? You're disgusting."

"No, Lenora. You are. What you're doing with that subhuman ain't right. It goes against nature." He licked his thin, cracked lips. "I'm sure I could find a judge who agrees with me. One who'll also agree that kind of environment's not good for a child."

The weight of the threat gave her pause. She knew Enoch Parrish would have no qualms about paying for a verdict in his favor. No judges worthy of their robes would rule that way, but there were others willing to bend laws for the right price. She had no doubt the Parrishes knew exactly who they could call.

Travis sauntered over, pausing beside his father. "Been a while, Leni."

"Not long enough. I can't believe they let you out early."

His face hardened. "Well, they did. And things are going to change around here now that I'm home. All I've thought about these past six years is my son."

She scoffed. "I'm shocked you could find the time, in between the bible studies you took up to impress the parole board and all the hours you've obviously spent working out in the prison gym."

"People can change, Lenora."

"Not you. And just to be clear," she added, "Riley's not your son. He never will be."

His hard expression turned stony. "We'll see about that."

At that same moment, Riley burst out of the restroom like the force of nature he was. "I'm ready, Aunt Leni! I even washed my hands two times."

"Good job, buddy."

Travis's big body went utterly still as his gaze lit on Riley. His breath gusted out of him on a low curse. "Shit. Look at him. He's so big. I kept picturing a baby in my mind."

Oblivious to the situation taking place across the diner, Riley skipped over to the back booth then halted. "Hey, where's my mac-n-cheese?"

"I've got it for you right here," Leni said. "Come around behind the counter with me, kiddo."

As reluctant as she was to bring him any closer to the Parrishes, she needed the reassurance of a solid barrier between her and Riley and the two men who were determined to take him from her. To her relief, he obeyed without a hint of resistance. Entering from the open end opposite her and his father, he shuffled up to her side. Leni wrapped her arm around his shoulders and drew him close.

Travis never took his eyes off him for a second. "Hi there, Riley."

"Hi. Can I have my mac-n-cheese now, please?" He tilted his face up at Leni, giving her a goofy grin.

She brushed some of his pale blond hair away from his eyes. "Yes, you can. Why don't you eat your lunch in the kitchen?"

"He's got his daddy's smile," Enoch said, patting Travis's hand, which was gripped on the edge of the counter.

"I don't have a daddy," Riley stated matter-of-factly. "I don't have a mom, either."

"You've got a mom," Leni countered. "You'll always have your mom. Remember what I told you about that?"

He nodded, touching the center of his chest. "She lives in here."

"That's right. Until we see her again, you need to keep her right there in your heart."

Enoch's airless chuckle rattled quietly. "Sweet sentiment. But I've always believed little boys need their fathers more than they need their mothers. Don't you agree, Travis?"

"Yeah. I sure do."

Leni bristled, her hold on Riley tightening. "Are you two going to order something? If not, I'll thank you both to leave so I can get back to work."

"Oh, hey." Travis snapped his fingers. "I just remembered. I brought something for you, Riley."

He stared at the stranger, confused. "You did?"

Before Leni knew what he was doing, Travis reached into his coat pocket and withdrew a shiny new phone. He woke the screen and held it out to Riley. "It's got some fun games on it, and if you push this button we can talk to each other anytime we want to."

"Cool."

Leni snatched it away before Riley had a chance to touch the device. She handed it back to Travis. "He's too young for a phone, and he has no reason to call you."

"I had a feeling you might say that." He stared at her for a long moment, then smiled. "So, I brought something for you too."

He pulled a white envelope out of his pocket and slapped it down on the counter. "It's a court order for a paternity test."

Riley glanced innocently up at her. "What's a perternity test?"

Travis gave her a thin smile. "Do you want to tell him, or should I?"

Leni glared at his smug expression as she picked up the plate of macaroni and cheese and handed it to Riley. "Go on, eat your lunch before it's cold. I'll bring your chocolate milk in. Just give me a minute, all right?"

He nodded, then pushed through the swinging door into the kitchen as she'd asked.

As soon as he was gone, she reached beneath the counter. Holding the envelope in one hand, the flaming tip of a long-nosed lighter in the other, she touched fire to the edge of the court order. She held Travis's gaze as she let the document burn.

He shook his head. "You shouldn't have done that, Leni. I thought you were the smart one."

She threw the burning envelope at him. He batted it away, then stomped it out with his boot when it drifted to the tile floor.

"Get out of my diner," Leni said. "Both of you, stay out of our lives."

Enoch sneered. "I told you, son. She's a dumb slut, just like her sister."

"Dumb sluts get hurt," Travis said. "Sometimes, they disappear."

"Are you threatening me? You're not out of prison two days and you're already itching so much to go back you're going to threaten me in front of half a dozen witnesses?"

He swung a glance at the diner full of people, all of them watching and listening now. Enoch curled his gnarled fingers in the sleeve of Travis's coat. "Come on, son. We're obviously wasting our time with her."

"Yes, you are," Leni agreed. "So, go."

They took their time about it, but after a few moments they were gone.

Leni sagged onto her elbows on the counter. What had she just done? She couldn't let them intimidate her, but dammit, she hadn't meant to escalate the situation, either.

Shuffling footsteps approached from the other side of the counter. Then a hand landed gently on her bent shoulder.

Old Claude heaved a long sigh. "Lenora, I'm worried for you. Don't you realize it's dangerous to draw a line in the sand with folks like the Parrishes?"

She lifted her head. "Yes, I know that. Maybe it's time someone did it anyway."

CHAPTER 18

L eni came back to the house just before sundown, carrying a sleeping Riley in her arms.

Knox met her at the back door. After prowling the confines of the house like a caged animal all day, he'd been counting down the seconds until nightfall when it would be safe for him to run out and hunt for a blood Host. Now that Leni was back, his only concern was the look of utter fatigue on her beautiful face.

The defeat he saw in her eyes disturbed him even more.

He'd never seen her so dejected, not even after his boorish behavior with her yesterday.

Worry pulled his face into a scowl. He reached out to take her burden. "Let me help you with him."

"No." A single word, crisp with finality. "I can manage. He conked out after supper in the diner. I need to put him to bed."

She walked past Knox without meeting his gaze. Her continued cold shoulder irked him, but the tension he saw in her spine and carefully schooled expression hinted at something more than just aggravation with him.

Knox's scowl deepened, along with his concern. "Did something happen today, Leni?"

"Nothing I can't handle."

With that quiet statement, she walked up the stairs to the bedroom on the second floor.

Knox waited below as the old floorboards creaked under her soft footsteps. After a few moments, he heard her make her way from Riley's room to the master bedroom at the other end of the hall. She closed the door behind her and didn't come out.

Ten minutes passed, then several more.

Knox swore under his breath. If she thought he was going to play along for another round of avoidance, she was sorely mistaken. If being near her without wanting to feel her in his arms was a torment he could barely withstand, being ignored by her was even worse.

And he couldn't deny the fact that he was troubled by her withdrawn demeanor.

Something was wrong.

Something had happened to upset her, and every combat instinct inside him was certain it had everything to do with Travis Parrish.

He took the steps three at a time, then stole down the hallway to her bedroom. His knock went unanswered. So did his low request for her to let him in.

Then he heard the faint sound of her hitched breath coming from somewhere inside. Followed by a muffled sob.

"Damn it." Knowing he had no right to barge into her private quarters didn't stop him from reaching for the doorknob. It was unlocked, though hardly an invitation for him to enter.

"Lenora?" He stepped inside, drawn to the hushed sounds of her crying inside the adjoining bathroom. She was still wearing her navy pea coat and boots, sitting on the closed toilet seat with her face in her hands, her body curved into itself as she wept. "Ah, Christ. Leni."

He crouched before her and gathered her into his arms. She didn't resist his embrace. All of the fight seemed gone from her as she continued crying into his chest.

"It's all right now. I've got you." It was a miracle his voice didn't sound more unearthly than it did. Rage poured through him at the feel of her trembling in his arms. "You heard from Travis today?"

She nodded, sniffling. "He came into the diner this afternoon with his father, Enoch."

The bastard had gotten within arm's length of her while he'd been holed up waiting for the sun to go down? Fuck.

Knox wanted to punch his fist through something—preferably, Travis Parrish's face.

"Tell me what happened, sweetheart." His reply was toneless with the depth of his fury. "What did he do? And God help him if he laid as much as a finger on you."

"No, nothing like that," she said, shaking her head. Her tears slowed as Knox caressed her back. She lifted her head, glancing up at him with red-rimmed eyes. "He's managed to get the law on his side now. He came in with a court order for a paternity test on Riley."

"Shit. Where is it?"

LARA ADRIAN

"I lit the damn thing on fire and threw it back in his face. Then I told him to get out of my diner and not come back."

Knox felt a smile tug at the edge of his mouth in spite of the gravity of the situation. "You're amazing, you know that?"

She frowned. "I'm only doing what I have to do. I have to keep Riley safe. I have to keep him out of the Parrishes' hands. For Shannon as much as anyone else, I have to do whatever it takes to protect him."

Knox didn't miss the fact that she was excluding him from that equation. Sometime between yesterday morning and tonight, she had determined she was on her own when it came to taking on Travis and his family.

It wasn't going to go over well when he informed her he'd arranged for a safe house without conferring with her. That the remote location a couple hours away from Parrish Falls belonged to the Breed warriors of the Order was only going to add a lot of gasoline to that fire.

"There's more, Knox." Leni's voice took on a strangled edge. "Travis said something to me before he left. Something indirectly about Shannon."

"What about her?"

Tears welled up in her eyes again, emotion choking her words. "He got mad after I burned up the court order. He told me I shouldn't have done it. His father called me a dumb slut. Travis agreed. He said, 'Sometimes dumb sluts get hurt.' Then he said, 'Sometimes they disappear.'"

Knox's growl vibrated deep in his chest. Not only because of the two men who'd spoken to her like that, but because of the threat those words carried.

And underneath the awful words was the intimation that Leni might have been right about the Parrishes' involvement in Shannon's absence.

Leni sagged against him, releasing a broken sob. "What if they killed her, Knox? Oh, God. What if she really is dead?"

He wanted that answer as much as she did. Maybe more than she did, because if it turned out Travis or any of his kin had anything to do with harming Leni's sister, he was going to kill every last one of them with his bare hands.

He pressed a kiss to the top of Leni's head. "We're going to find out what happened to her, I promise."

A small, pained moan escaped her.

"Don't do that," she whispered, pulling herself away from him even though it was clear to him that she needed the comfort. She frowned, shaking her head as she searched his gaze. "Don't let me think you care about me."

"I do care."

She drew back farther, then got to her feet and moved near the glass-enclosed shower. It was about as far as she could get from him without entirely leaving the room. She swiped at the salty streaks that wet her face. "Yesterday, you said you didn't want to add to my problems."

"That's right." He stood, but remained where he was because he had the feeling one wrong move would send his brave, beautiful Leni running from him now. "I don't want to do anything that's going to hurt you or make things harder for you."

"Don't you get it?" She scowled at him, looking cornered and afraid. "By being kind like this, you are hurting me. Just by being here like this, you're making things harder."

Fuck. He had felt like the worst kind of bastard yesterday. Now, his self-directed anger multiplied tenfold. "I'm sorry for what I said. For the way I acted. All of it."

She swallowed, her hazel eyes still wary and untrusting, still wounded. "I'm the one at fault. I asked something of you I had no right to—starting that first night when I assumed I could simply ask you to kill someone just to make my life easier."

"That wasn't why you asked me to deal with Travis Parrish. You were scared, Leni. By my guess, you were terrified of what he might be willing to do to take Riley away from you. After what he said to you at the diner today, I don't think you were far off the mark."

"But that's not your duty, Knox. Just like it's not your obligation to put your life on hold to help protect us—no matter what my Breedmate mark seems to make you believe."

He exhaled sharply. "Your mark isn't the reason I'm here now. It never was. I would've wanted to help you, protect you, even if I'd never seen it."

"I don't need protecting, remember? I don't break. Nothing can wound me, not even Travis Parrish."

"But I've wounded you," Knox pointed out. He let a curse hiss through his teeth. "I saw that yesterday when you offered me your blood and I refused it."

She gave him a withered look. "I don't want to talk about that right now."

"I do, Lenora." He took a step toward her. "You offered me a gift, a sacred one. I threw it back in your face. Not because I didn't recognize the honor of what you were willing to give me. I couldn't take your blood because I'm not deserving of your bond."

Her eyes held his solemn stare. She still looked as though she might bolt at any second, but she remained unmoving, watching him slowly close the distance between them.

"I don't know how to be what you need, Leni, what you deserve. You make me want to be something I've never been before."

Her brows knit over her uncertain gaze. "Not even with Abbie?"

"No. Not even with her." He reached out to Leni, smoothing an errant tendril of dark brown hair from where it stuck to her damp cheek. "Abbie and I didn't share a blood bond. She died on the night I planned to ask her to be my mate. Before her, I'd never let anyone in that close. Losing her gutted me."

Leni's breath sighed out of her lungs. "I'm sorry, Knox. I can't imagine how painful that must've been for you."

He nodded, recalling the depth of his anguish and his guilt. It had stayed with him for all of the past eight years. "The thought of hurting you has been its own kind of hell, Leni. So was not seeing you, not talking to you. Knowing I'd wounded your heart made me want to walk right back into the sun and stay there."

"Knox, no." Her expression softened along with her voice. She placed her hands on the sides of his jaw. "I hated seeing you in pain. It killed me to see your handsome face scorched so badly."

"I told you I'd recover," he murmured, her tender touch stirring his arousal. He hadn't followed her upstairs out of lust, but it was impossible to be anywhere near her and not burn with the need to touch her, to kiss her. He leaned forward and brushed his mouth over hers.

When he drew away from her lips, Leni gave him a sheepish smile. "I had planned to ask you to leave when I got home tonight."

He arched a brow, though he was unsurprised to hear the newsflash. God knew he'd earned it. "Is that still what you want?"

She shook her head. "I didn't really want it even then."

"Good."

He kissed her again, reveling in the feel of her mouth against his. As they kissed, he swept her winter coat off her shoulders so he could feel her body's warmth under his hands. She melted into his embrace, but there was no hiding the tension in the fine muscles of her back and shoulders.

The stress of her confrontation with the Parrishes was still riding her, and while he knew how to give her physical pleasure, what she needed even more than that was comfort and reassurance.

She needed someone to take care of her for a change.

Knox turned on the water in the shower, then began to undress her. She didn't ask questions, didn't reject his tender attention. He couldn't resist caressing her silky skin as he unwrapped her to his fevered gaze. Amber heat filled his vision as he removed her bra and panties.

He drew in a ragged breath through his teeth and fangs. "I couldn't tire of seeing you like this if I had a hundred years to look at you."

She held his transformed gaze, her eyes drinking him in. There was no fear in her face, only heat and desire. Only warm acceptance.

Knox undressed, then took her under the warm spray with him.

What he wanted to give her now wasn't sexual, despite his rampant arousal. She deserved care and compassion tonight.

He wanted to give her everything. Not only tonight, but for as long as she would have him.

That he cared deeply about her was no longer a shock for him to admit, at least to himself. But this other feeling was far more profound than simple affection.

In the short time since he'd met her, Leni had become the primary cause in his life. She'd become part of who he was. His heart had known it for a while now. It had taken his Hunter's coldly logical brain a bit longer to clue in.

He loved this woman.

The realization staggered him.

And it was piss poor timing, considering the phone call he'd made earlier today.

He soaped her shoulders and pretty breasts as she stood in front of him, wreathed in clouds of billowing steam. Her hands moved over him too, slick and warm, each stroke making the coil of need inside him twist tighter, more demanding.

He groaned when she reached down and found his jutting erection. "Ah, Christ, that feels too good," he admitted, his throat as dry as ash while she pumped him. "I promise, my motives were honorable when I brought you in here."

She leaned her head forward and took his nipple between her teeth. When she released it, her breath skated hotly against his chest. "That's too bad, because I need to feel you inside me, Knox."

Holy hell. His body responded with eager interest. The rest of him had equally tenuous resistance.

"Then turn around," he uttered thickly, his fangs surging against his tongue.

His fingers cleaved into the slick heat of her sex, readying her for him. He entered on a long, slow thrust. As hungered as he was, he took his time. She came twice before he let his own release roll over him.

Afterward, they lathered each other again, kissing and caressing until the water ran cold and they had no choice but to leave.

Knox could see the exhaustion still clinging to Leni even after they had toweled off. She was emotionally drained, half asleep on her bare feet.

"Come here," he said, scooping her into his arms.

He carried her to the bed and laid her on the cool sheets. Then he slipped in beside her.

He was still hard, never fully sated when it came to his desire for her.

A different hunger raked him as well, but the thought of leaving her side to feed held little appeal. He only wished he could claim the same about the steady drum of her pulse as she drifted off to sleep in his arms. It echoed in his own veins, a siren's call that took all he had to resist.

He needed blood after the recovery of his burns.

But there was something else he needed even more.

He had no doubt that the threat posed by Travis Parrish was only going to worsen. He had no intention of waiting for that to happen.

He was going to take great pleasure making that point clear.

Lenora Calhoun was his, and he protected what belonged to him.

CHAPTER 19

He hated the idea of leaving Leni and Riley unguarded, even for a minute.

Knowing they were both asleep in their beds, vulnerable to any threat, added urgency to Knox's lightning-quick pace across the frozen woodlands. He followed the river, heading for the large spread of forested land northwest of town.

He'd had several hours of daylight to wait out back at Leni's house today, and he had made use of it by doing a bit of internet reconnaissance on the Parrishes. He'd dug up a handful of interesting articles about their impressive twenty-eight-thousand-acre domain and the once-lucrative lumber operation that had been on a steady decline for the past decade.

Leni mentioned they were far from hurting financially, but it was clear their fortune was only a fraction of what it had been years ago. Public records showed they'd been quietly selling off parcels of the farmable timberland that had been in their hands for generations, relying less and less on the lumber that had made them rich and put their tiny, eponymous town on the map.

Hard times or not, long-widowed Enoch Parrish and his three sons evidently hadn't scaled back on their lifestyle as their business declined. Where the rest of the Parrish Falls' population lived in aged clapboard farmhouses, brick ranches, or mobile homes, the founding family resided in a palatial, well-secured compound adjacent to their lumberyard and sprawling forest land.

Knox stalked up to the electrified fence separating the house's long driveway from the snowy two-lane that rambled past the wooded property. The barrier wouldn't be enough to keep him out tonight, but he paused there for a moment and watched as a light-colored SUV roared to life inside the multi-bay garage.

Headlights pierced the darkness as the vehicle barreled up the drive toward the road. He melted into the shadows of the thick trees as the gate slowly opened to let the driver exit.

Knox had found an inmate photo of Travis Parrish online, and his blood seethed as he watched the newly freed son of a bitch roll out onto the two-lane.

He followed behind the SUV on foot, staying hidden on the tree-lined shoulder. He didn't have to run for long. About five miles up the road, Travis turned in at a squatty roadside tavern. The place was obviously popular, even in the dead of winter. Warm light and loud country music filtered out of it, the only signs of civilization for miles.

Travis drove the gold company vehicle around to the small parking lot in back. Knox crossed the road in a flash of motion, then casually entered the busy establishment from the front door and slipped onto one of the few empty barstools to wait for his target.

Travis Parrish's harassment of Leni today hadn't warranted a lethal confrontation, but that didn't mean Knox was going to let his threat of harming her go unanswered.

The bartender eyed him as the stranger he was as Knox placed an order for a beer he had no intention of drinking. Travis came inside through the back door reeking of cologne and dressed in stiff, new denim jeans and a sweater that strained across his puffed-up pectorals beneath his unzipped jacket. If the fresh clothes and penitentiary-short cut of his dark hair didn't give him away as a recent inmate, the harsh, predatory look in his eyes left no doubt.

Not that the tavern's patrons seemed to notice, or care. He was mostly greeted with friendly slaps on the back and fist-bumps as he cut his way through the cluster of patrons on his way farther inside.

A cursory glance bounced off Knox before Travis's attention zeroed in on a pretty young redhead seated with a friend at the bar. Emphasis on young. Neither one of the women looked old enough to be drinking, not that the small, far-flung tavern appeared to be living in fear of the law.

Travis sidled up to them, murmuring something to the man currently occupying the stool next to the redhead. The guy gave Travis a rankled look, but vacated his seat just the same.

Knox scoffed low under his breath as Parrish attempted to turn on the charm for the ladies. He was clearly on a mission, and the lecherous gleam in his dark eyes made it obvious that he'd come to the local watering hole to scratch an itch.

He ordered a round of shots for himself and the women. They had no sooner tossed back the first than he hailed the bartender for another. Then a third.

"Doubles this time, Steve-O. I've got a lot of partying to catch up on."

The women giggled. Travis wrapped his arm around the redhead, pulling her close.

He'd already made his choice. The new round of shots arrived and his hungry gaze stayed glued on her as she threw her head back and gulped the heavy pour. Liquor ran down onto her chin. She tried to catch the spill with her fingers, but her hands were clumsy, her reflexes slow.

Travis leaned over and licked some of the alcohol away. "You wanna get out of here?"

She shrugged, then the liquor seemed to wash away her reservations. With an apologetic look slanted at her companion, she hopped off the stool and let Travis escort her toward the back door.

Knox got up too.

He cleaved through the knots of humans like a blade, on Travis's heels before the door had closed behind the big human and the staggering young woman under his muscled arm.

Knox grabbed the back collar of Parrish's coat, nearly yanking him off his feet.

He wheeled around on an explosive curse, his hands curled into fists at his sides. Rage burned in Parrish's dark scowl as he took a threatening step forward. "The fuck you think you're doing, bitch?"

Knox ignored him, speaking to the young woman. "Go back inside with your friend. Now."

Eyes wide, she scrambled away to do what he ordered.

"You just made a serious mistake," Travis sneered, although some of his prison yard confidence leeched away when he saw the size of Knox. He was a big man by any standard, but he had nothing on the preternatural power and brute force of a Breed male.

Still, liquor and arrogance kept his mouth running. "You do not want to fuck with me, asshole. Do you have any idea who I am?"

"Yeah. I know exactly who you are. You're the worthless piece of shit who attacked Shannon Calhoun seven years ago. Same piece of shit who went into Lenora's diner today and harassed her with threats and a court order to take her sister's boy away."

Travis's liquor-soaked scoff scraped in his throat. "Am I supposed to know you?"

"Why don't you ask your brother Dwight about that?"

Realization drained some of the color from his face. "Holy shit."

"Surprise." Knox bared his fangs.

Travis bolted for his vehicle. Two steps and he ran right into Knox's chest. Staggering on his heels, he pivoted and tried to make a run for the tavern.

Knox was in front of him again in a fraction of an instant. He grabbed the human's throat in one hand. Travis sputtered under the hard grasp, fighting uselessly against the iron hold of Knox's fingers. He flailed and struggled, wild fear in his eyes as Knox walked him backward into the shadows of the small parking lot.

With his hand clamped around the human's neck, Knox's gift jack-hammered to life, as powerful as a kick to the gut.

Thick and oily, rife with the stench of corruption, Travis Parrish's sins poured through his senses. There were too many to sort or catalog. One after another, violence upon violence, and the sick enjoyment of the man who perpetrated them.

Shannon hadn't been the first woman Travis had brutalized. Nor the last.

Prison had put a halt to his sadistic pleasures, but he was eager for the chance to start again. The young woman in the tavern would have found that out for herself if she'd gotten into his vehicle tonight.

And there was more.

Knox squeezed harder, unable to rein in his own violence when he read the truth about Shannon's disappearance. Leni was right. Her sister hadn't abandoned her child. She'd been ripped away from him, drugged, then dumped with some bad people Travis knew across the border in Quebec.

"Where is she now?" he growled into Travis's terrified face. "While you were in prison serving your time, you arranged to have Shannon sent away. What happened to her?"

"I—I don't know." The words were choked, barely audible under the crush of Knox's hold. "I swear, I don't have any idea where she is!"

Knox believed him. He didn't want to, but he knew Travis would have already spat out the answer if he had it to give.

"P-please," he sputtered. "I can't—can't breathe."

"You want mercy from me?"

"Yes!"

"Then beg for it."

"Please," Travis whined. "Please . . . let go. I'll do anything! I'm begging you!"

Knox's head echoed with a dozen similar cries for mercy. All of them gone ungranted by the sick son of a bitch flailing in his punishing grasp.

He leaned his face down toward Shannon's assailant—her betrayer, who'd ruined her young life with drugs and abuse, then threw her away like garbage.

"No mercy for you," he uttered, not a trace of emotion in his voice, nor in his eyes.

Increasing the pressure on Travis Parrish's larynx, Knox watched with detached calmness as the man's life evaporated, second by agonizing second.

CHAPTER 20

Leni came awake to the gentle warmth of Knox's hand stroking her hair.

"Wake up, sweetheart."

"Mmm, that feels nice." She moaned in pleasure at his touch. Her heavy eyelids lifted as she slowly rolled over to find him seated on the edge of the bed. She blinked in the darkness of the quiet room. "What time is it? Why are you dressed?"

"I need you to get out of bed, Leni. Put some clothes on." His voice was grave. His expression was even more so.

She sat up, cool air chilling her naked skin, though not as much as the grim solemnity of Knox's entire demeanor. "What's wrong?"

"We have to leave. Now."

Confusion swam through her. The cobwebs of sleep fell away swiftly as she realized the urgency behind his steady voice. "What's going on? Where's Riley?"

"He's fine, still asleep."

"Then what—"

"Travis Parrish is dead."

"What?"

"I killed him tonight." Knox moved the sheets and coverlet aside, then stood up beside the bed. He took her hand and urged her to her feet. "It won't be long before his body is discovered. Before that happens, I need to get you and the boy away from Parrish Falls. I need to take you somewhere safe."

She struggled to process what she was hearing. Travis, dead. She felt no sadness over that fact, but it was impossible to hide her shock. And while Knox's emotionless confession didn't scare her, his obvious concern for her and Riley in the wake of the killing put a chill in her marrow.

"Now, Leni. We don't have a lot of time."

She hurried to get dressed while Knox turned on a light for her, then fetched her coat and boots. "Tell me what happened. Did you leave tonight looking to kill him?"

He shook his head. "I couldn't let his threat against you stand. But no, I didn't set out to kill him. I followed him to a bar several miles past the Parrish property. I confronted him, and that's when I realized I couldn't let him live."

Leni stared at him, realization settling over her like a cold rain. "You read his sins."

He gave a grim nod.

"What did you see?"

"Enough to know that you were right to be afraid of him." He handed her coat to her. "Pack some things for you and Riley for the next few days. I'll bring him downstairs while you get ready to leave."

When he started to head toward the door, Leni grabbed his arm. "There's nowhere to stay between here and the Canadian border, and the nearest hotel in the other direction is all the way out at the Interstate eighty miles away. Where are we going to go?"

Something unreadable flickered in his stormy blue eyes. "I've already made arrangements somewhere safe, somewhere no one will be able to find you. Pack your things. I'll be waiting with Riley for you downstairs."

He didn't wait for her to argue or to ask any of the dozens of questions swirling in her mind. With his brows knit, his expression grim with purpose and resolve, he stalked out of the bedroom like the soldier he was, leaving her to follow his sober instructions.

Leni raced for her closet and began filling a duffel bag.

~ ~ ~

Knox drove Leni's red Bronco as fast as the old vehicle could handle, following the GPS coordinates Razor had given him for the Order's safe house location about an hour northeast of Parrish Falls.

He didn't think the state of Maine could get any denser with forest than where he'd just left, but as the truck bounced and jostled over the snowy, unmaintained road, all he could see ahead of them was darkness and endless miles of tall evergreens.

Leni had kept quiet for the duration of the drive, but he could sense her unease over their sudden flight away from her home—and the reason for it. With Riley sleeping in the backseat, she hadn't said a word about Travis Parrish's death, but Knox knew her silence was filled with unasked questions.

Questions he would have to answer for once they were alone at the safe house.

As the Bronco rambled deeper into the uninhabited woodland, his phone announced they had reached their destination.

"I don't see anything but trees," Leni murmured from the passenger seat.

"Up there."

He pointed to the left where a narrow path broke off from the main road—if the narrow one-lane trail through the pines could be called a road. The entrance they turned on to was even less welcoming. Branches nicked against the windows as the truck pushed forward, moving at a crawl through the thick new snow covering the ground.

Although the terrain was forbidding and remote, he trusted Razor and the unmapped satellite coordinates he'd sent to Knox's phone after the Order had okayed the arrangement.

Leni glanced at him. "Where exactly are you taking us?"

"Somewhere safe," he said. "Somewhere the Parrishes and county law enforcement won't know to look for us."

It was the same answer he'd given her as they'd set out on their trek tonight. Eventually, before the night was over, he would have to tell her everything.

Based on the rustic condition of the road leading to the location, he wasn't holding out much hope for the safe house that was to be their hideout, even though Razor had told him the Order kept the property maintained and stocked on a monthly basis so it was always ready for use at a moment's notice. Knox expected to find a ramshackle bunker waiting for them at the end of the long, twisting approach. Instead, they drove up to a sprawling lodge-like mansion. One that looked capable of housing a small army.

Fitting, considering Razor had also told him the place had once been the Order's temporary headquarters.

"It doesn't look like anyone's been here for a while," Leni said, peering at the darkened residence at the end of the snowy driveway.

She was right that it hadn't been occupied for any length of time recently. It had been twenty-odd years since the warriors and their mates had made use of the place. According to Raze, the Order had been forced to relocate for a while from their Boston compound to this hidden corner of Maine's north country during the great war that led to First Dawn and the outing of the Breed to mankind. Their enemy at the time had been none other than Dragos, the Breed madman behind the Hunter program and a host of other twisted genetic experiments he'd conducted in his labs.

Leni stared at him from the passenger seat now, a look of confusion on her face. "How long do you think we'll have to be here?"

"A couple of days at most." Only until Lucan Thorne was able to send a team of his warriors out to collect Leni and Riley and officially move them into the

Order's protection. Knox parked in front of the lodge estate. "Stay put while I go open the house and make sure it's secure. I'll be right back."

She nodded, her expression anxious as he exited the idling Bronco to jog up to the timber-framed front door.

He disabled the locks with his mind as Razor told him to do, then pushed open the thick wood panel. The Darkhaven was cool and utterly quiet, obviously empty for some time. Only the fresh scent of pine from the polished floors and heavy timber ceiling beams and trim permeated the vast, vacant space.

Knox made a quick, but thorough check of the place, mentally cataloging the layout and the arrangement of the many rooms inside the expansive home. When he was satisfied the safe house was as secure as Razor had promised, he jogged outside to retrieve Leni and Riley.

"All clear," he said, grabbing her duffel and the small bag she'd packed for the boy from behind her seat in the back of the Bronco. He slung both over his shoulder, then led Leni to the house after she'd gone around the other side of the truck to extricate the sleeping child from his car seat and carry him in her arms.

Knox didn't miss her quiet gasp as they stepped inside the large foyer. Her wonder only multiplied when he flicked on a couple of lights and the soaring rafters and wide space of a beautiful great room illuminated before them.

"This is amazing," she whispered, careful not to wake the boy draped over her shoulder.

Knox gestured for her to follow him. He brought her into a cozy bedroom, the first one on the main hallway that spoked off the living area. He turned on a small bureau lamp, revealing an alpine-themed child's room with a double bed, a large cushioned chair in the corner and framed photos of woodland animals on the walls.

"I think he'll like this room," Knox murmured quietly.

Leni nodded, giving him a warm smile, the first she'd managed since their hurried departure from Parrish Falls tonight. "Thank you, Knox."

He set Riley's bag on the chair. "I'll go put some logs in the fireplace and get things warmed up in here. There's a bathroom two doors down on the right."

"Okay."

She came out a few minutes later. Knox had a fire roaring on the hearth, the flames' soft glow bathing her in golden light as she walked into the great room to join him. She took off her coat and folded it over the back of the large sectional in the spacious living area.

Knox faced her, watching her take in their new surroundings with an open sense of awe—and mounting suspicion.

"What is this place?"

"I told you. It's a safe house."

Her gaze landed on his. Wariness shadowed the curiosity that had been there a moment ago in those clear, intelligent hazel eyes. "I know what you told me, Knox. I'm asking for the truth now. All of it. This 'safe house' is more like a mansion. One that's apparently been unused for a long time, yet has recently been dusted, cleaned, and stocked like a luxury hotel. Who does it belong to?"

"The Order."

She drew in a breath. There wasn't a person alive in the last two decades, human or Breed, who was unaware of Lucan Thorne or the cadre of Breed warriors at his command. Their reputation for justice was practically legend, as was the dauntlessness with which they carried out their rule of law.

Leni stared at him. "You never mentioned you were associated with the Order."

"I'm not. My brother, Razor, in Florida has some inroads with them."

"They won't mind if we're using their property?"

He shook his head. "They agreed to let us come here."

"Why?"

"Because I had Razor explain to them that you were a Breedmate, and that you and Riley were in danger as long as you remained in Parrish Falls."

Her mouth tilted with wry understanding. "I guess being born with my mark does come with a few unwritten benefits. What did the Order have to say about Travis's death? Will they be able to help once law enforcement gets involved?"

"I haven't told anyone about the killing yet. Only you."

She frowned. "I don't understand. If no one knows, then when did you arrange for us to come to this safe house?"

Knox cleared his throat. "This morning."

"You mean before I told you that Travis threatened me in the diner?" Her frown deepened. "Before you went out and killed him, you had already made a call to the Order to arrange to move me away from my home?"

"I wanted to know I had an option to get you somewhere safe, Leni."

Her head slowly shook back and forth. "You went behind my back to do it. You knew you had done that before we made love earlier tonight. Before you comforted me and said all those kind things about how you cared and didn't want to hurt me."

He couldn't deny any of it, no matter how wrong or cowardly his actions seemed to him now. And as rightfully upset as she was to learn he'd arranged to take her out of Parrish Falls, he knew he had yet to explain what bringing the Order in truly meant for her and Riley.

For him too, when the time would come for him to let her go.

He cursed. "I needed to make plans for yours and Riley's protection. I only did what I thought was best."

"Right. And you didn't say anything because you knew how I felt about leaving my home. About not being there for Shannon if and when she comes home."

"Leni . . . about that." There was so much she needed to know. He had nothing but unpleasant news for her tonight, but out of all of it, the truth about her sister was a pain he loathed to deliver. "I know what happened to Shannon. I saw what Travis did."

Leni stared at him, her breath halting for a moment. Some of her anger gave way to her dread over her sister. "You read his sins. You saw how he brutalized her?"

He nodded. "She wasn't the first. He'd made a habit of hurting women, even young girls. He wouldn't have stopped. But he took it further with Shannon."

Leni swallowed. "What do you mean? Tell me."

"He arranged to get rid of her. You were right. She didn't skip town and leave you to look after her son. Travis had her taken."

"What?" Her hand came up to her lips, fingers trembling. "Where is she?"

"I don't know. Travis didn't know, either. He didn't care to know. All I was able to read was that he arranged for her abduction across the border in Quebec. He got rid of her in retaliation for her pressing charges against him."

"Oh, my God." Leni's face drained of color. "I knew he was behind her disappearance, but I didn't want to believe it. All these years, everything she's missed with Riley . . . all because of him."

"He won't be able to hurt anyone else now. And we'll find Shannon."

"How?" Leni lifted a bleak, imploring gaze at him. "She could be anywhere. By now, she's almost certainly dead, Knox. Or worse, in some awful situation somewhere, wishing she were dead."

"We'll find out what happened and where she ended up. I won't rest until we have those answers. And then, one way or another, I'll bring her home to you, Leni." He cleared his throat. "No matter where you are, I will bring the answers back to you."

"What are you talking about? Where do you think I'll be?"

He stepped toward her, each movement of his feet dragging like lead. "That's going to be up to the Order. You're a Breedmate. An unmated one who's in grave danger now. They'll want to move you to somewhere they can be sure you and Riley will be safe."

"Safe from what? Travis is dead."

"Yes. But you and I both know his family won't let his killing go unmet. They'll want blood now. If they were to realize you can't be injured, they'll want to harm you in any other way they can. You can't go back to Parrish Falls again, Lenora. I'm sorry."

She scoffed, her gaze turning brittle. "You're sorry? This is the outcome you've been after ever since you saw that damn mark on my stomach."

"All I've wanted is your safety. When I arranged for this safe house, I was only thinking of you and Riley. I only did what I felt was best."

"For who—yourself?"

"Is that really what you think?"

"I don't know what to think. When my sister became too unpleasant for Travis to deal with, he had her sent away. Now, you're doing the same thing to me."

"Like hell I am. I'm trying to protect you. I'm trying to protect you and Riley both."

"By foisting us off on the Order?"

He uttered a curse, knowing there was an element of truth to her accusation. As much as her wellbeing mattered to him, he had also been motivated by fear—his own. Foreign as it was for him to feel that weakness of emotion, he felt it to his bones when he thought about losing Leni. And he was losing her now, he realized.

"That's not what I want, Lenora. It's not what I wanted when I made that call this morning."

Her breast rose and fell with her rapid breaths as she stared at him. "Then what do you want, Knox?"

He considered every moment they'd spent together, from the minute he stepped into her diner and was greeted with her warm smile and kind heart. All of their conversations, both the combative and the tender ones. All of her breathless sighs and the pleasured screams he swallowed with his kiss.

What did he want?

All of it.

Forever, if she would give him that much.

But in killing Travis tonight, he had ignited the war he'd known was coming with the Parrishes. And in so doing, he had put Leni and Riley in the crosshairs along with him.

What he wanted now didn't matter.

She couldn't go back to her home, and for that she might never forgive him.

And he couldn't ignore what she'd said about Shannon. There were fates far worse than death or any depth of injury. Just because Leni's Breedmate gift shielded her from one kind of harm, there were other things that could be done to her that would make her wish she were dead.

The fear that thought brought with it chilled him to his marrow.

Leni stared at him in his tormented silence. She shook her head. "You can't even say the words, Knox."

He wanted to. Damn it, he wanted to tell her everything she made him want. Her forgiveness. Her trust. Her love.

Her eternal blood bond.

He wanted it all.

All the things he couldn't say right now swamped him like a tide.

A small cry sounded from the bedroom where Riley was sleeping. "Aunt Leni, where are we? I'm scared."

With one last look at Knox, she pivoted away and went to the child.

CHAPTER 21

S he stayed with Riley for a couple of hours, until his restlessness finally faded under the heavy pull of sleep and she was able to slip off the bed without making him startle or stir.

Leni was exhausted, not only from the upheaval of tonight's run from Parrish Falls, but from her clash with Knox. Especially that.

She couldn't deny her hurt over his apparent want to be rid of her, despite the fact that she could only blame herself for believing there was something real between them. Something that existed beyond his sense of duty toward a woman—any woman—born with a teardrop-and-crescent-moon mark on her skin.

She was the one who had made that mistake, allowing herself to care for him, to fall in love with him.

She had never been in love, had never felt the twisting ache of longing and affection that stirred within her whenever Knox was near. She had never felt the desire to make a place for someone beside her until she met him. Now that he was there, she didn't want to consider returning to the way things were before he came into her world.

But she would have to do more than consider it now. Knox himself had put her back on that path when he made the call to his brother. Sooner or later, the Order would be coming to ensure his wishes were carried out.

If Knox had simply walked away without any explanation it wouldn't have wounded her as intensely as his willingness to discard her.

Leni stubbornly swallowed back the raw lump that didn't seem to want to leave her throat. It had been there since she learned the truth about Shannon's fate at Travis's hands, and had only worsened in the hours since her confrontation with Knox.

She wasn't going to cry or feel sorry for herself. Not now, no matter how much she hurt for her sister and for what she thought she might have had with Knox.

She had Riley to think about. His safety, his future.

It had been enough for her before she met Knox. It would be enough for her again.

It would have to be.

Leni placed a light kiss to the little boy's brow, then quietly moved away from his bed. Closing the door silently behind her, she didn't realize Knox was outside the room until she lifted her head and her gaze collided with his solemn, stormy blue eyes.

She frowned. "How long have you been out here?"

"A while. Is everything all right?"

Nothing could have felt more wrong, but Leni knew he was asking about Riley, not the tumult of emotion swamping her as she stared at Knox's impassive, unreadable face. "He was anxious and afraid of being in a strange place. He's never slept anywhere but in his own bed at home."

Knox nodded soberly. "He's a tough kid. I'm sure he'll be okay."

"I guess he'll have to be, right?" She started to walk by, but paused when Knox pointedly cleared his throat.

"Razor heard from the Order. He told me they're sending a team up from Boston at sundown tomorrow. They should be here a few hours afterward."

The warriors were coming for her so soon? Leni lifted her chin, forcing a lightness into her tone that she didn't feel. "What a relief that must be for you. You barely have twenty-four hours left to suffer my company."

"Leni—"

She cut him off with a quiet scoff. "On second thought, why wait? There's no reason for you to be here now. Riley and I are in the Order's hands just by being in this house, aren't we? Feel free to leave anytime, Knox. In fact, I'll thank you to."

She started to walk past him again, but this time he stopped her with his strong hand on her arm. "Damn it, Lenora."

Rather than release her, he drew her closer to him. Close enough that she could feel the heat radiating off his big body, and she could see the flecks of amber igniting in his impatient, narrowed gaze.

"Let me go, Knox."

"I've been telling myself to do that from the minute I met you." Although his face remained harsh with throttled fury, uncertainty softened his now-blazing eyes. Reaching up with his free hand, he tenderly stroked the side of her cheek. "I don't know how to let you go, Leni."

His touch threatened to unravel all her strength. She wanted to savor the gentle warmth of his fingertips against her skin and the maddening pleasure of his caress. Instead, she tilted her head away from it.

"Christ." He blew out the rough curse through gritted teeth and fangs. His grasp on her arm tightened. "I don't want to let you go."

Leni steeled herself to the emotion in his voice. "Well, lucky for you, the Order's going to help you do that tomorrow night."

"I don't give a damn about the Order. This is about you and me, Leni."

"No, it isn't. Not anymore. You made sure of that when you asked your brother to help remove me from your life."

"That's not what I did. That's not what I wanted." Heat crackled in his transformed gaze as he stared at her. "I'm trying to tell you that I care about you, Leni. I care about Riley too."

"Don't." She shook her head, refusing to give in to the temptation of believing him. She couldn't afford to believe him when everything he said would have no meaning tomorrow night when the Order came to collect her and Riley. "That's easy for you to say now. Too bad you didn't feel that way before you brought me here and—"

"Damn it, woman, I'm trying to tell you that I love you."

Her inhaled breath sounded raw even to her own ears. Knox took both her arms in his hands now, holding in an unrelenting grasp.

"You belong to me, Lenora. When the Order gets here tomorrow, that's what I'm going to tell them. I'm not letting you go. Wherever they deem is safest for you and Riley to be, that's where I'm going too." His smoldering eyes searched her gaze. "The only question is, will I be telling the Order as your blood-bonded mate, or as the male who's going to do everything in his power to one day be worthy of that honor?"

God help her, she couldn't speak. All the sorrow and uncertainty she'd been feeling since they arrived at the Order's safe house melted away under the sincerity of Knox's words. Not only his words, but the solemnity of the vow she saw glowing in his eyes.

He reached up, tenderly cupping her face in his big palm. "I know what I've cost you, Leni. In killing Travis Parrish tonight, I've taken away your home, your business and livelihood . . . Christ, in telling you what I read in that bastard's sins, I've even taken away your faith in your sister's safe return."

"No, Knox." Leni gave a slow shake of her head. "I needed to know what you learned about Shannon. You didn't take away anything by telling me the truth."

He uttered a curse. "The point is, I want to give those things back to you. All of them. Instead, because of me, you've lost everything you once had."

Overcome with emotion, she lifted her hand to the rigid line of his squared jaw. "If being with you means leaving Parrish Falls for a future somewhere else— anywhere else—that's all I need. You, Knox. And that little boy sleeping in the room behind me." She slid her hand around to his nape and pulled him down for her kiss. "Knox, I love you. I started falling the moment you stood up for me in the diner against Dwight."

He growled in response, the amber fire in his eyes exploding into twin infernos of heat. She wasn't prepared for the possessiveness of his kiss. It seared her, igniting her veins and sending a hot spiral of need shooting into her bloodstream.

When he drew his mouth away from hers, his gaze nearly incinerated her. "You are mine, Lenora."

"Yes." It was all the breath she had in her lungs, the only word she could muster when her senses were consumed with the desire—and the love—she felt for this Breed male.

Hers.

Knox snarled in response, triumph gleaming in his eyes and in the brief flash of his diamond-sharp fangs. He lifted her into his arms and strode down the hallway with her, bringing her into one of the large bedrooms at the far end.

Far enough not to disturb the innocent child sleeping at the head of the long corridor.

With the door quietly closed behind them, Knox brought Leni to the king-size bed and undressed her with hands that moved with both precision and impatience. When she lay naked before him, he kissed every inch of her bare skin from forehead to toes, leaving her quivering and breathless, and so aroused it was a miracle she didn't melt right into the crisp, cool sheets.

His own clothes came off with equal efficiency.

Leni sat up, moving to the edge of the mattress as he disrobed for her. She couldn't keep the hunger out of her eyes, no more than she could resist reaching out to run her hands over his magnificent body and the beautiful patterns of his *glyphs.*

After dreading she might never be with him like this again, seeing Knox standing before her naked and pulsing with raw male power made everything female in her awaken with a fierce need to claim what was hers.

She stroked his heavy shaft, teasing the elegant arcs and swirls that tracked like multi-hued vines from the root of his thick cock nearly to its blunt crown.

Leni licked her lips, glancing up at him in fascination and overwhelming desire. "I love looking at you, Knox. I love knowing all of this belongs to me."

His reply was a groan that rumbled in his broad, muscled chest. It cut short on a hiss when Leni pulled him toward her and drew him deep into the heat of her mouth. The taste of his silky skin on her tongue lit a hotter flame inside her. The salty bead of wetness that slid down her throat as she took him all the way inside made the coil of hunger in her core twist into something ravenous.

She took her time savoring the feel of him moving over her tongue, filling her mouth and throat the way she knew he would fill the other part of her that ached to have him. His muscles bunched in her grip as she clutched his tight backside with one hand and stroked his length with the other.

He cursed, low and guttural, as a jolt traveled the hardness of his shaft. Power vibrated through his limbs and torso, his pleasure a jagged growl as his palm cupped the back of her skull while she licked and suckled and teased him.

"Fuck," he ground out hoarsely. "That feels too good, baby."

She wanted to keep going, take him right over the edge with her mouth, but on a tight groan he jerked out of her grasp. Then his hands were under her arms, lifting her up and onto the bed. He spread her legs with shaking hands, his dark head lowering between them.

Leni gasped as his mouth settled over her sex and he began a slow, merciless assault on her clit. She couldn't hold back the orgasm that had been building simply from the taste of him on her tongue. Now, that wave of arousal and need crashed into her. She bucked against Knox's mouth, her release engulfing her, pulling her beneath a velvet tide of pure pleasure.

When she opened her eyes moments later she found Knox watching her from between her thighs, a satisfied smile glittering in his amber-drenched gaze.

"I could watch you come all night," he murmured, his low voice thrumming all the way into her bones. "First chance we get to be alone, I'm going to do just that."

Leni smiled. "Promises, promises."

"I don't make them if I can't keep them." He smirked, rising up to cover her body with his. "Right now, I need to be inside you."

She nodded, then let out a shuddery gasp as he entered her body and seated himself to the root. With his eyes locked on hers, he began to rock against her, pushing impossibly deep, then withdrawing in a slow slide that drove her mad with need.

Each thrust and retreat made the fire in his transformed eyes burn even hotter, his irises as bright as lit coals. His pupils were thin and catlike, elliptical slits hardly discernible amid the intensifying glow that swamped them.

His *dermaglyphs* pulsed and churned with variegated colors, the intricate patterns filling with deep shades of indigo, burgundy, and gold. She'd seen these hues whenever they kissed or made love, and had guessed they were the emotional markers of Breed desire and arousal.

Yet there was another shade competing for dominance in Knox's *glyphs*.

Moving between dark reddish purple and inky black, this newer color seemed to sharpen by the minute. Knox's fangs had grown more pronounced as well, filling his mouth as he drove inside her body in a relentless rhythm.

His eyes had drifted away from her gaze, settled on the hammering pulse of her carotid.

She had read the torment in his handsome face as a purely primal one—and it was. Not only sexual need, but another need that was riding him as savagely as the other.

"Knox." She reached up to him, smoothing the backs of her fingers against his heated brow. "You haven't fed since your UV burns. Even longer than that."

His answer was a wordless snarl, his hips still moving against hers. He dragged his hungry gaze up from her pulse point, and she could see the depth of his thirst in the endless fire of his irises. He was starving.

She tilted her head on the pillow, baring the side of her neck to him. He snarled again, low, unearthly. Far from human.

"It's not sustenance I want from you," he uttered thickly. "I won't settle for anything less than your bond, Lenora. If you'll give it to me."

She smiled up at him. "It's been yours all along, Knox. In my heart, I know it always has been yours. I've just been waiting for you to come and claim me."

He let go of another wordless noise, one that sounded so possessive and exultant it astonished her. Though nothing could have prepared her for the feel of his mouth coming down hotly over her vein. An instant later, her tender flesh gave way to the razor-sharp points of his fangs. They sank deep, his bite an indescribable shock to every fiber of her being.

Pain and pleasure twisted into a glimmering cord of sensation as he drew her blood into his mouth. Her heart fed him, beat after beat, every vessel in her body coming alive under the erotic suction of his mouth.

"Oh, God," she gasped as he fed from her opened vein.

Instead of feeling drained, she felt energized by the act of nourishing him. She felt fulfilled.

Powerful.

And running undercurrent of those feelings was the incredible love she felt for the male who had just bound himself to her forever by blood.

"Knox," she whispered, overcome with emotion.

His tongue swept over the wounds he'd made in her neck, his breath fanning hot against her skin. "You taste so good. Your blood is as unique as you are. Crisp and fresh, like a cedar forest in winter, yet as warm and sweet as cream. I want to drink from you all night."

She wanted that too. She moaned at the loss of his mouth at her vein.

And she had a thirst of her own that was now beating like a drum in her marrow.

"I can feel you in me now, Leni. Your blood, your bond. Ah, Christ. It's amazing. So fucking bright and strong. Just like you." He lifted his head, searching out her arousal-drenched gaze. "I can feel your love. God knows I don't deserve that any more than I deserve the rest of you. But you're mine, Lenora. Mine."

He kept pumping inside her as he spoke, his tempo growing more urgent, fueling the fire in her. One that had only intensified under the feel of his bite. She closed her eyes, unable to curb the broken moan that leaked past her lips.

He gathered her close, thrusting deep. Leni arched with him, taking everything he gave her. She needed more. She needed all of him now.

As if she had spoken her desire aloud, Knox picked up his tempo. It was all she could do to simply hold on to him as he brought her past the edge of a blinding, soul-scorching release and into a pleasure that knew no bounds.

CHAPTER 22

He would never get enough of this woman.

His woman.

His Breedmate.

Drinking Leni's blood, feeling her bond take hold inside him, had been more than he'd imagined. More than he could ever hope to be worthy of, even if he had a hundred lifetimes to prove himself to her.

He had eternity now. He intended to use every second of it making sure she never regretted allowing him into her life.

Her love and forgiveness were two more gifts he hardly deserved, but was determined to keep.

Knox watched her spiral down from her release, his own veins echoing with the thrum of her pleasure as he moved inside her, still hard even after he'd come. Still craving more of the woman who had given herself over to him so openly, so honestly, right from the start.

When her eyelids lifted, her tender gaze held him as lovingly as her arms. She smiled up at him. "Is this what happiness feels like? I don't think I've ever really known it before."

He lowered his head and kissed her, unrushed, his hips still rocking against hers. "I don't know about happiness. It's never been something I wanted or needed. But I do need this. I want this, with you."

"You have me now," she said, her smile deepening. "And I have you, Knox."

"Yes, you do." He felt the depth of her vow in the bond that linked him to her. But as he stared into her beautiful hazel eyes, he slowly shook his head. "Growing up in Dragos's lab, I never knew what it meant to have a family. I didn't know how to feel anything. None of us did. We didn't want to feel, because in the Hunter program, emotion meant death. The only way to survive was to be a machine, so that's what I did. That's what we all did."

"I hate that you went through that," Leni murmured, caressing his face. "And I'm so very glad that you did survive, Knox."

Her sincerity—her tender compassion—wrapped its warmth around him through the bond. Where he once might have resisted the comfort, now he welcomed it. Hell, he needed it, more than he wanted to admit.

"I let someone in once," he murmured. "When she died, I fell back on my old ways. I closed myself off. I walled everyone out, including my brothers who'd escaped with me to build new lives outside the program. Over time, I had myself convinced I didn't need anyone, that I didn't want ties to any place or to any person. Then I met you, Lenora."

He smoothed his thumb over her soft lips, then couldn't resist leaning down to kiss her. She melted into him, her fingers tunneling into his hair and holding him close.

He let out a wry, airless laugh. "You ruined everything. You ruined me."

Her eyes widened under her furrowing brow. Doubt crackled through his connection to her and he wanted to kick himself for putting even as much as a second of uncertainty in her heart.

"What I mean to say is that you've changed me, Leni. You've done more than that. You've saved me."

She gave him a gentle smile. "You saved me too."

"No." He shook his head. "You were never the one in need of saving, and not just because of your mark. You are the strongest woman I've ever known. You have the purest heart. The most unshakable faith." He exhaled a hard sigh, feeling awkward for the fact that he couldn't even give her proper words to express all the things she made him feel. And yet he had just taken the one thing she couldn't share with another for as long as either of them drew breath. "You make me want to be the kind of mate you deserve. I want to earn the love and forgiveness I feel through your blood."

Leni frowned. "You don't have to earn anything, Knox."

"Yes, I do," he bit off sharply. "I've taken too much away from you tonight. I promise, I'll find a way to make it right."

Her fingers gently stroked the side of his face. "There's nothing more I want than what you've already given me. Your love, Knox. That's everything to me."

He kissed her again, each drumming beat of her heart pulling down the remnants of the walls that had served to protect him for as long as he could remember. With Leni, none of his walls had been high enough or strong enough to keep her from getting through, from getting into his blood even before he'd put his mouth to her vein tonight.

"You have my love," he murmured against her lips. "You'll always have that. You and Riley both. Tonight, I'm also offering you my bond."

She drew back, emotion glittering in her eyes. There was hesitation in her voice, and that note of uncertainty carved a hole inside him. "It's forever, Knox. If I drink from you, it can't be undone . . . not ever. I'll be a shackle you can't ever break."

Ah, Christ. His own words tossed back at him now, even as gently as Leni delivered them, struck him like a lash. He hated that he'd said them to her. He hadn't meant to be so cruel. Fear had done that to him, fear of what he was feeling for the extraordinary woman who had already given him more than he could ever want or need.

"Forever, my beautiful Lenora." He smoothed his fingers over the curve of her pretty cheek and delicate jaw line. "That's what the bond means. I know that, and I won't settle for anything less with you. If you'll have me."

Her soft gasp caught in her throat as elation poured through her veins. He felt it, reveled in it. Made a silent vow that he would love her with every breath in his body, right down to his last.

With his gaze locked on hers, he brought his wrist up to his mouth. His fangs sank into the flesh and muscle below his palm, piercing the vein that ran the length of his forearm.

Blood dripped onto her bare breasts as he waited for Leni to make her decision.

To his relief, she barely hesitated before taking hold of his arm and bringing the twin punctures to her mouth. The instant her lips closed over his wrist, his spine bowed. A strangled growl of pleasure boiled out of him, every sinew in his body going taut as Leni took the first sip of his blood.

Fuck, he'd had no idea what to expect. He wasn't prepared for the electric jolt that traveled through him as she drank and the bond between them fused into completion.

His veins were still lit up and humming with the power of her blood, but now a further energy coursed between Leni and him. He saw it in her eyes as she held his awestruck gaze and drew from his vein. He felt it in the connection that strengthened and pulsed with white-hot ferocity as the gossamer threads of their bond forged into an unbreakable, eternal link.

His love for her overwhelmed him.

His desire, which had seemed boundless before, now burned into an infinite need.

He thrust hard, groaning at the feel of her tight walls gripping him, milking him. She moaned as he rolled his pelvis against hers, each stroke more desperate than the last. He couldn't get close enough to her, couldn't go deep enough.

And through their bond, he could feel the same insatiable need in Leni.

On a ragged snarl, he drew his wrist away from the delicious suction of her lips and hastily sealed the wounds he'd made.

Lowering his head, he took her mouth in a savage kiss. "You're mine now. Forever."

"Yes," she whispered, her love wrapping around him from both the joining of their bond and their bodies. "And you're mine, Knox."

He growled his answer, too far gone to form words. All he knew was the pleasure of his female's body beneath his, her heat surrounding him, coaxing the explosive release he was powerless to control any longer.

Leni's climax crashed into him before his own had snapped its leash. Knox marveled at the feel of her surrendering to him completely.

Her body's delicate tremors would have been reward enough, but sharing her bliss through their bond made his own orgasm detonate with enormous force. He roared his pleasure, then rolled Leni over to start all over again.

"Mine," he rasped against the soft curve of her neck and shoulder as he entered her.

Leni let go of a shuddery sigh. "God, yes. Knox, don't stop."

He had no intention of it.

Possession poured over him, more powerful than any storm. She was his. Nothing—and no one—was going to stand in the way of that now.

Sooner or later, he still had to answer for Travis Parrish's murder, but he would gladly pay whatever price the Order or law enforcement demanded of him.

As for the rest of the Parrishes, they could burn in hell for all he cared.

And if they ever tried to lay a finger on Leni or Riley, Knox was prepared to send them there personally.

CHAPTER 23

The next morning, Leni opened the commercial-grade refrigerator in the safe house kitchen and peered inside at the plethora of choices. Anything she could possibly crave or need had been recently stocked ahead of their arrival and ready for use.

She'd found the same was true of the bathroom and shower. There was even a full wardrobe of brand-new casual clothes in various sizes in the bedrooms, and a mudroom closet outfitted with a variety of seasonal outerwear and boots. Even a few sized for a child.

Riley had spotted the winter gear before she had. His first order of business when he hopped out of bed was to wheedle a promise out of her that they would build a snowman after breakfast.

Leni retrieved a carton of milk and a package of eggs from the fridge. "What kind of pancakes would you like, kiddo? Blueberry or strawberry?"

"Blueberry!" Riley shouted from his seat at the island counter.

"Coming right up."

They were alone in the spacious kitchen. After an amazing night in Knox's arms, Leni awoke feeling as though she could take on the world. Not only because of the blood bond that still thrummed through her, strengthening every particle of her being, but because she also had the incredible gift of Knox's love.

Peace and contentment enveloped her as she gathered the ingredients and other supplies she'd need to make Riley's breakfast. As for herself, she had never felt so nourished or sated. She hungered for nothing this morning . . . except the next opportunity she had to lose herself in Knox's arms.

Her mate.

A slow smile curved her lips as she made Riley's pancakes, then delivered his plate to the counter where he waited. He practically pounced on the short stack, humming and bouncing in his chair as he ate.

"Take your time, little man. And don't forget to drink some orange juice too."

He nodded, reaching for the plastic glass with syrup-sticky fingers. A muffled musical tune drew Leni's head up a moment later. The noise came from her purse, which she'd left in the great room after they'd arrived.

Shit. Her phone.

She scrambled to answer, knowing by the ringtone it was Carla. "Hey. I was going to call you in just a minute."

"Where are you, Leni?" Her friend sounded more than concerned. "Is Riley with you?"

"Yes, he is."

"Thank God. It's Monday morning and when he didn't show up for school—"

"Shit." Leni winced at the curse that slipped past her lips in front of Riley. There were far worse things she needed to tell Carla right away too. Taking the phone into another room, she closed the door behind her and kept her voice just above a whisper. "Something happened last night."

"No kidding," Carla replied, anxiety lacing her voice. "Travis Parrish is dead, Len. The bartender at Tall Timbers found his body late last night in the parking lot behind the pub. Someone strangled him. From what everyone's saying, it sounds like someone wanted to make damn sure Travis was dead. His larynx was crushed like it had been in a vise and his spinal column was practically severed in the process."

Leni couldn't feel remorse for the brutality of his death. Not after what he'd done to Shannon. Not after Knox had told her about Travis's history of hurting women. All she felt was gratitude that no one else would ever fall victim to him again.

"I know he's dead."

Silence stretched on the other end of the line. "It was Knox, wasn't it?" Carla didn't wait for Leni to confirm. "Oh, God, Leni. Sheriff Barstow's got deputies crawling all over town looking for him as we speak. They're looking for you too. Are you and Riley okay? Where are you?"

"We're fine. We're somewhere safe."

Carla exhaled a relieved sigh. "Please stay there until this blows over. I'm worried about you. Dwight and Jeb Parrish are talking about organizing some kind of posse to search for you guys. Leni, they're out for blood."

Although it shouldn't have come as any surprise, hearing that Travis's brothers were already seeking retribution put a knot of cold dread in her veins. "They won't find us. Knox arranged for a safe house from the Order. The Order's sending a team up from Boston at sundown tonight to come and get us."

"The Order?" Carla's voice took on a soberer tone. "Where will you go?"

"I don't know yet."

"Damn, girl. This shit's really real, isn't it?"

"Yeah, it is."

"But you're okay?"

"I am," Leni assured her. "I'm better than okay, Carla. Knox and I . . . we're together. We're in love. Last night, he drank my blood. And I drank his."

"Holy shit. Do you mean you two are—"

"Blood bonded," Leni confirmed, giddy just to say the words. "In spite of everything else going on right now, I've never been happier in my life."

"I can hear it in your voice," Carla said. "Then again, I heard it in your voice the last time I saw you too. You deserve to be happy, Leni. No matter where you have to go to find it. I mean that."

"I know you do. Thank you."

She had been struggling to come to grips with the idea of leaving Parrish Falls, telling herself that no matter where she ended up she would be okay so long as she was with Knox and Riley. But the idea of leaving her best friend opened a fresh ache inside her.

"I'll be in touch as soon as I can, Carla. This isn't goodbye."

"It better not be, bitch." She laughed, knowing just how to take the sting out of any situation. "I'm going to be expecting an invitation to your wedding. Is that even a thing with the Breed?"

Leni smiled. "I don't know. I'll have to find out and let you know."

"You do that. And while you're at it, tell Knox to fix me up with his hottest brother as my date."

Leni laughed. "I love you, you know that?"

"Yeah, I do. Love you back, girl." She sniffled a little bit. "Miss you already."

"Same."

They ended the call, and when Leni walked back into the kitchen she found Knox waiting there with Riley. His handsome face was schooled into a calm expression, but she could sense the concern in him. She could feel it through their bond.

He came over to her and wrapped his arms around her. "Are you okay? I was on the phone with Razor when I felt your pulse spike. Riley told me you took a call from Carla."

"And she said a bad word," the little tattle-tale interjected.

"I'm fine," she assured her wary mate. "Amos Barstow is in Parrish Falls with some of his men. Dwight and Jeb Parrish are looking for us."

Knox grunted, unfazed. "You didn't say where we are, did you?"

"No. Only that we're in a secure location that belongs to the Order." She reached up to smooth the furrow that creased his brow. "Carla's my friend, Knox. I would trust her with my life."

He nodded, but his expression remained grim as he tunneled his fingers into her hair and pulled her deeper into his embrace.

Riley glanced up from his decimated stack of pancakes. "Is Aunt Leni your girlfriend, Knox?"

His answering chuckle vibrated against her cheek. "Yeah, buddy. She is."

Leni tilted her head up, smiling at her mate. She was rewarded with a tender brush of his lips against hers. The contact sent a fresh current of arousal through her veins and into her marrow.

From his perch at the counter, Riley smacked his hands over his eyes and exhaled a long, beleaguered sigh. "Are you guys gonna kiss all day?"

"Maybe," Knox growled. To Leni, he murmured, "You taste sweeter than usual."

"Blueberries," she replied. "This Darkhaven's kitchen is stocked with everything imaginable. Much like the rest of the place."

He grinned. "Interesting. We may have to sample a few other flavors later. Although, I doubt I'll find anything I like as much as cedar and sweet, warm cream."

His hand moved down to her backside, hidden from view of the impatient boy at the counter. There was no mistaking the hot glimmer in his stormy blue-gray eyes, nor the undeniable hardness of his body as he held her in his embrace.

"I'm finished!" Riley announced, pushing his empty plate away from him. "Can we go play outside now, Aunt Leni?"

Knox arched a brow at her. Although he didn't voice his disapproval, there was wariness in the subtle change of his expression.

"I did promise him," Leni said. "We'll be fine right out back. You know I will be, and I'll keep him close to me at all times."

He didn't look fully convinced, but he gave her a faint nod. She rose up and kissed the stern line of his jaw.

"Let's get you cleaned up, Riley."

In a few minutes, they both were dressed in snow gear, mittens, and boots. Leni took Riley out to the wooded backyard behind the wooden deck of the compound's sprawling house, where they proceeded to roll the body and head of a rotund snowman.

Leni didn't even hear anyone approach.

She didn't realize she and Riley were no longer alone until a snowball lightly hit the back of the boy's fluffy down-filled coat.

Startled, she whirled around to see where the playful assault had come from.

Knox stood on the deck behind her. He was covered from head to toe in UV-blocking black fatigues and gloves, with a Kevlar face mask and dark sunglasses to complete the look.

Leni smiled, instantly relaxed, and more than pleased.

"You're right," he said, gesturing to his daytime-proofed attire. "This place is stocked with anything we could possibly need."

He stooped down to pick up more snow between his gloved hands. The snowball he tossed came right at her, but Leni swiftly blocked it with the power of her gift. As if stopped in midair, the snowball bounced off the energy field that protected her and fell to the ground without making contact.

"You're no fun," Knox drawled.

She grinned. "That's not what you said last night."

Scooping up a handful of snow, she made her own projectile. She let it fly, even knowing she stood no chance of hitting him. He dodged it with effortless speed and grace.

Then he lowered his head and leapt off the deck to tackle her.

Leni shrieked, then dissolved into a fit of giggles as he took her down to the ground beneath him. With a battle cry, Riley piled on too, his own laughter joining hers and Knox's.

Leni clung to the normalcy of it all. To the perfectness of a mundane morning spent with the two people who mattered most in her life.

She clung to Knox, and to the promise she felt through their bond that somehow, no matter what, they were going to find their way through whatever waited for them on the other side of tonight.

CHAPTER 24

L eni dozed beside him on the large sectional sofa in
the great room, her head resting against his
shoulder. Her fingers had been twined with his since
they sat down a couple hours ago, as if she couldn't bear
to let go of him even in sleep.

Not that he was going to complain.

Leni's presence brought him more peace than he'd
ever dreamed he might know, and he was in no rush to
let any part of their perfect day slip from his grasp.

"She's missing the best part," Riley whispered from
the other side of Knox on the sofa.

The boy held a bowl of popcorn in his lap, his eyes
glued to the superhero movie playing on the big screen
TV above the fireplace.

The flames had begun to die down, but getting up to
tend them meant disturbing Leni and Knox was more

than content to let her relax against him for a while longer.

Forever, he thought, tilting his head to glance at the beauty of her freckle-sprinkled face as she slept.

Knox couldn't keep his gaze from drifting to the tall grandfather clock that stood in the corner of the room. Night fell early this far north and this deep into winter. It had been nearly three hours since the sun set, which meant the team from the Order's Boston command center was already en route. By now, they couldn't be more than a few more hours away from the safe house.

He had avoided thinking about that for most of the day. As the time drew nearer, he could focus on little else.

As he stroked Leni's arm, his preternatural senses picked up the low rumble of a vehicle's engine somewhere outside. He shifted on the sofa, suspicion crackling through his veins even before the glow of twin high-beams sliced through the darkness.

A large SUV approached on the drive.

The headlights loomed closer, blindingly bright, as the dark vehicle rolled toward the house. "Wake up, baby."

Leni moaned quietly, her head lifting off his shoulder. "Someone's here? Is it the Order so soon?"

"No." Gently, but firmly, he moved her off him. "It's too early to be the Order. Stay put."

She sat up at once, reaching for the remote to silence the movie. When Riley protested, she hushed him, asking him to be quiet for a minute. "Someone must've gotten lost on the roads, kiddo. Knox will handle it, and then we'll go back to the movie, okay?"

But it wasn't a lost driver.

Knox knew it, and so did she. He felt Leni's trepidation—her bone-deep fear—as he walked toward the front door prepared to dispatch whoever had managed to find them from Parrish Falls.

Even if it meant using lethal means.

The vehicle's engine idled just outside, those glaring lights shining into the great room through the front window, illuminating Leni's anxious face.

Knox reached for the latch on the heavy front door.

His fingers hadn't closed around it before the entire entrance exploded inward, the door blasted open by a force that knocked him backward off his feet.

A massive figure stepped inside, moving swiftly and certainly straight for Leni and Riley.

They didn't see the Breed male.

He moved with inhuman speed, no more than a flash of dark, deadly motion.

But Knox saw him.

He saw enough to realize this was a Gen One like him. A fellow Hunter.

He saw the large pistol in the assassin's hand too.

With equal speed and reflex, Knox leapt up and sprang for the intruder.

The staccato report of gunfire rang out at the same time—two bullets, squeezed off in rapid succession. Both of them aimed point-blank at Leni's head.

No. *Damn it, no!*

Knox's roar reverberated in his skull. His fear was too immense to be contained. So was his rage.

But even as his body sailed forward in a streak of motion, he watched in stunned amazement as the killer's rounds hit the shield of Leni's Breedmate gift and bounced uselessly onto the hardwood.

The assassin recovered from the setback without missing a beat, making a lightning-fast grab for Riley.

His hand collided with the unseen wall of Leni's ability.

Holy shit. Her protective energy enveloped not only her, but the boy as well.

Knox had no time to process the miraculous change in her gift. At the same instant, he slammed into the bastard who'd come to kill them. The force of his impact knocked the weapon out of the Hunter's grasp. It clattered to the floor and spun away.

The male was more than his equal match in terms of size and strength. On a bellow, he threw Knox off his back. Fangs bared, eyes on fire with amber rage, he let his fist fly, hammering hard into Knox's face. Knox went down, the sharp crack of shattering bones echoing in the awful quiet of the large room.

Leni's horrified scream rang out.

Knox hated that she and Riley were there to witness this side of him. He hated the cold terror this struggle was causing in her as she held on to her crying nephew. Her fear leached into him, adding fuel to the inferno of fury boiling in every fiber of Knox's body.

As the male came for him again, he planted his bare foot in the center of the bastard's torso and kicked the vampire back. As his opponent staggered, Knox leapt to his feet. He threw a punishing volley of blows to both sides of the assassin's face and skull.

Bone and cartilage snapped. Blood gushed from split skin and fractures that protruded out of the savage wounds Knox delivered.

And still the other Hunter kept coming.

Relentless. Unstoppable. A machine programmed for one purpose: Death.

He swung at Knox, both males dodging and striking, both determined to be the last one standing. That was their training. The thing Knox had in common with all of his half-brothers who'd been born and reared in Dragos's hellish lab.

"Who sent you?" he demanded, even though he didn't need the Hunter to confirm what he already knew.

His ability to read the male's sins had awakened the first instant his fists made contact with him.

The Parrishes had hired this killer.

He didn't want to think how the Breed male had managed to locate them so easily. But as he drove another punch into the assassin's face, the prickle of misgiving he'd had about Leni confiding in her friend came back to him with bleak certainty.

Like Leni, he hadn't doubted Carla's loyalty.

This Hunter would have killed her whether she told him what she knew or not.

And all the assassin would have needed was the woman's phone in order to trace her call to Leni's location.

Knox's boiling rage shifted to cold fury when he thought about the anguish Leni would feel over the senseless loss of her friend. He landed another brutal blow, then grabbed the male's arm and violently twisted the limb around to the vampire's back.

The Hunter quickly pivoted, using his disabled arm as a lever to flip around in Knox's grasp. The move freed him just long enough to throw Knox onto the coffee table in front of the sectional. The heavy wood-and-glass piece shattered beneath him, crashing Knox to the floor.

The Hunter grabbed for the stand of metal fireplace tools near the hearth.

With one of the iron pokers in hand, he came back at Knox, his long fangs dripping with blood and saliva, murder blazing in his fiery eyes.

He brought the sharp end of the tool down like a hammer. Knox rolled out of the way, then back the other way as the vampire tried once more to skewer him.

Knox swatted the poker away, then leapt fluidly to his feet.

No sooner than he had, the big male wrestled him into a headlock. Knox fought the relentless hold with all he had, finally managing to break loose. On a snarl, he shoved his opponent across the room.

The vampire flew backward a few feet, then skidded to a halt on his boot heels. Panting, his eyes on fire with animal rage, he lowered his head like a bull and came at Knox on a feral, unearthly cry.

Knox scrabbled for the poker on the floor beside him. As soon as his fingers closed around the handle, he drew it back. Then he drove the weapon right through the center of the charging Hunter's skull.

The blow was catastrophic, even for the most powerful of his kind. The big male crumpled to his knees, dead even before his body hit the floor.

CHAPTER 25

Leni stood rooted to the same spot, her arm still wrapped tightly around Riley and holding him close to her, after Knox removed the body of the slain Breed male and took it outside.

"The sun will do the rest in the morning," he told her when he came back into the house.

She nodded, not yet able to find her voice.

Riley clung to her, his little body shaking nearly uncontrollably. The poor child was obviously in shock, terrorized by what he had witnessed. Leni didn't feel all that stable herself.

She didn't think she would ever be able to purge the memory of staring into the Breed assassin's cold eyes while he pulled the trigger on the pistol he'd aimed point-blank at her face. Even though she had been secure in the power of her gift to protect herself from injury, it hadn't lessened the horror of the attack.

And she was still trying to reconcile how she had been able to shield Riley at the same time.

In spite of her terror, Leni had felt a new strength surge within her. She felt it now too. It lived inside her, thrumming with energy, even at rest.

She felt the incredible presence of the blood bond she shared with Knox. That hadn't left her for a second, not during the attack or now. Knox's strength fed her own. His love galvanized her. Tonight, it had saved her life.

He had saved all their lives.

As remarkable as her ability was, how long could she have held out against a relentless killer with the brute force and lethal skills of ten mortal men?

Knox closed the damaged front door, then strode toward her. "It should be secure enough until the Order arrives." Drying blood and dark, swollen bruises marred his handsome face. One of his brows was split open, his eyes still smoldering with banked fire. Behind his torn upper lip, his extended fangs gleamed long and sharp from the depth of his battle rage.

But his touch was infinitely gentle as he gathered her to him, pressing a kiss to the top of her head. "Are you all right?"

"I am." Her reply was a choked whisper. She lifted her head, her heart breaking as she took in the awfulness of his injuries. "I'm fine, Knox. Riley and I are both unharmed. But you—"

Frowning, he shook his head. "Don't worry about me. I'll heal soon enough."

And so he was, she realized. The lacerations and shattered bones of his cheeks and jaw were mending before her eyes.

"That's the power of your blood inside me, Leni." He brushed his mouth over hers. "My blood will make you stronger too."

"It already is. That's how I was able to shield Riley with my ability, isn't it?"

He nodded. "And thank God you did."

The gravity of his deep voice only confirmed just how close they'd come to losing the boy.

They all had come terribly close to losing everything tonight.

In a dread-filled corner of her heart, she knew the worst of it wasn't over yet.

Knox crouched down onto his haunches in front of Riley. "How're you holding up, buddy?"

Instead of answering, the boy sidled around to the back of Leni's legs, his small hands clutching the loose fabric of her pajama bottoms.

"Hey," Leni said, reaching around to coax him out of hiding. "You don't have to be afraid of Knox, honey. He's not going to hurt us."

"Never," Knox vowed. "No one means more to me than both of you. You believe me, don't you, Riley?"

His pale blond head bobbed in mute agreement. He stared at Knox for a long moment, then stepped forward and wrapped the big male in a tight hug.

Relief washed over Leni as she watched the tender exchange between them. But it didn't diminish the panic that had taken up residence in her breast.

When Knox rose, she saw the same bleakness reflected in his grave stare.

"What if there are more of them?" she asked woodenly.

He gave a grim shake of his head. "There was only the one. The Parrishes hired him. I read it in the bastard the instant I touched him."

It didn't shock her to hear Travis's family would send an assassin out to kill them. She was fresh out of shock after what happened in this room tonight. But confusion gnawed at her.

Confusion and a cold, dawning realization she didn't want to acknowledge.

"How did they know where we are? How could they know how to find—" The words jammed in her throat, trapped there by a knot of anguish.

Oh, God. Carla.

She didn't have to say her friend's name out loud. If she had, it only would have added to Riley's trauma. Knox's bleak expression confirmed what she couldn't bear to say.

Carla was dead.

"You're sure?" she asked, her voice breaking with grief.

Knox acknowledged with a sober nod. "The Parrishes sent the Hunter there first. She didn't volunteer anything, Leni. But it wouldn't have mattered if she had."

Leni didn't want to believe it, but the truth was there in Knox's solemn gaze.

Her friend was gone.

"It's my fault. I shouldn't have said anything to her this morning. If I hadn't—"

Knox shook his head. "It wouldn't have changed a thing. Hunters hunt, Leni. All that matters to them is eliminating their target. They don't give a thought to the carnage they leave in their wake."

She didn't have to ask how he could be so certain. It was impossible to think of him in the same cold business as the Breed male he'd killed tonight, but she knew Knox was lethal. Now, she had seen it firsthand.

And while she loathed the sick madman who'd kept her mate a prisoner of his brutal program for so many years, she had never been more grateful for Knox's deadly talents than she was right now.

If only there had been some way to protect her friend too. Leni wanted to crumble as he drew her into his tender embrace, but she had to hold herself together. For Riley. For Knox.

She had to hold it together for Carla, too, because Leni knew her best friend would demand it of her.

Inhaling a fortifying breath, she drew out of the comfort of Knox's arms. "What are we going to do?"

"The Order should be here in three to four hours. I need you to stay put with Riley and wait for them. I'm going to leave you my phone. There's a number stored in it that will put you in touch with my brother Razor in Florida. If you need to reach the Order's team before they get here, he can make that happen."

Leni didn't like the way this was sounding. "What about you?"

A tendon jerked in his healing jaw. "I'm taking this war to the Parrishes' doorstep. And I'm going to end it, once and for all."

CHAPTER 26

It would have been faster to make the trek back to Parrish Falls on foot, but far less satisfying than rolling up to the Parrishes' property in the black SUV that belonged to the killer they'd hired.

Knox had made the drive in record time. Fury seethed in his veins as the miles fell away between the hidden safe house where he'd left Leni with Riley and the Parrishes' compound estate on the edge of town.

Before leaving Leni, he'd taken Riley aside and erased the boy's memory of the attack. Mind-scrubbing was an ability all of the Breed had, though Knox used it sparingly. It felt invasive to him, stealing a piece of someone's past, but in Riley's case there was no question it was a mercy.

No one should have to live with a reminder of the ugly brutality that existed in the world, least of all an innocent child.

Knox only wished he could have done the same for Leni.

If it were in his power, he'd remove every pain she had ever endured and shield her from any in the future.

Tonight, however, he'd have to make do with cold vengeance.

He slowed the vehicle, tires crunching in the rutted snow and ice as he approached the closed gate in front of the Parrishes' home and business. The big house glowed peacefully in the winter darkness, warm yellow light spilling out from behind curtained windows.

One of the Parrishes—a man too young to be the family's patriarch and too short and thin to be Dwight— worked outside near the adjacent lumberyard. He stood on the broad side of a tractor trailer loaded with fresh-cut timber, evidently checking that the cargo was secure.

His breath steamed under the pool of illumination pouring down from a pair of flood lights mounted on the outbuilding.

He glanced over his shoulder, peering through the distance at the SUV now waiting at the gate. The man's hand went up, a welcoming wave for what he apparently presumed was the lethal Hunter returned from his mission.

Well, he was half-right.

Knox smiled behind the dark-tinted glass of the windshield. He flashed the high-beams in reply, then watched as Travis Parrish's brother jogged into the outbuilding and hit a button that operated the gate remotely.

The metal grate slowly swung open.

Knox drove through, a growl rumbling in his chest.

As skilled and experienced as he was, he had never

particularly relished the act of killing.

Tonight he would make an exception.

CHAPTER 27

Knox had barely been gone an hour, but the waiting felt like an eternity.

The fact that Riley had no memory of the attack made the entire ordeal somewhat more bearable for Leni, but nothing would ever erase her grief over Carla's death.

Or her worry for Knox.

He had to be back in Parrish Falls by now. She knew he was alive. She felt his vitality like a balm through their bond. She also felt the coldness of his fury, and Leni almost pitied the men who'd found themselves on the receiving end of it tonight.

Almost.

The Parrishes had earned every bit of Knox's wrath for what they did to Carla.

Leni's veins boiled when she thought of her friend's final moments of fear and suffering. Carla had lost her life simply for being Leni's friend. Despite Knox's effort to assuage her guilt, she didn't know how she would ever forgive herself for putting her friend in the crosshairs of her war with the Parrishes.

As for Riley, he was still at the center of that battle.

Now more than ever, after Travis's murder.

And when she considered the possibility that the innocent little boy might have fallen into that family's hands tonight, her blood seethed with outrage. If not for Knox's lethal skills and the enhanced strength of her ability thanks to the bond she shared with him, Riley would be long gone.

Instead, he sat on the large sectional playing with Fred and a shoebox of action figures he'd found in one of the bedrooms.

Leni had hurriedly cleaned up the great room while Riley slept off the effects of the mind scrub Knox gave him before he left the safe house. The bloodied rug was rolled up and stashed in another room. The broken debris from the smashed coffee table was swept away.

Riley had lost interest in the movie they'd been watching before the attack, so Leni had turned on a local news station instead. She kept the volume low, just enough to chase away the silence of the big, empty Darkhaven.

Sitting beside him while he played, she couldn't resist reaching out to brush some of the pale blond hair from his brow. He was so much like Shannon. Bright and funny, a charming little imp with her sister's big blue eyes and silky hair.

It hurt to see him growing up without her.

And as much as she grieved for Carla, part of her heart would always mourn Shannon too.

All the things her sister would never see, never know about her wonderful son.

Leni cleared her throat. "You've been playing for a couple of hours, kiddo. Why don't you take a little break and I'll make you a sandwich?"

"Okay." He blinked up at her with wide, innocent eyes. "Do you think they got peanut butter here?"

Leni smiled. "Oh, I imagine they do."

"And grape jelly?"

"Why don't we go find out?"

She got up from the sofa and started walking toward the kitchen. She went a few paces before she realized Riley wasn't following her. Alarmed, she glanced back and saw his attention was rooted to the TV over the fireplace.

"Rye?"

She drifted back to him, her own gaze drawn to the news coverage playing on the big screen. It was from the local station, a breaking story about a young girl who'd apparently gone missing from Quebec almost two weeks ago. A snapshot of a preteen girl with light-brown hair and a shy smile dominated the display.

"That's her," Riley said, turning to look at Leni.

"That's who, honey?"

"My friend. The one Fred and me met in the woods down by the river."

A chill moved through Leni's bloodstream. "What do you mean, you met her? Are you talking about the imaginary friend you mentioned that morning you left the house without telling me?"

He frowned, shaking his head. "Not 'maginary. She's real. But I don't know her name, cause—"

"Because she ran away when you tried to talk to her," Leni replied, her voice wooden as she recalled what the boy had told her that day. The report she had dismissed as fiction because she was upset and scared and had no patience to play games with him.

Had there been a missing girl on the run in the woods in Parrish Falls?

If so, how on earth had she gotten so far away from her home?

Leni grabbed the remote and turned up the volume. The photo of the shy child was replaced with recent video file footage of law enforcement officers cordoning off a stretch of woods above the river outside Parrish Falls while a coroner's van waited on the snow-covered road.

"Authorities in Canada say the girl, whose body was found in the Penobscot River yesterday, was last reported seen at the rest stop near St. Zacharie. It is believed the twelve-year-old French-speaking victim may have been at risk for trafficking," the female anchor reported soberly. "If anyone has further information, you're asked to please contact law enforcement."

"What's trafficking?" Riley asked.

Leni couldn't answer. Her head filled with a sick suspicion—and a cold, niggling sense of alarm.

What was a child who'd gone missing from the border at St. Zacharie doing in Parrish Falls?

As she considered it, Knox's account of what he'd discovered when he read Travis Parrish's sins came back to her with terrible clarity.

Travis had arranged to send Shannon away. No, not sent away.

Taken.

Abducted across the Canadian border into Quebec.

Travis, who had a habit of hurting women, Knox had said.

And young girls.

She thought back to the odd reaction that passed between Travis and his father in the diner Sunday afternoon, when Enoch had mentioned Dwight and Jeb had a delivery to run to St. Zacharie. An urgent delivery made on the worst road conditions of the season.

Money doesn't wait for good weather.

Enoch Parrish's remark, and the strange look he'd exchanged with Travis suddenly took on a sinister new meaning.

Could the Parrishes be involved in something so heinous?

After everything she'd learned about them these past few days, nothing was beneath them.

Knox needed to be warned.

With the Order still hours away from the Darkhaven safe house, they would arrive too late to help him. Knox's brother Razor was even farther away than that. Her only other option was to report her suspicions to the county sheriff's department.

Muting the TV, she ran to retrieve her phone and tapped the number she saw every day on a fridge magnet in the diner.

The dispatcher answered and Leni took the call out of Riley's earshot. She hastily relayed everything she knew and suspected, from the girl Riley had seen in the woods and the strangely urgent trip the Parrishes had made to the border. Then she told the operator what had been done to her sister.

"There's more," she said to the silence on the other end. "The Parrishes tried to kill me tonight. They hired a Breed assassin. They murdered my friend Carla Hansen and then—"

There was an odd click on the line before a familiar voice intercepted the call.

"Lenora?" Sheriff Barstow's smooth baritone skated into her ear. He sounded concerned, but she didn't miss the edge of surprise in his voice. "Are you all right? I've got the whole damn department looking for you."

"What for?"

"What for? Haven't you heard? Travis Parrish was murdered in cold blood last night. We've got witnesses who've ID'd his killer, Leni. It was that homicidal vampire that's been sniffing around your skirt lately."

She cringed at the vulgar expression, coming from a law officer she'd known since she was a child. "Knox is my mate. All he's done is protect Riley and me."

"He's a killer, plain and simple. The way you and the boy vanished from town, I've been afraid the son of a bitch might've left you both for dead somewhere too."

"No, Amos. Knox isn't the dangerous one. The Parrishes are. They sent a Breed assassin out to kill Knox and me and take Riley. My friend Carla's dead now because of them too. The Hunter they sent after me killed her first to find out where I am."

The old sheriff went quiet for a long moment on the recorded line. "These are very serious charges, Lenora."

"It's the truth. Send someone to Carla's house if you don't believe me."

"I will do that," Barstow replied, his tone grave. He let go of a sigh, a heavy sound, full of contemplation.

"What about the other Breed male . . . Knox. Is he with you now, Leni?"

"No."

"Where is he?"

She was sure it wouldn't take the cagey old law officer more than a second to answer that question for himself, but she wasn't going to give it to him.

"You've been through quite a lot, Lenora. I know you must be scared, but this will all be over soon, I promise." Barstow's voice took on a soothing tone that for some reason made the fine hairs at the back of her neck stand on end. "Stay where you are. I've got deputies on the way to bring you here to the station as we speak."

That prickle of unease went cold now. "I never told you where I am, Amos."

Before he could sputter in response or try to calm her with more false concern, she ended the call. Her phone was no use to her now. All it would do was help lead Barstow and his men to her and Riley.

She tossed it away, then dashed back to the great room to get the boy.

They couldn't wait another minute for the Order to arrive.

They had to leave now.

Somehow, she had to find a way to warn Knox about everything she'd just learned.

She only prayed she could do that before Sheriff Barstow and his men caught up to him first.

"Riley, we have to go now, kiddo."

He must have seen the urgency in her face. Grabbing Fred, he hopped off the sofa and ran to her. Leni grabbed their coats and her purse, then hurried out to her Bronco parked outside. With Riley strapped into his

249

seat in back, she climbed behind the wheel and started the engine.

As the old truck rumbled to life, she pulled out the phone Knox had given her and hit the number he'd told her to call.

A low voice answered. "Too early to be hearing from you, brother. This can't be good news."

"Hello . . . um, Razor?" She held the phone between her ear and shoulder as she gunned the gas and roared out to the road. "My name is Lenora Calhoun—"

"I know who you are. Tell me what you need, Leni."

CHAPTER 28

Knox kept the Parrish man in the beams of the headlights as he drove up the length of the driveway. The urge to hit the gas and ram the conspiring bastard against the trailer and the tons of timber stacked on it was nearly overwhelming, but he kept a lock on his rage as he approached.

When the SUV slowed to a halt, Parrish strode up to the driver's side. He rapped his knuckles on the glass from the outside, an invitation to roll down the window. "Dwight and Pop are waiting for you in the house. They'll handle paying you the rest of your mon—"

The human's expression went slack as the dark glass slid open and he stared into the face of a stranger instead of the paid killer he'd been expecting. Knox's amber-hot irises and bared fangs sent Parrish back on his heels.

"Oh, fuck."

Knox wrenched open the door, knocking the man to the ground. Parrish's boots moved as if he was running even though his ass was planted on the snowy driveway.

Knox climbed out of the vehicle.

"Holy shit!" Parrish clambered to his feet and started sprinting away. He managed to fumble a pistol from the pocket of his jacket and pivoted to fire a wild shot. He missed. He fired a couple more, his skinny legs pumping as he fled for the cover of the outbuilding.

He didn't get that far.

Knox flashed from his position a few yards behind Parrish to the space directly in front of him.

He didn't waste another second's effort or thought on the man. Grabbing his skull in both hands, Knox gave the fragile human neck a hard twist. The corpse dropped at his feet with a muffled thud.

At the same moment, Dwight Parrish burst out the side door of the house. He stood on the covered porch, a large semiautomatic pistol in his hand. "Jeb?"

Knox stepped out of the darkness and into the pool of light from the floods overhead.

"Jeb's dead. So is the Hunter you hired." He started walking forward. "You're next."

Dwight raised his weapon and shot off a seemingly endless hail of bullets. A few of them hit, though not enough to stop Knox. He stalked across the driveway, heading with deliberate purpose toward the house.

Dwight had about two seconds to decide between continuing his useless barrage of gunfire or running for cover. No surprise, the coward chose the latter.

On a panicked curse, he pivoted back into the house and bolted the door behind him.

Knox kicked it off its hinges and stepped inside.

He caught the flash-fire of a shotgun blast in the corner of his eye barely an instant before the spray exploded toward him. He dived out of the way, though not before he saw that the shooter wasn't Dwight, but an old man.

Enoch Parrish.

The hunched, gray-haired patriarch of the family fled like a rat through the hole Knox had made where the side door had been. He let the scurrying bastard go—for now. Enoch wouldn't get far.

First, Knox had some payback to deliver on the old man's son.

He pounced on Dwight's retreating bulk, taking him down to the floor. Flipping him over, he pinned him with his hand clamped hard over the front of Parrish's throat. The instant his hands made contact, the bombardment of Dwight's sins and ugly truths seeped through the connection.

The suffering of countless young women and girls.

Abductions. Sexual enslavements and imprisonment. Unconscionable physical abuse that had ended in murder too often for Dwight to keep an accurate count.

And while some of those sins were decades old, many of them were fresh.

Knox glared down at the face of the human monster. "You sick fuck. I should've killed you that first night. I should have killed all of you that night."

Dwight snarled, his voice throttled under the pressure of Knox's grip. "Go to hell!"

"You first," Knox said.

He reached for Parrish's dropped pistol and put it under the bastard's chin. Then he pulled the trigger, blowing away Dwight's final words and taking half his skull along with them.

In the lumberyard outside, the semi's engine fired up.

Knox rose and calmly headed out to deal with the last of the Parrishes.

Enoch sat behind the wheel of the tractor trailer, exhaust spewing in a gray cloud as the old man revved the engine. Knox was there before the truck lurched into gear.

He ripped off the driver's side door and yanked Enoch out of the seat, throwing him to the ground. The old man had a gun too. Knox batted it out of his feeble grasp like he was swatting a fly.

He didn't have to guess at Enoch Parrish's guilt. That he had participated in the decision to send the Hunter out to kill Leni and him in order to take Riley was not a question. But Knox couldn't kill the son of a bitch without being certain of everything he'd done.

The old man made a frantic attempt at escape, crab-walking backward while Knox loomed over him. Knox brought his boot down on Enoch's chest, savoring the brittle pop of aged ribs giving way beneath his heel.

"Get up." He backed off slightly, glowering at the man. When Parrish only wheezed and sputtered, refusing to comply, Knox reached down for a fistful of his flannel shirt and hauled him up to his feet.

Parrish howled in agony.

The scream cut short under the punishing crush of Knox's fingers, now wrapped around the old man's throat.

"Holy hell," he hissed through his teeth and fangs as the floodgates opened on Enoch Parrish's nearly eighty years of corruption, criminality, and unspeakable cruelty.

If Dwight and Travis had committed hideous acts, their father's sins made them pale in comparison.

A lifelong abuser, Enoch's brutality had known no bounds. His wife and children. Local girls in Parrish Falls and elsewhere. And it hadn't stopped there.

Christ, not even close.

Enoch Parrish was the leader of a twisted ring of fellow offenders, who, like him, got off on preying upon young females who lacked the power or resources to stop them. Indigent women. Runaways. Vulnerable girls with no one to turn to, no one to help them.

Parrish had been trafficking and trading in human flesh most of his adult life, but had stepped up his operation once the family logging business had begun to decline.

He and his sons, along with a secret cabal of repugnant cronies, were still enslaving helpless young women to serve their sick pleasures.

Knox slammed the old man's spine against the rough timber logs stacked on the trailer behind him. "Where are they? The girls you're currently holding. Goddamn it, tell me where you're keeping them."

The blare of sirens screamed in the distance. Swirling lights broke through the trees as what appeared to be an army of law enforcement vehicles sped along the two-lane toward the Parrish property.

Enoch struggled against Knox's grasp, but his craggy old face remained shuttered, his thin mouth stubbornly silent.

Knox wanted to kill the bastard. God knew he did.

But he needed the information first.

He needed to be able to save Enoch Parrish's victims.

"Where are they, you miserable fuck?"

Then he heard it. A soft, muffled cry coming from within the outbuilding. He heard pounding. The sound would have been undetectable to human ears, but Knox's Breed senses latched on to it at once.

Behind him now, half the county's sheriff department swarmed onto the property. Snow and ice kicked up as the fleet of vehicles poured in to block any escape. Officers leapt out with guns in hand, all of them trained on Knox.

A voice came over a bullhorn—Amos Barstow, demanding Knox's surrender. "Turn around, and put your hands where we can see them."

Spotlights hit him from behind at the same time, lighting up Enoch Parrish's grinning face.

"Now, you're done for, vampire."

Someone fired a warning shot. Knox glanced back and saw it was Barstow.

"Bastard."

"Let him go," the sheriff shouted over the PA.

"You heard my friend." Enoch cackled. "Let me go."

Knox sneered. "All right."

He dropped him, at the same time reaching for the side rail release lever on the trailer's payload. Enoch Parrish screamed as twenty-plus tons of heavy timber avalanched down on top of him, burying him alive.

Amos Barstow's voice bellowed to his men. "Kill that son of a bitch!"

An explosion of gunfire erupted from the army of cops behind Knox.

CHAPTER 29

"Oh, my God. No!"

Leni pulled through the gate of the Parrishes' property just in time to see dozens of sheriff's department officers open fire on Knox. Throwing the old Bronco into park, she leapt out and ran toward the line of cops whose vehicles were fanned out like they had come prepared for war.

"No! Stop shooting at him, please!"

But they didn't stop. Amos Barstow was in charge and his voice rose over the din of the gunfire.

"Where'd that bloodsucking son of a bitch go?" he shouted to the other officers. "Don't let him get away!"

Leni couldn't tell where Knox had gone, either. He'd moved with all the speed he had at his command, vanishing into the darkness as nothing more than a blur of shadow.

But he hadn't escaped without injury.

She could feel his pain through their blood bond.

Some of the rounds had found their mark. But he was alive.

He was alive, and he was furious with a rage she could hardly fathom.

"Stop," Leni pleaded. "You've got the wrong man. Knox isn't the enemy."

"Stay out of this, Lenora." Barstow swung a contemptuous sneer in her direction. "You'd say anything to protect your lover. It won't work. That vampire's gonna die tonight. We just watched him kill my good friend Enoch Parrish in cold blood."

"You mean, the way you and the Parrishes killed my friend Carla Hansen? The way you would have killed me too?"

The gunfire died down, then ceased altogether. Some of the other officers stared at her in confusion.

"It's true," she said, addressing Barstow's colleagues. "Enoch Parrish and his sons hired a Breed assassin to get rid of me and Knox so the Parrishes could take my nephew. Sheriff Barstow was going to let it happen. And that's not all they've done. The Parrishes are running a human trafficking ring. It wouldn't surprise me for a second if Amos isn't also aware of that too. He may even be participating in it."

The sheriff sputtered. "You've lost your mind. Those are vile lies you're spouting, Lenora. Dangerous ones."

"Leni is right."

Knox's deep voice rang out, coming from the direction of the lumberyard outbuilding. He stood inside the open entrance of the steel barn, immense, fearless in the face of so many weapons trained on him. His transformed eyes glowed like hot coals. Blood dripped from the numerous gunshot wounds that had managed to hit their mark.

"The Parrishes are responsible for the abuse and murders of dozens of young women. Children too," Knox announced grimly. "Their evil ends tonight."

"Holy shit," one of the sheriff's deputies gasped. "He's not alone in there. Look!"

From behind Knox, a frail woman in soiled, tattered clothing stepped forward. Another followed. Then another, her arm sheltering the thin shoulders of a crying preteen girl. More females emerged, one by one, all of them looking haggard and abused.

The most recent victims of the Parrishes' sick ring of terror.

"Knox." Leni sucked in a stunned breath. Then she ran to him.

He caught her in a brief embrace, then took her hand in his. They walked out together, leading the group of traumatized survivors.

"Hold your fire," one of the law officers commanded. "Let them all come out."

The unit obeyed . . . all except Amos.

On a mad bellow, he raised his weapon and squeezed the trigger.

A rapid stream of bullets tore across the distance—only to collide with the unseen barrier of Leni's gift.

She wrapped the whole group in her shield. Knox and herself, the terrified women and girls who had already endured more than anyone should have to bear.

Amos's spent rounds dropped to the snow like metal raindrops.

And in that next instant, he dangled aloft in the vise of Knox's fist.

"You did know," Knox growled as he held the sheriff two inches off the ground. "You've been part of this for decades, along with your father before you. You helped the Parrishes bring their victims over the border. You took your cut out of the flesh of innocents."

"Lies!" Amos wailed. "It's all lies!"

"Ask any of those females if it's a lie," Knox snarled. "Who else was in on this with you?"

"Knox," Leni said, glancing around her at the near dozen women who watched in silence. A few of them had lifted their fingers to point at two of Amos's fellow officers.

They pointed at Amos too, united in their condemnation.

While one of the deputies ordered some of the men to apprehend the pair who'd been identified, Leni's pride surged.

She wasn't only proud of her incredible mate and his actions which had saved so many lives tonight, but for the resilience she saw in the faces of the women and girls who were getting their first taste of freedom, of triumph, over such an unspeakable suffering.

It would take time, but they were alive. They were going to be okay.

Thanks to Knox, they all would be.

A pair of big officers strode over to Amos with grave purpose. The one in charge nodded in approval, clapping Knox's shoulder in acknowledgment. "We'll take it from here."

Knox let go of Amos, turning him over to his colleagues who immediately slapped their former commander into handcuffs and led him away.

Only then did Leni let go of the cry that was trapped in her throat. Then she strode forward, into her mate's open arms.

CHAPTER 30

Knox pressed a kiss to the top of Leni's head as the unit from the sheriff's department wrapped up at the scene.

Amos Barstow had been put into the backseat of a squad car along with the two other officers implicated in his crimes. Also nearby, a pair of ambulances had arrived a few minutes earlier to look after the women and girls who'd been freed from their imprisonment inside a cage the Parrishes had constructed under the floor of the lumberyard outbuilding. Now the group of survivors were seated inside the heat of the vehicles, wrapped in blankets and being tended by a team of paramedics.

Standing next to Knox, Leni was wrapped in a blanket too, holding Riley inside the warmth with her.

One of the emergency medical staff came over to check on them. The male attendant had already given Riley a snack and some water. Now, his concern was on

Knox. "You're sure there's nothing we can do for you, sir? Sounds like you took on some heavy fire tonight."

"I'm fine," Knox replied.

And he was, more than fine. He was already healed from the worst of the gunshot wounds, and he had his Breedmate secure in his arms. He couldn't think of anything else in the world he might need.

As if she could feel the depth of his contentment, Leni smiled up at him.

Because, yes, of course, she could feel that.

She had to feel just how desperately he loved her too.

The paramedic cleared his throat. "All right then. We'll be heading out shortly."

As he returned to the ambulances, another vehicle rolled through the open gate of the property. The large black Land Rover with Massachusetts plates came to stop not far from Knox and Leni.

A pair of Breed males in patrol gear climbed out. The passenger had the demeanor of a leader, his ice-blue eyes shrewd beneath the military-cut of his golden hair. His companion behind the wheel was ebony-haired and immense, an obvious Gen One soldier with the catlike prowl of a stealth killer. A former Hunter, Knox had no doubt.

He stiffened. "What's the Order doing here?"

"I asked Razor to send them to Parrish Falls," Leni said. "I called him as I left the safe house to come after you."

Part of him was grateful for his mate's smart thinking. Another part of him would have been happy never to see the Order at all. If the two warriors had any doubts about his fitness to look after Leni and Riley, or had thoughts about removing them for their own safety, there would be a second battle yet to come tonight.

The lighter-haired warrior strode toward them, his expression grave. "You must be Knox. And Lenora."

"Leni," she said, offering the male a kind smile.

"I'm Sterling Chase, commander of the Order's Boston operation." He gestured to the formidable male beside him. "This is my team captain, Nathan."

Knox nodded at them both.

"Looks like we arrived too late," Chase said, glancing at the scene. "You handled this all on your own?"

"No." Knox shook his head. "I had a partner. My mate, Leni."

The commander's mouth tugged into a faint grin. "Good work. Both of you."

The Hunter called Nathan extended his hand. "Good to meet you, brother."

Knox took it, exhaling the tight breath that had been dammed up in his lungs. "You too."

A history of sins and regrets spilled through the brief connection with his fellow former assassin, but they were old scars on Nathan's soul. What he saw in the warrior's steady gaze was honor. He saw an unspoken understanding there as well, a kinship. One that only Knox and another of his laboratory-born brethren could share.

Nathan's glance slid to Leni. "It appears my brother is well-mated."

"Thank you," she murmured, her arms going tighter around Knox. "I'm well-mated too."

Chase nodded. "Razor briefed us about the situation along the way here. The Order is grateful for your work and intel, both of you. Not only have you saved the lives of those victims tonight, but we're hopeful you can help us and law enforcement dismantle this ring all the way to its source."

"I'll be glad to do whatever I can," Knox replied.

Maybe if they could follow the trail from the Parrishes to whomever they were working with across the border and elsewhere, they might also find the truth about what happened to Shannon.

After the ugliness of what he'd read in each of the Parrishes' hearts, Knox loathed to think where those answers might lead. But he knew Leni needed them.

In time, when he was old enough, Riley would need them too.

"Much appreciated," Chase said. He held out his big hand to Leni first, giving hers a gentle shake. Then he offered the same to Knox. "You have our thanks. That's coming all the way down from Lucan Thorne as well."

Knox gave the commander a sober nod.

"You know," Chase added, as he let go of his hand. "I'd be more than willing to make a place for you on the team in Boston. Or put a good word in for you with the Commander of operations in Montreal, if you prefer."

Knox chuckled. "Thanks, but no. I've already found my place." He lifted Leni's chin on the edge of his fingers. "It's here in Parrish Falls, with my extraordinary, beautiful mate."

EPILOGUE

Six months later . . .

"Claude, would you like more coffee?" Behind the counter full of diner patrons, Leni held the fresh pot in her hand. She winked at the old man's wife, Mable. "How's that blueberry pie?"

"Best in the whole state, honey. Your mom and gran sure would be proud."

Leni smiled. "I'll swing by with some more vanilla ice cream. That slice looks awfully lonely, if you ask me."

Mable chuckled. "That's only because my husband stole the first scoop from right under my nose."

She squawked as Claude reached over and gave her a playful pinch.

Leni left the elderly pair to their flirting and made a quick final round to the rest of the patrons before it was time to start closing for the night.

It was a glorious, warm August evening, the sun having set just a few minutes ago. She loved the blue hour between sundown and nightfall. Not only because of the soothing way it painted the summer trees outside the diner in a cool shade of twilight, but because it also meant it was nearly time for her evening escorts to come and walk her home to the house.

She couldn't curb her smile as the bell above the door jingled with Knox and Riley's arrival.

The little boy from just half a year ago had somehow grown a full inch during summer break. He had since retired Fred and the rest of his imaginary friends, moving too quickly from the whimsical child he'd been to an inquisitive, sensitive youth who absolutely adored and idolized his current best friend, Knox.

But he still gave the best hugs Leni had ever known.

She wrapped her arms around his shoulders as he ran to her in greeting. "You're getting really fat," he declared, resting his head on the rounded swell of her belly. "How long is that baby going to take to get here, anyway?"

She laughed. "Only a few more months now."

Knox strode up and tilted her face for his kiss. "Hello, love."

She melted into him, as always. After the trauma they had come through together, she savored every second of every day she shared with Knox. And the nights.

Especially the nights.

He broke their kiss on a low growl meant for her ears only. His strong arms enveloped her, the heat and scent of him driving her mad with desire. Even heavy with his child, she couldn't get enough of her blood-bonded mate.

"Do I look fat to you?" she whispered.

He shook his head, amber sparks dancing in his stormy blue-gray eyes. "You look beautiful. So beautiful, I think I might keep you pregnant for the next ten years."

"What does pregnant mean?" Riley asked, hopping onto one of the empty stools at the counter.

Leni and Knox both laughed, along with several of her customers.

She didn't doubt for a minute that her mate was fully capable of keeping her knocked up. God knew, they spent enough time practicing for it.

Given his background, she had worried that Knox might be reluctant to start a family. Instead, it had been his suggestion. He wanted to put down roots with her, make a life together in the town that had been her home from the day she'd been born.

Now, in just three months' time, they would welcome their son in Parrish Falls too.

Knox stroked her unbound hair, drawing her against the hard ridges of his warm, all-too-sexy body. "Have I told today you that I love you?"

"You have," she murmured. "But by all means, don't let that stop you."

"I love you," he said, his gaze so earnest and solemn, it made her heart squeeze in her breast.

"I love you too, Knox. Forever."

Riley heaved a dramatic sigh. "Oh, geez. There they go kissing again."

Knox chuckled. "Get used to it, buddy. Kissing your Aunt Leni is my favorite thing to do." His eyes flared, and behind the lush curve of his lips, the points of his fangs gleamed. "One of my favorite things, that is."

He lowered his mouth to hers again, but paused as a large black Rover turned in to the parking area in front of the diner.

"That's the Order," he said, tension seeping through their bond.

"Were you expecting them?"

He shook his head. "No."

They had been in regular contact with Sterling Chase from Boston, but the big blond warrior who stepped out from behind the wheel of the SUV outside was a different male. He was accompanied by a tall, stunning woman with a chin-length, raven-dark bob. The female carried herself like a warrior too, garbed in black leather the same as her companion. Except she held an infant in her arms.

And then, from out of the backseat, another woman appeared.

Petite, fair-haired. With bright blue eyes the exact shade of Riley's.

Leni's breath seized in her lungs. "Oh, my God. It can't be . . ."

But it was.

"Shannon."

Leni wanted to run to her. She wanted to race outside the diner and pull her sister into her arms and never let go again. But her feet stayed rooted to the floor. Her heart hammered with uncertainty in her breast as she watched the frail woman take a few hitching steps away from the vehicle.

It had been so long.

Shannon had been through so much.

Knox had been working with the Order in Boston and Montreal, doing what he could to help the warriors piece together what had happened to her sister, and where she had ended up after Travis arranged for her abduction.

They had told Leni not to get her hopes up, that finding Shannon alive, let alone in any shape to resume a normal life, were likely slim to none.

But now, here she was.

Home. At last.

Knox drew Leni close to him, a fortifying presence as she waited the eternity it seemed to take for her sister to step inside the diner with the couple from Montreal.

The bell jangled. Shannon flinched at the sound.

Then her eyes lifted, meeting Leni's tear-filled gaze.

"Leni." Shannon's hand trembled as it came up to her cracked, pale lips. A jagged cry tore out of her. She took a step, then another. Then ran forward and clutched Leni close.

"Oh, Shannon. I've missed you so much."

Her sister wept, and Leni did too. It seemed as though they clung to each other for an endless time before Shannon's hold finally loosened.

She drew back, looking at Leni's belly, then up in question at the massive Gen One Breed male at Leni's side.

"This is my mate, Knox."

Knox smiled, his deep voice gentle and soothing. "I'm honored to meet you."

Shannon gave him a faint nod, then her red-rimmed gaze slid toward the counter. To the grown-up seven-year-old she hadn't seen since he was a baby, but who could never be mistaken as anyone's child but hers.

The sound she made was a mix of elation and abject sorrow.

"Riley," Leni said softly. "Didn't I promise you she would come home one day?"

"My mom?"

Leni nodded. Riley's sweet little face crumpled for a moment, then a smile burst through his tears. He jumped off the stool and ran to his mother, wrapping her in one of those hugs of his that had always managed to make all of Leni's problems disappear.

She hoped her sister felt some of that healing power too.

Leni moved closer to Knox as they watched Shannon reunite with her son.

Shannon had Riley again, and she was home.

As for Leni and Knox, they had all they would ever need too.

Family, home, and a love that would last forever.

~ * ~

ABOUT THE AUTHOR

LARA ADRIAN is a *New York Times* and #1 international best-selling author, with nearly 4 million books in print and digital worldwide and translations licensed to more than 20 countries. Her books have regularly appeared in the top spots of all the major bestseller lists including the *New York Times*, USA Today, Publishers Weekly, Wall Street Journal, Amazon.com, Barnes & Noble, etc. Reviewers have called Lara's books "addictively readable" (Chicago Tribune), "strikingly original" (Booklist), "extraordinary" (Fresh Fiction), and "one of the consistently best" (Romance Novel News).

Visit the author's website at
www.LaraAdrian.com

Find Lara on Facebook at
www.facebook.com/LaraAdrianBooks

Coming Soon!

Have fun and exercise your brain with this exciting new way to enjoy the Midnight Breed Series. Makes a great gift!

Midnight Breed Series Word Search

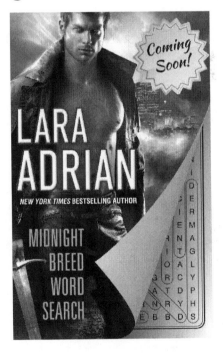

December 2019

Look for it in paperback online or ask for it at your favorite bookseller.

Coming Soon!

Watch for a sexy new contemporary romance standalone set in Lara Adrian's 100 Series!

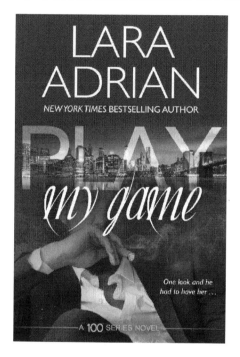

Play My Game
Available Spring 2020

"Lara Adrian not only dips her toe into this genre with flare, she will take it over... I have found my new addiction, this series."
--*The Sub Club Books*

www.LaraAdrian.com

Never miss a new book from Lara Adrian!

Sign up for Lara's VIP Reader List at
www.LaraAdrian.com

Be the first to get notified of new releases,
plus be eligible for special VIPs-only exclusive content
and giveaways that you won't find
anywhere else.

Sign up today!

Discover the Midnight Breed
with a FREE eBook

Get the series prequel novella
A Touch of Midnight
FREE in eBook at most major retailers

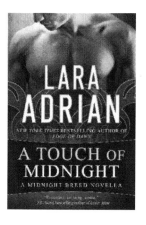

After you enjoy your free read, look for Book 1 at a special price: $2.99 USD eBook or $7.99 USD print!

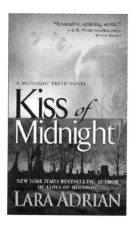

The Hunters are here!

Thrilling standalone vampire romances from Lara Adrian set in the Midnight Breed story universe.

AVAILABLE NOW

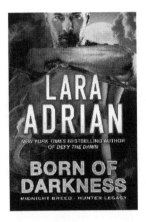

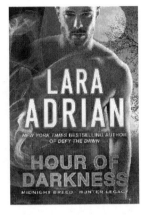

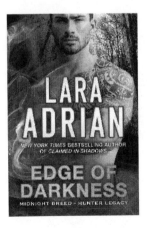

Turn the page for an excerpt from the
newest story in the Midnight Breed
vampire romance series

Break the Day

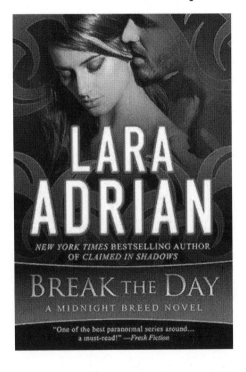

**Available now in ebook, trade paperback and
unabridged audiobook**

For more information on the series and
upcoming releases, visit:

www.LaraAdrian.com

Lara Adrian's New York Times and #1 international bestselling Midnight Breed vampire romance series continues with Break the Day, an adrenaline-laced, passionate new novel of paranormal adventure.

After a shocking betrayal nearly killed him and the people he cares about the most, what Breed warrior Rafe wants more than anything is revenge against the insidious brotherhood called Opus Nostrum. But to achieve that goal, he must turn his back on the Order and infiltrate a dangerous gang with ties to Opus. Risking everything to redeem himself and carry out his deep-cover mission, Rafe will let nothing stand in his way-- least of all his desire for one of the loyalists he should despise, a mysterious, dark-haired beauty named Devony Winters.

But Devony has secrets of her own to protect, as well as a personal duty she will do anything to fulfill. And as a daywalker passing herself off as human to the gang she's been embedded with for months, the last thing she needs is a dangerous former member of the Order unraveling all her hard work. Her plans depend on keeping Rafe at arm's length, but if she surrenders to the dark need he stirs within her, will her heart pay the ultimate price?

"Sexy romances, alpha heroes, strong heroines, and great story lines never fail to keep me occupied way into the night! And with a couple of surprise twists and plenty of action, Break the Day *was a fabulous addition to the Breed series!"*

—Jewls Book Blog

Chapter 1

Rafe stroked his fingers over tender female flesh, his thumb lingering at the carotid, where the human's pulse pounded as hard and fast as her panting breaths.

As blood Hosts went, this one was more than willing to give him her vein. She either didn't notice or didn't care that they were seated at the bar in full public view of the other patrons at Asylum tonight.

Which suited Rafe just fine.

Lowering his head to the side of the woman's bared throat, he took a long moment to savor the scent and sound of coppery red cells rushing just beneath the surface of so much fragile skin. His fangs elongated in reflex, pushing out of his gums in anticipation of the first bite.

"Feeding curfew ended at midnight, warrior."

On a growl, Rafe paused and swiveled a dark look at the bartender who'd issued the warning. The man was Breed, like him. A big male with a shaved, tattooed head and shoulders as wide as a tank.

Asylum mainly catered to a human clientele, given that the Breed had only one drink of choice: blood taken from a freshly opened vein. Still, in the twenty years since Rafe's kind had been outed to man, the tavern in Boston's old north end had become a popular gathering place for members of both races.

At this late hour, the place had thinned out to a few dozen diehards and the usual smattering of inebriated newcomers who'd evidently grown tired of the flashy dance clubs and sim-lounges in the tourist areas and had wandered deeper into the city for a taste of the local color.

From time to time, Rafe and his teammates from the Order had hung out here as well, sharing some laughs together after their patrols.

Damn, how long had it been? A few months by now. Not since the summer, when he'd been pulled off all Order missions.

Not since his epic fuck-up in Montreal.

Worse than a fuck-up, the near catastrophe had almost killed him. And it might also have cost the lives of everyone closest to him if Opus Nostrum's beautiful, but treacherous, mole hadn't been stopped by Rafe's best friend and comrade, Aric Chase.

Rafe had been played for the worst kind of fool, blinded by a pretty face and a seductive mouth that had spewed nothing but lies.

Never again.

He shook off the bitter reminder with a curse uttered low under his breath. Self-directed anger put an even sharper edge to his voice as he glared at the big bartender. "Why don't you do us both a favor and get off my dick? I don't hear the lady complaining about feeding curfews."

The male scowled. "Listen, man, I don't make the laws."

Rafe grunted. "Neither do I."

"Yeah, but isn't the Order supposed to enforce them?"

"He ain't Order. Not anymore. Rumor has it they bounced his ass."

The comment came from a group of Breed civilians from area Darkhavens occupying one of the tables behind him. Affluent and useless in their polo shirts and khakis, they were the vampire version of rich frat boys. Rafe had earned the scorn of the five young males the minute he arrived and the human blood Host they'd been plying with alcohol for most of the night decided she'd rather spend her time in Rafe's lap.

He swung his head around to glance their way now, sensing the contempt simmering at his back. A couple of the ego-rankled boneheads actually looked stupid enough to want to take him on.

Rafe had to curb his smile. He was ready for a fight tonight.

Hell, it was the reason he was there in the first place.

"My father works in law enforcement," the mouthpiece of the Darkhaven males added helpfully. "He says it's been all over JUSTIS for weeks that Golden Boy here got his ass handed to him by Lucan Thorne and they cut him loose. Evidently 'gross insubordination and conduct unbecoming' isn't a good look, even for the members of the Order."

"That true? You're not one of the Order's warriors anymore?"

Rafe pivoted back to the scowling bartender. "Do I look like I am?"

He knew damn well he didn't. His blond hair was grown out in loose waves that broke at his shoulders, windblown from the ride on his motorcycle, which he'd parked outside the bar. Thick whiskers shadowed his face and jaw. He hadn't put on the Order's black fatigues and weapons belt in months.

Tonight he was dressed in jeans and a dark T-shirt under his black leather jacket. He more resembled one of the cluster of menacing-looking gangbangers playing pool and slamming back shots near the other side of the room than a member of the elite warrior team from the Order.

The humans in studded black leather had been watching him since he walked in, mistrusting and cautious. Rafe felt their eyes on him now, in particular the muscled, goateed man lording over the bunch, and the sole female of the pack, a tall, leggy brunette with an angel's face and mouth-watering curves beneath her biker's leathers and black turtleneck sweater.

As for Rafe, his rough appearance was as deliberate as his presence in the bar tonight.

All part of the plan. Just like his removal from his team's patrols after he returned from Montreal, and the more recent, carefully constructed rumor that had been allowed to spread like wildfire through both human and Breed law enforcement communities that he had been dishonorably ousted from service.

Only a few in the Order who knew the truth. Namely, the architects of Rafe's current deep undercover mission: Lucan Thorne at the D.C. headquarters; Gideon, the Order's technology genius; and Sterling Chase, the commander of the Boston operations center.

Lucan had agreed on one concession at Rafe's insistence—his parents, Dante and Tess. Although Dante commanded the Seattle operations center for the Order, there would be no keeping him away from Boston if he truly believed his son had strayed so far off the path.

Allowing his parents to think the worst of him would have been hard, but it damn near killed Rafe to be required to keep the truth from his teammates and friends Nathan, Elijah, and Jax. He could only imagine what they thought of him now.

Letting Aric Chase believe he was a washout and a failure was even worse. Especially when he owed his life to his best friend. Fortunately, the male was still in Montreal with his new mate, Kaya. The pair were busy recruiting a new team for the Order, one comprised of daywalkers, those few and rarest of the Breed like Aric and his twin sister, Carys, and their mother, Tavia.

Rafe only hoped that once the dust settled after the solo operation he was launching tonight, he'd be able to redeem himself in everyone's eyes.

Not just for his covertly orchestrated fall from grace with the Order, but for the very real one that had preceded it.

Ironically, it was the shame he brought down on himself in Montreal that made him the only suitable candidate for this mission now.

And he would not fail.

Not this time.

Even if it meant staking his last breath on that vow.

Behind him, Big Mouth from the Darkhaven only seemed emboldened by the fact he wasn't getting more of a rise out of Rafe. "I don't know, boys, he doesn't seem like such a hardass to me. Guess he ain't so tough without the other Order thugs around to back him up."

Rafe exhaled a heavy sigh, if only to mask his satisfaction at the predictability of his target tonight.

Calmly, he moved the clinging woman off his lap and onto the stool beside him. Then he tossed a sneer at the table of civilian vampires. "You know the best thing about getting axed from the Order? Not having to treat entitled Darkhaven fucks like you as if you matter."

A couple of them scoffed at the insult. Rafe heard the abrupt scrape of a chair in the instant he turned his attention away from them. He knew the attack was coming even before he felt the shift in the air as one of the Breed males launched himself at him from behind.

No surprise, it was Big Mouth. And shit—the asshole had a knife. It would have been buried in Rafe's back if he hadn't dodged the strike in the same moment his attacker lunged. Rafe grabbed the male's wrist in the vise of his fist and twisted hard.

The male screamed and let go of his weapon.

Rafe caught the blade in his free hand, using the other to wrench his assailant's arm around to his back. He could have snapped the limb with a flex of his wrist or turned the knife on its owner, but he wasn't looking to do real harm to the Darkhaven punk or his friends, no matter how satisfying it might be.

He had escalated the situation for an audience of one.

And he had the guy's full attention too.

While half of the bar cleared out in a hurry, a few panicked tourists shrieking as they fled to the street outside, the gangbangers remained. From Rafe's peripheral, he saw their goateed leader watching as he calmly continued his game at the pool table.

Rafe increased the pressure on Big Mouth's elbow joint, making him squawk for good measure. And yeah, because the bastard deserved a little pain.

He was just about to toss the male back at his companions when the bar's front door opened. Another pair of Breed males strode inside, no doubt alerted to the trouble by the crowd pouring out of the place moments ago.

Rafe groaned inwardly.

Ah, fuck. Just what he didn't need.

Jax and Elijah.

His two teammates—former teammates, as far as they knew—were suited up in patrol gear and armed to the teeth. Whatever they thought of him now, they were clearly shocked to find Rafe standing in the middle of Asylum holding a whimpering Breed civilian in one hand and a dagger in the other.

"What the fuck's going on in here?" Eli's low, Texas-tinged drawl was practically a snarl.

Jax's ebony brows were drawn together over his dark, almond-shaped eyes. "This is the last place we expected to see you, Rafe."

"No shit." Last place he expected to see them too.

He didn't miss the fact that one of Jax's razor-sharp hira-shuriken glinted in the warrior's hand, ready to let fly.

The move to palm a throwing star was pure reflex for the lethal male, but this was the first time Rafe had ever stood in the crosshairs of his comrade's cold skills.

Fortunately, the pair had arrived without Nathan, the team's captain. As much as Rafe dreaded the thought of a confrontation with Eli or Jax, his odds of walking away in one piece would diminish drastically if the former Hunter were standing here with them.

"Good thing you showed up," the bartender muttered from behind the counter. "This one's been itching for a fight with someone since he got here."

Rafe couldn't deny it. The plan had been to cause a ruckus in front of the gang, make it known in a very public, even violent, way that he was no longer on the right side of the law.

He kept his hold on Big Mouth, only because his mind was busy formulating the best way to defuse the situation without unraveling his sole purpose for being there tonight.

Meanwhile, he was caught in an unwanted standoff with the two warriors he still considered his brothers.

"Let him go, asshole!"

The shouted command didn't come from Eli or Jax, but rather one of Big Mouth's buddies.

And the dumbfuck had the poor judgment to draw a gun from somewhere on his person. The shiny stainless-steel semiautomatic pistol wobbled in his grasp as the civilian vaulted up from his chair and squeezed the trigger at Rafe.

Or, tried to.

In that same moment, Jax's hira-shuriken zipped through the air. It ripped into Dumbfuck's forearm, knocking his aim off.

The weapon fired a short spray of rounds toward the ceiling, the ricochets ringing over the beat of the music thumping on the sound system.

The two Order warriors moved quickly on the table of Darkhaven males. In seconds, they had them rounded up and searched for other weapons.

Eli strode up to Rafe and pulled Big Mouth out of his grasp, shoving the male over to his friends. Then he grabbed the dagger from Rafe.

"You're already walking a razor-thin line, man. Don't do something you can't take back."

His deep voice was level, but there was no mistaking the warning it carried. He turned back to the Darkhaven males. "As for the rest of you ladies, get your asses home before some jackass like the one over here wastes you just for being stupid."

Rafe watched as Big Mouth and his friends shuffled out of Asylum. Jax followed behind them, but Eli lingered for another moment. He pinned Rafe with a grave stare.

"You know if the command ever comes down from Lucan to deal with you, we're gonna have to carry it out."

Rafe held his comrade's sober gaze. He knew how he had to act right now, what he had to say. But knowing it and pushing the words off his tongue were two different things.

"You think I actually give a fuck anymore?" His mouth twisted from the bitter taste of the lie.

"No, man. I guess I don't." Eli frowned, then slowly shook his head on a curse. "So you'd better fucking watch yourself."

He turned away then, and stalked out of the bar without a backward glance.

A few seconds after the Order was gone, a pained groan drew Rafe's attention to the area near the pool table. One of the gangbangers pawed at his midsection in a frenzy, his face going ashen with shock.

"Oh, fuck! Cruz, I think I'm hit. Son of a bitch, I'm bleeding!"

The olfactory punch of fresh hemoglobin hit Rafe's nostrils at the same time the scrawny man tore off his leather jacket to reveal a blooming red stain across his stomach.

Just fucking great.

Rafe's fangs erupted in response. It was next to impossible for a Breed vampire not to react to the sensory blast of spilled blood. His eyes burned amber, his vision sharpening with the vertical narrowing of his pupils as everything Breed in him came to dangerous life.

The gangbanger's wailing intensified. A couple of his companions gathered around him, including the one in charge. A few others moved farther away, including the pretty brunette who averted her gaze from her wounded comrade and wheeled away from the others as if she were on the verge of throwing up.

Behind him, the Breed bartender growled through his fangs. "Fucking hell. That son of a bitch is gonna bleed out in another minute."

Rafe couldn't pretend he actually cared. He glanced back at the human with the likely mortal gut wound and the grave faces of his comrades. A few more seconds was probably all the life their friend had left.

Rafe had been studying the hard-partying, petty-thieving crew for weeks, looking for a way to win their attention—and their trust. The plan he'd put together with Lucan and Sterling Chase required patience he didn't really have. Maybe this unscripted opportunity might be his best chance to grease the wheels of his mission.

Rafe glanced down at his hands. He'd been born with his mother's gift for healing. As much as he hated to use his personal ability on vermin like these, it would all be worth it if it got him closer to his ultimate goal: the destruction of Opus Nostrum and everyone loyal to their cause.

The bartender uttered a harsh curse. "If that human dies in my bar, I'm holding both you and the Order personally responsible, asshole."

Rafe shook his head. "He's not going to die."

Fisting his hands at his sides, he headed across the bar.

BREAK THE DAY

is available now at all major retailers in eBook, trade paperback, and unabridged audiobook.

Watch for the next Midnight Breed novel coming in 2020!

Thirsty for more Midnight Breed?

Read the complete series!

A Touch of Midnight (prequel novella)
Kiss of Midnight
Kiss of Crimson
Midnight Awakening
Midnight Rising
Veil of Midnight
Ashes of Midnight
Shades of Midnight
Taken by Midnight
Deeper Than Midnight
A Taste of Midnight (ebook novella)
Darker After Midnight
The Midnight Breed Series Companion
Edge of Dawn
Marked by Midnight (novella)
Crave the Night
Tempted by Midnight (novella)
Bound to Darkness
Stroke of Midnight (novella)
Defy the Dawn
Midnight Untamed (novella)
Midnight Unbound (novella)
Midnight Unleashed (novella)
Claimed in Shadows
Break the Day

. . . and more to come!

If you enjoy sizzling contemporary romance, don't miss this hot series from Lara Adrian!

For 100 Days

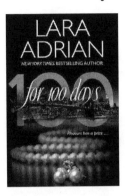

The 100 Series: Book 1

"I wish I could give this more than 5 stars! Lara Adrian not only dips her toe into this genre with flare, she will take it over . . . I have found my new addiction, this series." --The Sub Club Books

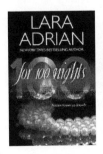 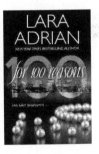

All available now in ebook, trade paperback and unabridged audiobook.

Combat vet Gabriel Noble barely survived the war overseas, but now the stoic Baine International security specialist's honor is put to the test bodyguarding beautiful Evelyn Beckham.

A 100 Series Standalone Romance

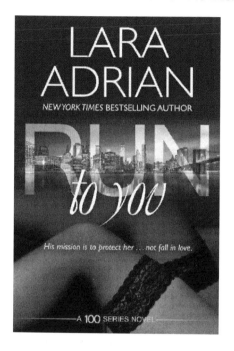

Available Now

eBook * Paperback * Audiobook

"Lara Adrian has managed once again to give us a story with heat, high emotion, and angst that touches our heart. I absolutely loved it."
—*Reading Diva*

Award-winning medieval romances from Lara Adrian!

Dragon Chalice Series
(Paranormal Medieval Romance)

"Brilliant . . . bewitching medieval paranormal series." –Booklist

Warrior Trilogy
(Medieval Romance)

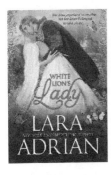 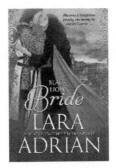 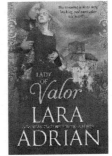

"The romance is pure gold." –All About Romance

A dark knight abducts the daughter of his enemy
as the price of her father's sins. Can the bold but
innocent beauty tame the beast?

Lord of Vengeance

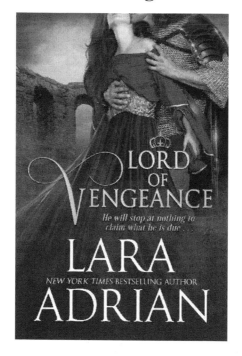

Available Now

eBook * Paperback * Audiobook

"A truly wonderful read."
—*All About Romance* (Grade A / Desert Isle Keeper)

Connect with Lara online at:

www.LaraAdrian.com

www.facebook.com/LaraAdrianBooks

www.goodreads.com/lara_adrian

www.instagram.com/laraadrianbooks

www.pinterest.com/LaraAdrian

Made in the USA
Columbia, SC
14 January 2020

86787099R00186